Praise for Gina Robinson's
DIAMONDS ARE TRULY FOREVER

"A fast-paced and exciting thriller. Jam-packed with funny dialogue and hot sex . . . There's never a dull moment. [This] is one book you definitely will NOT lose interest in; instead you will be unable to put the book down. Excellent and innovative read!"

—*Fresh Fiction*

"Readers are in for a fun, rollicking read with *Diamonds Are Truly Forever* . . . If you love a romantic suspense that is long on funny situations and romantic to boot, then you'll love [this book]."

—*Romance Reviews Today*

LIVE AND LET LOVE

"Secret agents, mysterious identities, and a love that just won't die make for a sweet, clever escape from reality."

—*Kirkus Reviews*

"Robinson's action-packed tale doesn't shy away from the fact that the hero is an assassin. Featuring plenty of interesting gadgets for spying and killing, as well as some delightful dogs—and a good dose of humor and suspense—this book ensures readers will race to the perfectly fitting finish."

—*RT Book Reviews*, 4½ stars

"Gina Robinson is a talented writer . . . if you are a fan of her stories . . . this book is worth adding to your wish list."

—*Night Owl Romance*

THE SPY WHO LEFT ME

"This first Agent Ex novel is good, old-fashioned fun. Full of laughter, intrigue, and, of course, steamy spies, it's a great weekend escape. Robinson knows how to balance a book with lighthearted romps and serious romance."

—*RT Book Reviews*

"At times laugh-out-loud funny, Robinson's foray into the world of James Bond has its poignant side, assuring that readers will be back for more." —*Booklist*

"Punctuated with Bond-worthy downhill car and bike chases and near-death surfing parties, Robinson's clever concoction of lust and longing is a refreshing tropical cocktail." —*Publishers Weekly*

"Mystery, mayhem, sexy spies, and lots of laughter. Gina Robinson writes a damn good book!"

—Christie Craig, award-winning author

"The action is fast and furious and the plot twists turn on a dime. Ms. Robinson seamlessly adds humor to her story that will keep the reader laughing as things keep going wrong." —SingleTitles.com

ALSO BY GINA ROBINSON

Love Another Day

GINA ROBINSON

St. Martin's Paperbacks

This is a work of fiction. All of the characters, organizations, and events portrayed in this novel are either products of the author's imagination or are used fictitiously.

LOVE ANOTHER DAY

Copyright © 2014 by Gina Robinson.

For information address St. Martin's Press, 175 Fifth Avenue, New York, NY 10010.

ISBN: 978-1-250-03301-7

Printed in the United States of America

St. Martin's Paperbacks edition / March 2014

St. Martin's Paperbacks are published by St. Martin's Press, 175 Fifth Avenue, New York, NY 10010.

10 9 8 7 6 5 4 3 2 1

For My Sister, thanks for all the support!

CHAPTER ONE

CIA HEADQUARTERS, LANGLEY, VIRGINIA

Being called into the chief's office was something Malene Cox looked forward to. A special missive commanding her attendance in a solo meeting with the notorious Emmett Nelson, head of National Clandestine Services, the spying arm of the Central Intelligence Agency, meant a plum assignment. Something filled with intrigue, and she hoped, lots of shopping.

As head of NCS's cover life department, Malene lived for these moments. She smelled a sweet professional challenge. It was just too bad she never got to talk, and maybe brag just a bit, about her top secret work for NCS with anyone outside of the Agency.

Her friends and family believed she was wasting her considerable artistic design talents on a boring, though adequately paid, facilities position with the CIA. Working for the pension and the government benefits. Yes, working for the CIA did have a certain cachet attached to it. But when you weren't a spy, only a drone who bought office furniture, as her former mother-in-law liked to call her? Well, that killed any mystique, status, and prestige that might have been attached to working for her secretive employer. Malene always had an underlying sense that she should be offended that no one considered her spy material. She could be just as sneaky and secretive as the next person.

Besides, if she were a spy, would she really tell anyone? But no one seemed to think of that, and for some reason, it rankled her.

Of course, if she did tell anyone what she *actually* did for the Agency—designing and coordinating cover wardrobes, furnishing and setting up cover homes, setting up social media and creating convincing documentation for NCS's agents—no one would ever believe her. Hers was a job that didn't exist, not to the general public. Didn't anyone wonder about the cover part of being undercover? What did people think—that these things just sprang into being fully formed? That the spies took care of these details *themselves*?

Now that was laughable. The spies she knew, and she knew all the Agency spies, including her ex-husband, Tate, couldn't be bothered with tasks as menial and mundane as setting up their own cover lives. Which left it to Malene to coordinate with senior field agents, handlers, and the top brass at NCS to get their secret agents comfortably settled into any new cover that was demanded.

It was challenging and creative work that required a deep knowledge of personalities and personality traits, psychology, history, and a myriad of cultures. Malene had trained at Central Saint Martins College in London, where she'd dabbled in fashion design, interior design, and psychology, and had eventually graduated, married Tate, and joined the CIA. Ironically, though he'd never had much appreciation for the work she did for the Agency, Tate had been the one to bring her to Emmett's attention. He was, in essence, her recruiter.

Malene had talent. She had the eye, an eye few people had. Her coworkers told her she should have worked in movies. She'd make an excellent wardrobe designer, set director, or location finder. But Malene loved what she did. She reveled in keeping secrets and being responsible, in some small way, for protecting and defending her country.

She was definitely not a thrill-seeker, had never wanted to be at the wrong end of a gun or an antiballistic missile. Now, a little covert shopping, that was another thing. She loved the secretive element of her job—the fear that she could be found out as she set up a life. The joy of imagining lives that could be and bringing them into being without anyone suspecting. Of shopping at everything from exclusive shops to tag sales. Her job was simply, and absolutely, perfect.

The chief's door stood open. Malene knocked lightly on the door frame.

Emmett Nelson looked up from his laptop and smiled at her. "Ah, Malene, there you are. Come in."

It was amazing there was any room on his desk to set his computer. Emmett's office was renowned in the Agency for being cluttered with the eclectic—tiny figurines, airplane models, McDonald's toys, miniature gadgets, puzzles and mind-benders, abstract art, energy-drink cans, bottles in odd shapes, and just about anything else a person could imagine. Probably including a few deadly weapons disguised as toys, compliments of the research and development department.

Emmett called his eccentricity and habit of collecting interesting odds and ends from across the globe and displaying them in his office the sign of a creative mind. The clutter inspired him.

The disorder offended Malene's sense of design, but she understood Emmett's love of it. Her fabric samples, paint chips, and magazine clippings inspired her in much the same way.

"You wanted to see me, Chief?" She slipped into the room and closed the door.

It went without saying that you closed the door when having a meeting with Emmett. Everything in this building was top secret, even what the chief had for lunch. The entire building was shielded and protected by scrambling equipment and signal-blocking machinery. Every type of cloaking device imaginable protected the clandestine missions being planned inside the building and the intel that protected the country. Emmett's office was triple shielded. Topping the airline industry, the Agency believed in triple redundancy. Double redundancy was not enough.

There was a saying among spies, "Trust no one." And that was never truer than inside agency headquarters. You never knew who might have turned, or was a plant, or a mole, or a double agent. The paranoia could drive a normal person crazy. It certainly did its best to make Malene berserk. She would have appreciated a little trust, even just a smidgen.

"Have a seat." Emmett gestured toward the impressive deep-brown leather guest chair.

Emmett had some of the best furnishings in the Agency. He had to. He never knew when the director, a five-star general, or the president would stop by. Malene had picked out most of them herself. The Agency couldn't trust an outside design firm with the details or layout of Emmett's office. Loose lips and all. And people willing to take payoffs.

Emmett wore an immaculately tailored suit that fit his sleek, athletic frame as if it had been made for him. And it had been. She'd designed and ordered it herself. It was darn good work.

Today Emmett looked every inch the government professional, a politician, the boss—handsome and stately. Which was her intended effect when she'd designed the suit. Emmett could appear any way he chose. He was also one of the world's finest masters of disguise.

Malene tried to digest what it meant that he was looking bosslike this morning. Did that bode ill, or not?

Not, she decided. If he looked too friendly, it meant he was up to something. Always be suspicious if the boss offered you a drink as soon as you walked in. If he appeared too sympathetic, it meant he had bad news to relate. Bosslike couldn't possibly mean anything other than he had an exciting assignment for her, something to be taken seriously. She was Emmett's go-to cover-life girl. Maybe it even meant a raise. She'd been doing some fine work this past year. She was due one soon.

She sat and relaxed into the plush, buttery leather of the wingback chair.

"A high-priority job's come up," Emmett said without preamble. "I need my best personnel on it."

Malene clasped her hands in her lap and smiled back at him. "I'm your woman." She certainly was. She wasn't vain, but she wasn't falsely modest, either. She worked hard and excelled at what she did—she was quite simply the best.

Emmett gave her a half-smile and cleared his throat. "I appreciate your enthusiasm and loyalty, but let me give you a piece of advice—never agree to a deal until you've heard the details, large and small."

"Read the fine print, right. Got it." She felt duly chastised, but it didn't kill her enthusiasm. She'd accept no matter what.

"I need absolute subjectivity and impartiality for this job," he said, peering at her piercingly. "You've always been a consummate professional. I've never had any complaints there. But I know better than anyone there's a limit to a person's ability to remain impartial where emotions are involved. Personally, I have my doubts about whether you'll be able to separate your personal from your professional life during this project." He sighed and shrugged. "But I'm up against it.

"I'll understand your objections completely, and allow you to withdraw your agreement. No black marks on your record." His eyes twinkled with tease.

Malene was smart enough to know there'd be no way to decline, but she listened politely as a sick feeling settled in her stomach. Personal from private? That didn't sound good. Not at all.

"I'd like you to think it over and give my proposal a fair shot. As head of the department, it falls under your jurisdiction. You'll ultimately be in charge, but you'd have a little distance. But I'd like, I need, your personal hand in this. *If* you think you can handle it." He ran his hand through his salt-and-pepper hair as if he was struggling with his decision.

But Malene knew the boss too well to be fooled. He'd just issued a challenge—one he was certain he'd win.

She was on extreme alert now. What was the chief hinting at? Tate was about the only thing that would sour her on an assignment. *Oh, damn.*

"With Kendra out on maternity leave, I know you're swamped. Her absence is partly why I'm asking you to attend to this matter yourself."

Emmett was usually direct. Malene grew distinctly anxious, and that sick feeling turned into a roiling knot, as he hedged. The mention of Kendra also made her sit up straighter. Since Malene had divorced Tate over his mission-related infidelity, Kendra handled all his cover-life needs. Not that there were many—Tate never went undercover as anything other than himself—Tate Cox, software guru, son of deceased Senator Burrell Cox and wealthy socialite Lenora Andrews Cox, and international playboy.

Heaven knows there was a time or two when Malene had been itching to get her hands on one of his assignments.

For one, Tate got some of the most interesting missions in the Agency. And two, well, she wasn't usually a vindictive woman, not where anyone but Tate was concerned. But she wouldn't have minded a little bit of good fun and innocent revenge for the emotional travails he'd put her through during their marriage. These days they were cordial, polite, distant, with an underlying sense of seething when their paths crossed. What would it hurt to mix things up a bit?

She knew all the little ways to make him squirm and she wasn't above using them. Emmett, however, had been sharp enough never to give her the opportunity. Until now? This must be important stuff.

"This must be Tate's mission." Though her heart raced, she tried to remain calm, and sound almost bored. "He doesn't usually present much of a challenge for my artists."

Emmett laughed. "Ah, but this time he's taken on a rather unique, and extremely dangerous, situation."

"That's so like Tate." So she'd been right to be leery.

Emmett picked up a wooden puzzle cube and rolled it in his palm. "Careful what you say. Objectivity, remember? This could be a career-maker for you. A mission so delicate, there will be a rare amount of active fieldwork involved."

Fieldwork? Now he really had her attention. As long as she wouldn't be looking down the barrel of anything stronger than a beer . . .

"I need someone nimble and adaptable. Someone who thinks on the fly. Someone with connections all over Britain and Europe. Someone whose presence won't arouse suspicion."

Malene took a deep breath. "What has Tate done now?"

Emmett raised a brow at her skeptical question.

Malene was Kendra's supervisor. She knew a great deal more than most people about the trouble Tate could get into.

"An enemy agent has apparently fallen in love with him. So she claims."

"What!" She recovered from her shock quickly and shook her head and laughed. "Poor thing."

She could handle this. She hoped. Where Tate was concerned, she still had a decent amount of unreasonable, unfathomable jealousy. "Well, it's not the first time. He can turn on the charm when he wants to."

She didn't really feel much sympathy for this poor, vulnerable, "loses her heart too easily" foreign agent who'd fallen for Tate's act. "I'm guessing Nicole isn't too thrilled about this news."

Tate had been dating Nicole Arceneau, a French actress, for the past six months. Malene had heard rumors Tate was thinking of marrying her, mostly from their five-year-old daughter, Kayla, who guilelessly spilled her daddy's secrets. He'd never mentioned it when he'd picked Kayla up for one of his custodial visits. But then, he and Malene never talked much. It was more of a "grab the kid and dash" situation.

Malene didn't relish sharing Kayla with Nicole. If she had her way, Tate would remain single until Kayla was grown. She didn't need an evil stepmother interfering with her parenting. It was bad enough she had Tate to contend with.

"Didn't you hear?" Emmett said a little too casually. "Nicole broke it off. Rather suddenly. She's taken up with a French director and eloped." Emmett grinned. "Guess she chose career over pleasure."

Malene was stunned. Why hadn't she heard? She was supposed to be in the intelligence business.

For the past week, Tate had been in town between assignments. He'd had Kayla with him several days and she hadn't spilled a word about his breakup. Usually her five-year-old would blab news like that to her the minute Tate dropped her off. She wondered what he'd bribed her with and why the media hadn't picked up the story.

"Actresses can be fickle. Tate must be heartbroken." Served him right. Then she felt herself grinning. One bad stepmother avoided.

Emmett shook his head. "He bounces back quickly."

That was true, too. But she had the feeling Emmett was teasing her, either that or trying to get an obtuse point across. "When did this big breakup happen?"

"A month ago, while he was still in Monte Carlo. We've had a hell of a time keeping it under wraps."

That explained things. Malene frowned. Sneaky bastard. She really *was* out of things. She made a mental note to get some new internal informants and either teach Kayla how to pry better or outbribe Tate for the intel her daughter was keeping from her.

"And now he's taken up with this foreign agent on the rebound? As much as he loves women, that doesn't sound like Tate. He'd never purposely date the opposition unless it's his mission."

She hadn't heard about this new love affair, either. Or mission, if that's what it was—a way to infiltrate the enemy camp and get human intelligence, humint? As she knew all too well, Tate wasn't above prostituting himself for a mission. But she still should have heard about it.

She hated to ask the next question. "And by enemy agent, I assume you mean RIOT?"

The Revolutionary International Organization of Terrorists was NCS's main adversary. A group of terrorists bent on creating worldwide anarchy and ultimately installing their leader, Archibald Random, as grand poobah and supreme leader of the world. Random had a genius

IQ and some days seemed unstoppable. His terrorist network included organizations from street gangs to the Mafia and Al Queda. Each group acted in their own interests, but ultimately he controlled them. He also had his own team of spies and personnel who worked directly for him.

Tate, and therefore Malene, always wondered whether these groups knew they were expendable to Random. Random was a terroristic genius, strategically minded in a frightening and accomplished way.

Emmett nodded. "Yes, RIOT, of course. And it *will* be his mission."

She sighed heavily. "I'm confused. You'd better give me the mission details. And not to contradict your authority, Chief, but are you sure sending Tate out to date the enemy is a good idea? He falls in love so easily." She couldn't keep the bitterness out of her voice. "The last thing I need is to share custody of Kayla with Tate and his evil RIOT mistress."

Nicole was starting to look pretty good in comparison. Damn that French director.

Emmett gave her a crooked smile. "That's why I need you for this job. Tate has to seduce this young woman and convince her to come to our side—without losing his heart in the process. I need you along riding roughshod to make sure the mission goes as planned.

"You're extremely valuable to the Agency and know too much about too many Agency operations. If the terrorists got hold of you . . ." He shrugged. "It's dangerous to send a senior official like you into the field. Under normal circumstances, I'd avoid it."

Oh, boy, Malene thought. She didn't like the sound of this at all. "Let me get this straight—you want me to stop Tate from falling in love with a RIOT agent who's in love with him? What makes you think I have any influence over him?"

Emmett shrugged again. "I'm not sure you do, but you have something more powerful—a vested interest in the outcome. And that's the best I can shoot for right now. You're my best hope."

She pursed her mouth to one side and made a look of doubt. "Hope you're not betting on this one, Chief. The odds are long."

Emmett laughed. "But the payout will be tremendous. I'd bet on a mamma bear protecting her cub any day."

Malene couldn't help smiling back. He had a point. "Okay, give me the details—how has this woman fallen in love with him? When did they meet? What's the plan?"

"That's the crazy thing—they haven't met."

"What?"

Emmett nodded. "She worked as a clerk in RIOT's records department while completing her Ph.D. in mathematics and fell in love with his picture, the surveillance videos of him, and his dossier when she came across it."

Malene was taken aback and let her surprise show. She didn't know what was worse—a girl mooning over Tate, or the fact that RIOT had a dossier on him and Emmett seemed unconcerned. Maybe the dossier shouldn't have surprised her. Tate had dealt RIOT some heavy blows over the years; of course they'd be watching him. A man as handsome and outgoing as Tate wasn't easily overlooked, she grudgingly admitted to herself.

"Really? She fell in love with his picture, like a groupie, or a stalker fan? Spies have them?" It gave her the creeps thinking of some girl kissing Tate's picture good night.

Emmett nodded. "Something like that, though I'm guessing it was more like looking at points of compatibility on an online dating site. Sophia is a sharp girl. Has a high IQ. She's sized up Tate's dossier and seems to think he can save her. Or, at least, he's her best chance."

"That's not love. That's a schoolgirl crush. Tate's good enough looking, but, really? How old is she?"

"Twenty-four."

Too young, Malene thought, with a tinge of jealousy even though she hadn't a clue as to what this girl looked like. She could be a two-bagger for all Malene knew. But Malene was thirty-three, the same age as Tate. And irrationally, she didn't like the competition of youth.

"Well, her youth and inexperience certainly show, falling in love with a picture and a dossier persona." She shook her head. "What does she want?"

"She wants to defect from RIOT, escape and start a new life."

Malene fought to keep her jaw from dropping. "Is she completely crazy? *No one* escapes from RIOT. They'll send their death squad after her. SMASH has a one hundred percent kill rate. She understands that?"

This was going from bad to worse. She *really* didn't need Tate falling in love with someone who had SMASH on her tail.

Emmett nodded. "She's a mathematician. She knows all too well the odds she'll survive in the long run are incredibly stacked against her. But she's also desperate. Sophia's not a RIOT agent. Not a spy. She's a civilian who works for them. And she had no choice in that.

"Her parents got involved with RIOT when she was two. They were true believers in RIOT's cause and involved her in their activities from the beginning. Indoctrinated her. She grew up not knowing any other kind of life or belief system existed. From the time she was a toddler she was in too deep to escape.

"She grew up, went to college, got a doctorate in mathematics at the tender age of twenty-two, and was moved from the records department by Random to join RIOT's elite encryption team.

"But the more she saw of the operations, the more her conscience struck her. She realized she was on the wrong side, the side of evil. She couldn't leave as long as her father was still alive. She has no siblings and her mother died when she was ten. Her dad just passed away two months ago, freeing her to risk escaping from RIOT's Soviet-like grip.

"She came across Tate's files during the course of her work in college. Saw how many times he was suspected of thwarting RIOT's plans, and knew that if anyone could help her, Tate was the guy. She developed a sort of hero worship. She's been in love with Tate for some time."

Malene shook her head, resisting doing a lot of tut-tutting. "She missed a key point of compatibility—she must not have noticed Tate's an only child, too. There's a combo rife with the potential for disaster and head-butting. One of the absolute worst birth order combos. Never marry an only child."

Malene let out a breath, wishing she hadn't made that mistake, she with her training in psychology. And further wishing her daughter wasn't an only. She planned to find the right man and rectify that, make a sibling for Kayla. "The little darlings think they're the center of the world, always want to take charge, and haven't a clue about how to deal with the opposite sex. Not in the long run. I can only imagine the horror of two of them trying to get along."

"Her full name is Sophia Ramsgate. Her mother was Swedish. Her dad a good old American mutt, an expat who preferred Sweden and England to the good old U.S. of A. Sophia grew up in Sweden and Great Britain." Emmett grinned and turned his laptop around for Malene to see.

A stunning twenty-four-year-old beauty with deep blue eyes, lush blond hair, and a figure to die for, smiled out at her. A femme fatale of just the type to catch Tate's eye.

Malene involuntarily gasped. Was it just her imagination, or did Sophia look like a younger, prettier, more glamorous version of herself?

"She's certainly . . . Tate's type," she said slowly, frowning. It seemed a little too opportune to Malene that a sexy woman practically designed to catch Tate's eye suddenly wanted his help escaping from RIOT. She latched on to her professional control and spoke dryly. "RIOT does realize that Tate and I ended badly?"

Emmett cocked a brow and laughed. "You see the resemblance, too."

Malene was glad she wasn't the only one. "It's hard not to. If only I'd been that gorgeous." She shook her head.

She wasn't begging for a compliment and the chief didn't give her one.

"Don't let her looks now fool you—like I said, she's smart. In the last six months she's sexed herself up and made her looks over to attract Tate." Emmett hit a button on his laptop and brought up a photo of a slightly younger Sophia—plain, but with good bone structure, no makeup, bad haircut, unstylish, baggy clothes, unflattering glasses, and a few pounds overweight. Certainly not the svelte, toned creature from the first picture of her he'd shown Malene. "This is her a year ago. She's been following his career for years. She knows what kind of women Tate likes. Why wouldn't she give herself the best chance of success?"

Mal frowned at the before shot of Sophia. "Has *she* remade herself? Or has RIOT done it for her? That's an exceptionally professional makeover. In my expert opinion, too professional." She looked at the chief. "I smell a setup. You don't think this is all just a little too convenient, that Sophia is simply too tempting a treat for Tate to resist? What are the odds?"

She stared at her boss. The Agency wouldn't risk helping a young woman escape from RIOT out of the goodness of their hearts.

His grin deepened. "I appreciate your concern. We all feel the potential for a setup. But what would RIOT gain? We've checked her out thoroughly and her story holds water."

"And?"

"In exchange for exfiltrating her successfully and providing her with a new identity and protection, she has promised to share her inner knowledge of how RIOT's encryption squad works. Their encryption techniques, their encryption philosophy, the works. With the intel she could give us, we could put a serious dent in RIOT's operations."

Malene understood the temptation for such valuable intel. But she didn't like the risk to her family. "And if she double-crosses us and feeds us false intel?"

"How? Our encryption experts will obviously check out anything she gives us before we act on it. She can't go back to RIOT. If we cut her loose, she's a dead woman."

What the chief said made sense, but Malene was still wary. "When and how do you plan to exfiltrate her?"

"RIOT is sending her to the Cheltenham Festival of Science as a guest speaker. The science festival is a big summer tourist event, half entertainment, half serious science. It's the perfect spot to make an escape. Lots of people in town and ways to blend into a crowd and assume a new identity."

Malene's heart skipped a beat. She knew all about Cheltenham. Tate had taken her on vacation there when they were dating.

"As you know, Britain's Government Communications Headquarters, GCHQ, is in Cheltenham. What else is RIOT up to? Are they trying to infiltrate Britain's top codecracking institution?" Emmett said.

"Sophia initiated contact by approaching one of our

agents in London and outlining her plan and demands. Ironically, at the Tower of London. Nice place to meet spooks, one of the most haunted places in England."

Yeah, Malene knew all about meeting spooks at the Tower. That's where she'd met Tate.

The chief winked. "She won't defect for anyone other than Tate. She has it all figured out—she wants Tate to meet her at the festival and spirit her away."

Malene frowned. She felt a lot of things about Tate, most of them distinctly not nice, but she didn't want her daughter to be fatherless at five years old. Tate had made a solemn promise he'd be around to pay for Kayla's college and walk her down the aisle, and Malene meant to hold him to it. "And Tate rushed to take this assignment, despite the risks and potential for walking straight into a trap?"

Emmett's look said everything. "You know Tate. He loves a challenge."

"And beautiful women." She shook her head. "Does the man have a death wish?" Sometimes she suspected he did—it was called a thrill-seeker gene and not a day went by when she didn't worry that he'd passed it on to Kayla. She was already showing signs . . .

"Tate thinks the payoff's worth the risk. You can see why I need my best team on this assignment," Emmett said. "Meaning you, with your vested interest in making sure Tate comes home alive with his heart intact."

"And the fact that I look like Sophia." Malene knew how the chief's mind worked. "I can go along with Tate with my authentic paperwork and simply switch identities with her, allowing her to escape on my passport with Tate while I disappear."

The chief just smiled. "What do you say?"

"How are you going to sell this "take your ex-wife on assignment" to Tate? I'm not an agent and he doesn't need much cover-life help."

Emmett's eyes danced with malicious delight. "That's where you're mistaken—the girl is nervous about Tate's being recognized and being put under tight surveillance. She stipulated that he must spirit her away *undercover*."

Malene's heart raced with real professional excitement now. This was getting more and more interesting by the minute. Tate undercover? That was simply delicious.

"You sure know how to twist a girl's arm." Malene bit her lip and smiled to herself as one evil thought after another occurred to her. "Can I make him gay?"

That might keep him out of Sophia's bed and prevent him from falling in love with this girl. She really didn't like the vision of Kayla walking down the aisle as a flower girl in Tate's wedding to a RIOT mathematical genius. Or the thought of seeing the beautiful babies Tate and Sophia would make.

Emmett laughed. "I already said Tate's job is to seduce her. Hard to do if he's gay. Sophia's expecting a charmer, even if he is undercover."

Malene shrugged. It had been worth a try. "But you will let me torture him a little?"

"No torturing. I can't afford to have him distracted in the slightest."

"He's going to be distracted no matter what we do. You're absolutely no fun sometimes, Chief." Against orders, or not, she was going to dress Tate in the itchiest wool sweater she could find. Wool irritated Tate's skin. Other than in a suit, he never wore it.

Tate had a lot of itches she planned to interfere with, including an insatiable sexual appetite. For now, wool would have to suffice as her weapon of choice.

"You'll take the assignment?" Emmett said. "You'll have to be away from Kayla on location in Great Britain until we have Sophia safely hidden away."

"Do I have a choice?" She smiled back at Emmett's

smug smile. He knew he'd won. The thought of fieldwork and creating a cover life for Tate was simply too enticing. And messing with Tate and saving him from himself? The thrill of that went without saying.

"I'll do it. Mom will take Kayla. She loves having her." She bit her lip and shook her head. "The things a mother does for child and country."

Emmett laughed. "I need you to get on it immediately."

Malene nodded. "Sure thing, Chief. What do you have in mind? What's my cover story?"

The chief arched a brow. "Don't you mean Tate's?"

"No, mine. I've never had one before. Mine's going to be a lot more fun."

CHAPTER TWO

Tate sat in Dulles International Airport, outside the security check, waiting for his ex-wife, Mal, to arrive. They were traveling together to Cheltenham, England, as mathematics professor Tate Stevens, Ph.D., and his trusty graduate student and research assistant sidekick, Mallie Green.

What the hell had Emmett been thinking assigning her as his cover-life artist for this mission? And insisting she go into the field with him—lunacy. First of all, Tate worked alone. He certainly didn't need Mal, or any woman, for that matter, tagging along to scare Sophia off. It was going to be dicey enough convincing her he was falling in love with her so he could bring her in. He didn't want to give her any reason to bolt.

Second, he and Mal got along now about as well as the Agency got along with RIOT—they generally wanted to kill each other. He blamed himself and Mal's jealous nature. He'd thought when he married her that she understood that sometimes sleeping with other women was simply part of the job.

Third, while Mal was an excellent cover-life artist, she wasn't a trained agent. Oh, she could shoot with the best of them, but a gun wasn't her most efficient weapon. No, she wielded words like a pro, cutting as efficiently as if using a stiletto. He knew—he'd been the recipient of her knife's edge too many times. He didn't want her sharp tongue anywhere near Sophia.

And last—she was a horror at math. Could barely balance a checkbook. He wasn't a math genius, but he had a degree in computer science and knew math as well as any engineer. What he didn't know, his eidetic memory would help him fake his way through. Without one, how was Mal going to convincingly play a mathematics grad student? He shuddered as he thought about how he'd have to cover for her. Could he claim she was mute?

Tate had reasoned, begged, and even pleaded with the chief to let him go solo. He didn't need a cover-life artist. He didn't do disguises when he went undercover. He was an out-in-the-open agent.

"You do this time," Emmett had said. "Our contact in London says Sophia insisted she will contact you. Not the other way around. She's nervous about being discovered and killed. Very skittish.

"You're to go to Cheltenham undercover as Dr. Tate Stevens, professor of mathematics. She specified the name. That way she'll know whom to contact. She says you're too well-known in RIOT circles as yourself. She can't be seen anywhere near you. You'll have to go undercover and in disguise."

Emmett had given him an up-and-down look and scowled. "It's too damn bad you've never taken the trouble to learn how to use a disguise. They can be extremely useful."

Emmett was a master of them.

"She also said you're to dress the part of a geek to throw RIOT off. There will be plenty of them around." Emmett shook his head. "I need you to be a sexy geek. There's no way you can carry that off without help. Malene's your only hope."

Tate had sighed deeply and resisted pounding the arm of the chair he sat in. "Let her pack me a bag, but does she have to come with?"

"She does. She's your master of disguise in case things go wrong and you need to escape without attracting notice. Malene can get you new IDs, new costumes, new identities by wiggling her little finger. You need her on-site this time." Emmett looked amused at Tate's discomfort.

The chief was well aware of why Tate's marriage to Mal had failed. This mission was like rubbing it in her face and Tate knew it.

"Then assign someone else for the fieldwork. *Anyone else*. Call Kendra back from her mommy leave. Tell her I need her. Offer to give her a nice bonus, whatever it takes."

"And be slapped with a lawsuit?" Emmett's eyes twinkled. "She's not leaving her weeks-old baby to dash off to England, no matter what I offer her. I can guarantee that.

"This is a delicate operation. I need my best personnel on it and Malene is it. Besides, her resemblance to Sophia plays in our favor."

Tate had scowled. It was hard to argue with the chief's points. "How am I supposed to seduce a twenty-four-year-old RIOT agent with Mal watching my every move?"

"I doubt she'll be watching you *that* closely." Emmett had laughed. "Learn how to use a disguise. And maybe next time I'll think about letting you go solo." And then Emmett had dismissed him, sending him to research and development to pick up his gizmos.

Tate had an uneasy feeling about this whole operation and setup. He believed in his sex appeal—he had as healthy a male ego as the next guy—but a college girl falling in love with his picture and file? It seemed a little *too* fantastic to him. It could happen, he supposed. But he didn't trust RIOT. Were they behind this? And if so, what mayhem did they have up their sleeve?

The brass and intel and data crunchers at Langley had run through all the intelligence and data. Done thorough background checks. Sophia checked out in every regard. Her father *had* recently passed away. It was the perfect time to break away and escape RIOT's death grip on her life.

If she was genuine, she was still taking a horrendous chance with her life. RIOT's assassin squad, SMASH, would track her down and kill her no matter how long it took. She could live to be one hundred and they wouldn't give up. Was a life spent in constant fear of discovery worth living?

On the other hand, constant fear pretty much described a life in RIOT's service. Maybe it was a wash.

However, if she *was* part of a plot by RIOT, what could they be up to? If they wanted him dead, it was easy enough to send a SMASH assassin to take him out. They didn't need to lure him out with a girl. He knew intelligence secrets, true, but nothing he could think of that could be seduced out of him by a woman. They'd have to torture them out of him, and again, sending SMASH to kidnap him seemed like a more efficient plan. Neither he, nor Emmett, nor any of the heads of departments could think of a reason to send a girl to get to him.

Tate could have refused the assignment. Emmett gave him every opportunity to turn it down, had even tried to talk him out of it. But the opportunity to bring in such a valuable informant, one who could open up RIOT's entire encrypting algorithm, was too tempting to pass up.

"Tate!"

Hearing his name being called startled him out of his thoughts. He looked up to see Mal wheeling a suitcase the size of a small travel trailer behind her. Seeing her, he felt his heart stop. When it banged back into action, it beat infuriatingly fast.

She was dressed casually in a tight-fitting dark denim miniskirt, thick, opaque tights, ankle-high brown leather boots with a low heel, a cream blouse, a long, loopy gold necklace, and a reddish-orange military-style jacket with gold buttons and leather trim. Her blond hair fell in loose waves around her face. Her makeup was light, fresh, and natural looking. Except for her lips, which were deep red-brown, moist and glossy, the very look and color he found so hot. The way they'd looked when they first met. Mal had the most kissable, perfect mouth—full and lush, with a delicate bow in the middle. She looked as if she was still in college herself. One of the hot college girls all the guys chased. Why hadn't Emmett commanded her to de-emphasize her looks, to shoot for dowdy?

Now *he* was going to have to tell her to tone it down and give her the satisfaction of thinking he wasn't over her. And maybe that was the truth. Maybe he wasn't. Hell, he didn't know. He'd been trying to get over her since she'd thrown him out after discovering his infidelity. Lately, he'd grown tired of playing around. Even his affair with Nicole had been an attempt at finding someone to settle down with again. But when she'd left him for the French director, he'd been more relieved than upset.

Damn his body for reacting to Mal. He wasn't prepared for the impact a college-age Mal made on him. She looked so much like she had when they first met. More updated college style, but still as young and tempting.

He tried not to scowl. Mal was the queen of putting together disguises and cover-life personas. She could have downplayed her looks and gone for major nerd, too. But she'd let her pride get the best of her.

"Traveling light, I see." He stood as she approached.

She arched a brow, which transformed her into a cynical

thirty-three-year-old. Thank goodness. His attraction evaporated. It was easier to keep his distance this way. If he was already reacting to her, what would he do when they reached Cheltenham, the site of their first romantic vacation together?

"Nice to see you, too, Dr. Stevens." Mal leaned in and whispered to him, "Stop daydreaming and pay attention. We're supposed to be undercover already.

"I called out to Dr. Stevens three times and only got your attention when I used your first name."

"What can I say? I'm an absentminded prof. And I just decided—we're casual at the university. First-name basis only." He cut her off. He didn't want her arguing.

"Works for me, Tate. Especially since we're supposed to be lovers going on vacation together. Just thought we were keeping it on the down low around home. Isn't that part of the cover dossier? Have you even read it?" She took him in with the look of a tailor eyeing her work. Finally she shrugged and smiled, obviously pleased with herself. "You look good in nerd glasses and three-day growth."

He appreciated not having to shave regularly. But he had perfect vision. He didn't need the damn heavy black plastic-rimmed glasses. The frames interfered with his field of vision. He wouldn't have worn them at all, but the tech department had outfitted them with a concealed camera and rearview capability that made them halfway acceptable.

"Where's your bag?" she asked. "Have you checked in already?" She smiled sweetly.

She'd picked out his suitcase, bought everything in it, packed it, and had it delivered to his place minutes before he had to leave for the airport. Worse yet—she'd locked and booby-trapped it so he wouldn't tamper with it. There was no trust in the Agency. He pulled his luggage receipt from his pocket and waved it for her to see.

"Good. Now you can help me with my suitcase. It's too heavy for me to lift onto the scale. I have our . . . research materials inside." She wheeled it toward the check-in stand.

Tate followed her. He could hardly imagine all the torturous things she had in there. He was certain she was going to try to exact some kind of revenge on him for any number of perceived slights over the years.

They walked up to the check-in counter. "Tate? Would you?" She nodded toward the backbreaker she called a suitcase.

He sighed and hefted the behemoth onto the scale. The bag weighed more than it should have, even given its size. He hoped R & D hadn't given her anything too dangerous.

The casual leather laptop bag he had slung over his shoulder housed a host of goodies. Two magazines of bullets were sewn into a clever hidden and shielded compartment. He also had a stash of gold coins and currency of various kinds in the false bottom. The handle contained two lethal ceramic fighting knives. And, of course, he had his laptop, iPad, and iPod, along with an assortment of bugs and listening devices.

The baggage handler weighed Mal's bag and charged her for the overage. Within a few minutes she was finished checking in and they were on their way to the security checkpoint. Tate had a special air marshal waiver to get him through security. Mal was on her own.

They were supposed to be undercover, but as they walked side by side toward security, he had to ask about Kayla, innocuously, of course. "How's the kid?"

"Great. She's with my mom for the duration."

Tate frowned. "Yeah, I heard."

He leaned in and whispered in her ear at an angle none of the security cameras could catch to read his lips. "My mom wasn't happy. She'd like her turn. Kay's her only grandchild, probably stay that way. The least you could do is let her see Kayla once in a while. Take her off your hands for a few days. She and your mom could share."

Tate was an expert at reading microexpressions, tiny involuntary muscle movements that gave away emotions. Though Mal looked calm enough to the casual observer, she was pissed.

"You divorced me, not Mom," he said.

Mal looked at him and rolled her eyes. "I wish. When I divorced you, I was hoping to be done with that witch."

"Hey." Tate grabbed her arm and stopped, pulling her around to face him. He was sure there were no cameras that could catch what they were saying. "Show a little respect. Kay and I are all the family Mom has. All she wants is a little time with her."

Mal's eyes narrowed. She glared at him. "And to turn her against me.

"I'm always the bad guy. The girl who stole her little boy from her. The evil villain who keeps her from her granddaughter."

"If she showed me some respect, I'd show her some. As it is, she's threatening to petition the court for visitation rights. I suppose you put her up to that?"

He ran his hands through his hair. His mother could be a handful. She always had been. She and Mal had never gotten along, which put him in a horrible bind in the middle. "I tried to talk her out of that."

Mal shot him a look that said she didn't believe him.

He *had* tried. "I did."

"Dr. Stevens, you say the most amusing things." A look of hurt swept across her face. Then she pinched his cheek and kept walking.

Damn, he didn't want to fight with her. He'd never wanted to fight with her. But she never understood that he'd promised his dad he'd take care of his mother, no matter what. And he'd never understood the rivalry between his mom and Mal. His mom was one of their irreconcilable differences.

He couldn't fight with Mal now even if he had wanted to. In their cover story, Dr. Tate Stevens and Mallie Green got along famously, were a real team, and were engaging in a sizzling secret affair. He had to hustle to get back in step with her.

"Yeah, I'm a real card."

They reached the security line.

"This is where we part company." She smiled sweetly at him.

He wondered whether there was any way he could rig the security screening so she failed.

"Don't even think about it," she said as if she'd read his mind. "I have Emmett on speed dial and permission to use his red phone number."

Shit.

"See you on the other side." She winked at him and joined the line.

That woman was enjoying this way too much. He wondered what delights she'd filled his suitcase with. He knew that gleam in her eyes and it meant trouble—for him.

CHAPTER THREE

Tate nestled into his business-class seat with its luxurious twenty-two inches of space and cocooning privacy walls, which mercifully shielded him from his ex-wife in the next seat over. He was used to first class, but business class would have to do. Fortunately, the Agency had a policy of sending agents business class on overseas flights. Given that they were living the right cover life, of course.

The famous spy Dusko Popov, the model for James Bond, had it right when he'd said that a spy lives the life of his cover. If your cover is a dishwasher, you wash dishes. In this case, if your cover was a dishwasher, you flew economy. As a respected professor, he flew business. As himself, international playboy, he would have traveled first class. Yes, he and Dusko had been lucky. They had the best covers imaginable—playboys and big spenders. Except when their ex-wives were tagging along with them on a mission.

Tate settled back against the memory-foam headrest. Despite what Mal might have thought, he wasn't sure, when it came right down to it, that he could prostitute himself this mission, even for his country. It was one thing to seduce beautiful women when you were attracted to them and out for some fun. It was another thing entirely to be commanded to do it. Had he slept with women for the sake of the job? Yes. But Mal hadn't been tagging along, looking over his shoulder. Despite what she believed, he'd never wanted to hurt her. He still didn't.

He adjusted his personal reading light and privacy screen. The flight attendant came by and poured him a nightcap—a nice glass of brandy.

"Would you like a bedtime snack, sir?"

He'd signed up for sleeper service, planning to get a good night's sleep and arrive refreshed for this mission. It might be the last decent night of sleep he got for several weeks.

"No, thanks. I'm fine." He held up his glass of brandy and grinned, only slightly flirtatiously.

The attractive flight attendant returned his smile. "Very good, sir. I'll return with your blankets when you're finished with your drink. Ring if you need anything."

He nodded and watched her walk off to attend the next passenger before returning to his ruminations. The truth was, Mal was the only woman among the many he'd known that he'd ever loved. Really loved and wanted to make a life with. And three years after their divorce, he was still trying to find a new love to replace Mal. Still kicking himself for losing her. For putting the job first. For not coming clean to Mal before they married about what the job might require of him.

He'd been so damn afraid of losing her. And young and naïve enough to think he could hide it from her. The day she threw him out, she'd screamed at him that the lies had hurt the most. That he should have trusted her with the truth.

If only that damn Italian socialite, he couldn't even remember her name at the moment, hadn't gotten jealous and sent Mal evidence of his one-night stand with her. He would have been a dead man if he hadn't had sex with her. So would have several other agents he'd been protecting, and a major covert military operation thwarted. But losing his marriage was a hell of a price to pay.

Tate knew about, and even privately laughed at, the idea that he fell in love easily. Yes, sure, he fell into flirtations easily. But love? He'd thought about proposing to Nicole. Had even been happy to let the rumors float about that he was going to. But he hadn't been heartbroken when she'd left him for that director. His pride had been wounded, some. And he was lonely again. But mostly he was relieved and his heart was remarkably intact. Only Mal had ever been able to smash it and there were times when he believed she'd done irreparable damage. He seemed patently unable to ever truly love again.

He had himself to blame. The breakup of their marriage had been his fault. He'd always been ambitious. Mal, with her obvious ties to the Agency, cramped his spying style.

Emmett had recruited him at eighteen, at his father's urging, just after he graduated from high school. Dear old dad wanted him to follow in his spying footsteps and Tate had been game for the experience. He knew the rules—you don't fall in love and get married. And at eighteen, when marriage seemed almost a repulsive idea, something an old man did, he was happy to accept them.

His dad complained bitterly of the problems of maintaining a happy wife and child and keeping them safe while living the life of intrigue. Of keeping a marriage on solid ground when traveling so much and keeping secrets from his wife. Of being limited in the kinds of covers he could use. Like Tate, he'd used his real-life job as his cover, until he'd been elected to the Senate, when he'd had to take a hiatus. Tate's mother had never known that either he, or Dad, were spies. She still didn't.

But all the fatherly warnings and knowing the rules

hadn't stopped Tate's twenty-year-old heart from giving itself to Mal, from naïvely thinking that if she worked for the Agency, too, there would be no objections to their marriage, no secrets between them, no problems. It had been a brilliant, if doomed, plan. And sometimes, he was still amazed at his powers of persuasion to talk Mal into it. At other times, he felt guilty for diverting her from her dreams and the fame and fortune she could, and should, have had.

So, yes, he'd chosen career over Mal and Kayla. But only because he'd thought he could have it all. If given the choice again?

Mal sighed as she relaxed into her seat and sipped her preflight champagne. What was she doing on a mission with Tate? Why was she tormenting herself? To protect Kayla, sure, but . . .

She hadn't expected him to look so good. She'd even given him glasses. Not just because it would annoy him, or because glasses were all the rage among the nerd crowd. Many guys with perfect vision wore them with empty frames or plain glass lenses as a fashion statement. She'd given him glasses hoping they would make him less attractive, not just to her, but to this reckless girl, Sophia.

But Malene was too good for her own good. She'd picked out the glasses without even looking at a photo of Tate. She knew his face, every inch of his perfect bone structure, from memory—the strong curve of his jaw, the plane of his cheekbones, the depth, shape, and exact shade of brown of his eyes, the swarthy tone of his skin, the perfect oval of his face, and that dark stubble that used to scrub her face when he kissed her—

Stop that, she scolded herself. She was trying to think of Tate as unattractive, not remember the sexy times they'd had and what an excellent kisser he was.

She blew out another breath, reached for her cocktail napkin, and dabbed her lips. She looked at the lip print on it and frowned—Carnelian Kiss—that was the shade of lipstick she wore, covered with a shiny coat of clear gloss. Carnelian Kiss was the color she wore when she'd first met Tate. These days she had to order it online and pay a premium price. But it was worth it. It made her feel young and powerful, luscious, and . . .

It may have been a mistake to wear it. She may have given Tate the wrong impression. What was she thinking?

And now, here she was, going back to London with him, the very city where they'd met, to help him seduce another woman, a traitorous girl barely out of college.

Remembering how she'd met Tate, she scowled, picturing Sophia's response to meeting him—pure animal attraction. Tate photographed well, but a flat picture did nothing to showcase his charm and personal magnetism. The girl would go down, hook, line, and sinker, as her grandpa liked to say.

Malene had only been twenty herself, an American student at London's Central Saint Martins College when she met Tate while visiting the Tower of London. She'd gone by herself, taken the tube. The day was sunny, blue sky. She was homesick, tired of British accents and longing for a good old American twang, drawl, or intonation as she wandered around by herself. Though why she thought she'd particularly find one at the Tower, she didn't know. It seemed as good a tourist place as any to try. Later, she thought it must have been fate. Now she thought it was fate playing a cruel joke.

She'd simply been hoping to run into a tourist from home, and by home, she meant from anywhere in the U.S. Male, female, old, young, she wasn't particular, though she was hoping for a grandmotherly type. Someone chatty and nonthreatening. She really didn't care what kind of American accent as long as the person behind it originated from one of the fifty states. Her friends still laughed at that—wasn't she enchanted by the way the Brits spoke?

Oh, she had been. For a while. But she reached a point where she needed a sound from home, the feeling of a compatriot right there with her. Someone far from home, too, and willing to laugh about it. She was tired of being an expatriate.

She walked around the Tower Green, staring up at the Queen's House, shuddering as she remembered her history—Anne Boleyn had been executed here, as well as sixteen-year-old Lady Jane Grey, the Nine Days Queen.

Not being much past sixteen, she found it hard to imagine dying, having her head lopped off, facing it bravely with dignity. How could those people of old have been so cruel? Why kill a teenager simply because her dying young cousin the king had named her his successor? That wasn't her fault. Poor thing, she'd been damned if she did and damned if she didn't take the throne. History wasn't exactly as romantic as a fairy tale. Of course, after years in the Agency, Malene had lost her innocence. People killed for much less than a threat to their power.

She was so lost in her thoughts and used to ignoring the sounds of tourists around her, she didn't hear Tate walk up on her right.

"The Queen's House is the most haunted place at the Tower." His intonation was brilliantly American. His voice young and sexy.

She felt almost rapturous, as if she'd conjured him up herself. "Oh, thank goodness! Someone from home." As she turned to look at the young man, she was thinking he'd never live up to that voice and wonderful East Coast accent of his. Really, she could have almost kissed him just because of that.

But his voice was nothing to the way he looked. Over six feet tall. Broad shoulders. Slender, but taut and fit, with enough bulk to impress. Dark brown hair. Deep brown, laughing, intelligent eyes. She fell in love in that moment. Love at first sight. Why not? She'd been primed for it.

"I call Virginia home. You don't sound like you're from there," he said, cocking a brow.

Her California-girl accent had slipped through. "Maybe I should have said, 'from the homeland.'"

"That sounds a little too Bolshevist." He looked around. "No friends with you? Family? Overprotective fathers?"

"Nope. I'm by myself."

"I hope you at least have some pepper spray on you. You really shouldn't tell strangers you're alone and vulnerable."

"Who said I'm vulnerable?" She shot him a flirtatious smile and made a girlie fist, the kind with her thumb wrapped inside, ready to get broken if she tried to smack someone. She knew better. She knew how to fight. Her brothers had taught her. She was just pulling his chain.

He laughed again. "Vicious, but that's not going to do much to scare off a ghost. You really should be careful around here. You never know when you'll run into a spook."

Her turn to look around. "What about you? Where's your entourage?"

"I was hoping you'd be it." He winked. "Anyway, don't worry about me. I can spot a spook a mile away. You'll be perfectly safe with me. How'd you like to hang out? Let me show you the Crown Jewels."

"As long as you mean *the* Crown Jewels."

"What else would I mean?"

Uh-huh.

"You could be a psychopathic serial killer," she teased back.

He shrugged. "At least I'd be a good old American

killer. You look thirsty. Let me buy you something to drink. And maybe a biscuit to go along with it."

"Please tell me you mean a cookie. I could really go for a great, big chocolate-chip cookie." And she really wanted to get to know him, and listen to that sexy American accent of his for as long as she could.

That was their start, the beginning of the end. Later, when she found out he was working for the Agency when they met that day at the Tower, she finally understood his inside joke about spooks. She'd thought at the time he was just being glib.

She also later learned that he'd been at the Tower meeting a contact. He'd been high with adrenaline after receiving some vital and privileged intelligence from a RIOT double agent.

Thinking about a chocolate-chip cookie made her stomach growl. She should have signed up for the sleeper service, as Tate had, and had dinner before they departed. But, to be honest, she hadn't even thought about it. Now, she'd have to raid the larder as soon as they took off and the captain turned off the FASTEN SEAT BELT sign.

Half an hour later, her stomach was still growling, and she got her wish. The captain's voice boomed over the passenger address system, "You're now free to roam about the cabin."

About time. They fed you pretty well in business class, but the dinner cart hadn't yet made an appearance. Malene unbuckled her seat belt, stood, and stretched. When she glanced at Tate, his chair was fully reclined flat. He wore his headphones. All of his lights were off. His blindfold was on. And he was snuggled beneath a particularly soft, comfy-looking blanket and out cold.

Curses on that man. He could sleep anywhere, just drop off in mere seconds. She, on the other hand, usually took at least half an hour to fall asleep under the best circumstances. She never slept well on planes, trains, or in cars. Trying to was practically a lost cause. She was not lulled off to dreamland by the white noise of an engine. And she couldn't afford to take a sleeping pill, which made her groggy. Tate, on the other hand, was in for a nice, long sleep until breakfast. While she'd arrive at Heathrow with bags beneath her eyes to face the beautiful, *young* Sophia.

Tate didn't so much as stir as she scooted past him on the way to the larder. He didn't look like he was on alert at all. Any old terrorist could probably walk up and off him.

She resisted sighing. *Top secret agent, my hind foot.* Now she'd have to watch his sleeping backside.

The larder, as the British liked to call a pantry or snack cupboard, was located in a middle section of the business-class cabin. It was a waist-high cupboard; a platter of fruit, cheese, and crackers sat on top. Bottled water—still and sparkling—sat next it.

Malene frowned. She needed chocolate, something sweet and sinful to take her mind off Tate and the current situation. Fruit wasn't going to do it.

A flight attendant walked by. "Not satisfied with what's out? Open the cupboard doors and help yourself. We keep all the good stuff behind closed doors." She winked and walked on.

Why not?

Malene opened the polished stainless steel doors and sighed with happiness as she caught a glimpse of an assortment of Cadbury chocolate bars, and British biscuits. And another of American junk food—chocolate bars, packages of chocolate-chip cookies, potato chips. She kneeled down to get a bird's-eye view of the selection, being careful to make sure her tiny denim skirt still covered her butt. She'd half forgotten what it was like to wear the tiny things. As she was squatting, she pulled a basket of cookies out from the shelf and a reflection in the open stainless steel cupboard door caught her attention. A man was staring at her from behind from the first row of business class behind the larder.

Malene wasn't trained in the art of surveillance, but she was observant and she'd lived with Tate long enough to pick up some of his habits. The staring man was good, not too obvious, but he was watching her all the same. The hair on the back of her neck stood up. This wasn't a "you're such a hot chick" perusal. Or an "I wonder if there are any good cookies in that cupboard?" glance. Or even a "pardon me but your slip is showing" look. This man was watching her, confidently, and he had a "thrill of the hunt" look in his eyes, from what she could tell through the skewed optics of the stainless steel door. She needed a closer look and a picture to send to HQ.

She rummaged through the basket of cookies, keeping her eyes averted as she studied the man's reflection. She pulled her phone from her skirt pocket. Malene's expertise was costuming and dressing. This man was dressed like a business traveler in jeans, a light blue dress shirt, and leather loafers. But something felt off about him.

She needed a closer look. Fortunately, a round, wrapped package of wine gums was just the tool she needed to get up close and personal with the watcher. She managed to snap a quick picture of the reflection in the door at an angle she hoped he couldn't tell what she'd done. Then she picked up a basket of candy from the shelf, tipped it in the guy's direction, and "slipped," sending several rolls of wine gums bowling toward his feet.

He stopped one with his size-thirteen loafer as she scrambled after her rolling candy on her hands and knees. A woman in the seat to his right stopped two packages and handed them to her as she crawled past her.

"Sorry." Malene winced. "Thanks! I'm such a klutz."

Her target leaned down and picked up the roll of candy just as she crawled to his feet. The nails on his beefy hand were chipped and dirty. He had a callus on the top of the first finger on his right hand between the first and second knuckle—the trigger finger. The callus was the sure sign of a practiced shooter, someone who shot high enough caliber bullets to deliver a good recoil on the rifle. The man was a sniper or she missed her guess.

As he held the candy out to her, she smiled up at him, avoiding his eyes as if she were embarrassed. "Thanks."

He grunted. "Welcome."

Huh, normally pitched male voice, neither high nor low, just average. No special accent she could peg with just the single word.

He had a full beard and mustache. It was a very convincing fake. But Malene knew her costume and stage makeup, and a fake it was.

She took the roll of candy from him and inched away, back to the larder, where she stuffed the jar back into its spot, stood, and closed the cupboard doors.

She had to talk to Tate and warn him about this guy. *Now.* Even if she had to wake him up to do it. A task she didn't relish. Tate wasn't exactly Mr. Sunshine when he first woke up.

Tate was nestled snuggly in his bed, dreaming a confused, and sensual, dream about a mission where he was assigned to seduce a college-age Mal. She wanted him to rescue her, take her away with him.

He pressed her up against the outside wall of an ancient stone tower. In a garden, with blue sky above and the sun shining warmly. Music played in the background, soft, dreamy music. His hand slid up her smooth, firm, yet incredibly soft and creamy bare thigh, beneath her tiny skirt. He used his other hand to prop himself against the wall, leaning heavily on it. His pulse raced. He wanted to take her, right there. And she was willing.

She looked up at him with passion and desire in her eyes, begging to be kissed. He lowered his lips to hers—

"Tate! Tate, wake up. I have to talk to you."

Disoriented, he squinted as he opened his eyes. Mal squatted next to him, holding his headphones away from his ear as she hissed at him.

What the hell? This wasn't the willing Mal he'd been dreaming about.

"Mal?" He frowned at her, glad his involuntary arousal was covered with a blanket. It was quickly wilting. "You better have a good reason for waking me up." And interrupting a romping round of sex with a college-age you.

"I need to talk to you."

He detected the worry beneath her calm voice. He propped up on his elbows and studied her. "So talk."

"In private."

He arched a brow. What could the woman want now? If she'd been a trained agent, she would have known to use a code phrase if this had to do with their mission.

"The only private place around here is the bathroom," he mouthed back to her.

She shrugged. "Fine with me."

He sighed, sat up straight, ran his hands through his hair, and reached into his private storage compartment and retrieved his signal jammer. He slid on his in-flight slippers and stood. "You do realize what it will look like?"

"Mile-high with my professor. I get it. Just don't get any ideas."

"After you." He followed her down the aisle to the business-class bathroom. Personally, he was impressed she hadn't flinched at his suggestion of the bathroom. She

did hesitate a moment at the door, even though the UNOC-
CUPIED sign showed.

He pushed the crease of the folding door, banging it
open, and held out his hand in that gentlemanly gesture
meaning "ladies first, after you." However, if a gesture
can be sarcastic, then his was. He was mostly impatient.

Airplane lavs, even business-class lavatories, are notori-
ously tiny. Mal stepped in, turned to face him, and backed
in as far as she could, and he still barely had room to
squeeze in. It took some jiggling and rearranging to get the
door closed. Finally, they stood breast to chest, toe to toe,
and Tate was finding things getting hard for him.

Mal had a nice pair, always had. And right now, they
were rubbing up against the thin cotton of his T-shirt. She
looked so young and sweet, so almost vulnerable and in
need of protection. So tantalizing. So much like she had
in the dream she'd woken him from, the one he was still
trying to shake. Why did dreams have to hang on and feel
so real? Why couldn't he shake the emotions he'd felt—
the desire and need?

He looked into her steely eyes, and even their hardness
and the fear he saw didn't cool his ardor, though it should
have.

She opened her mouth to speak. He held up a hand to
silence her and activated his signal jammer. When he was
satisfied it was working, he nodded for her to go ahead.
"This had better be good," he whispered.

She frowned slightly. "Would I pull you out of a deep
sleep if it weren't?"

"You really want an answer?" She would definitely have
woken him if she'd known what he was dreaming about.
Hell, he would have woken himself. If dreams really do
reveal subconscious desires, he was in deep trouble.

She grinned. For just a second, she was that girl from

his dreams. "If you hadn't been out of it and totally vulnerable, you would have noticed—we have a tail."

"What?"

"There's a bearded guy in business class just behind the larder in seat 6A. He's dressed like a business traveler, but the beard is a fake and so is he. He's been watching me."

Tate pursed his lips. "You're wearing a short skirt and look like a college girl, of course he's watching you."

"Flattery will get you nowhere." She took a deep breath. "Didn't you hear what I said—the beard's fake and this isn't Halloween. It's a very good fake, too, not many people besides an expert would notice. Now, why would a man be wearing a fake beard if not to be able to lose it and make a quick escape unnoticed?"

She had a point. "You mean like after he's committed a heinous crime?"

She nodded. "He's an assassin—"

"Wait a minute. Fake beard to assassin, that's a huge leap in logic—"

"He has a callus on the outside of the first finger of his right hand between the first and second knuckle."

"Damn."

The plane hit a small pocket of turbulence. Just enough to bounce Mal's breasts and distract Tate from clear thinking. He and Mal had always had chemistry. That had never been their problem. Until now. There was no way he was giving her any ideas about how attractive he still found her.

Mal let out a cute little squeak, and arched back and grabbed the counter for support. Which had the effect of pushing her breasts more firmly against his chest.

"What are we going to do? What if we've already been discovered? Should we call Emmett and abort—"

"Are you crazy? No aborting." He had to think fast.

Mal pulled her phone from her pocket and turned the screen toward him. "Recognize this guy? Is he one of your RIOT buddies?"

Tate studied it for a while. "Is this his reflection in a pantry door?"

Mal nodded.

Tate frowned. "Not from these distorted optics. But I like the fake beard. Wouldn't mind one myself."

She rolled her eyes. "Be serious—what's our next move?"

He was thinking fast. "I'm going to have to get rid of him."

Her eyes went wide. "You're going to kill him?"

He sighed. "You know what I do for a living."

She shook her head. "Don't mistake me for squeamish. I know what all our agents do. I've enabled you to do it. I'd agree with that course of action if we had more definite data. But what if I'm wrong? What if he's really an innocent air marshal traveling undercover?"

"Then why would he be watching you? You don't exactly fit the profile for a terrorist."

She bit her lip. Apparently, she had no answer.

He shook his head. "Look. I'm going to disable him for a while is all. Search him. See if he's sent off any damning evidence. Find out what he's about, and send him on a ride somewhere so we can escape without him following us."

She nodded just as the aircraft hit another patch of turbulence, throwing her into Tate and slamming them both against the closed door. In the next instant, the plane pitched in the opposite direction, tossing him into her, and the FASTEN SEAT BELT sign lit up. She landed on her butt on the closed toilet seat with him perched over her.

Her breasts were heaving. Her lips moist. Her eyes wide. Her legs spread and her skirt hiked up. She looked exactly as she had when they'd been young and fallen in love. Tate swallowed hard, trying to fight off the memories and the way his body was reacting to hers. He'd had other women during these past three years. None of them had turned him on as she had, though he'd never admit that to her. He barely admitted it to himself.

He and Mal had been wild, unable to keep their hands off each other, making love in all kinds of crazy, dangerous places. Doing it on an airplane had been on their sexual bucket list. He wondered whether she remembered and if she'd be game for checking that one off the list—for old time's sake.

This was the perfect setup to join the mile-high club, and damn, with those memories assaulting him and the aura of danger in the air, it was taking every ounce of restraint he had to resist her. The turbulence only added to the thrill and the challenge. Hell, wasn't turbulently the only way they'd made love those last months together, anyway?

The plane dropped suddenly. Mal seemingly rose in the air to meet him as he was flung upward toward the ceiling. Her eyes were wide and her pupils dilated. She was either hot for him, or afraid. Maybe both. "Brace yourself."

CHAPTER FOUR

They came down with a clunk, landing on the toilet seat, Tate sprawled over Mal. She braced her hands against his chest. *Nice,* he thought. Until she spoke.

"Off!" Mal shoved him with the strength of a black belt.

He grinned at her futile efforts, but he wasn't taking any chance she'd use her infamous karate chop on him. He pushed off her and leaned back against the lav door. "Okay, here's the plan. You leave the lav first before we hit any additional turbulence, go back to your seat and buckle in for safety. I'll go disable the bad guy. We'll rendezvous when our would-be assassin is out and the turbulence has passed." Like the turbulence between them would ever pass. "Sound good?"

"Peachy. Just watch yourself. Turbulence can be deadly. And messy. I imagine there's a lot of spilled milk, coffee, and liquor out there."

I'm facing a hard-core, hardened RIOT assassin, and she's worried about atmospheric instability. How sweet.

He opened the lav door and let her out, closing it behind her and staring at himself in the mirror. Damn, his eyes were dilated beneath the clear glass lenses of the glasses that were purely for show. They may have made him look intellectual, but he hated them all the same. He wasn't a bookish kind of guy. Or nerdy, even though he was a software guru.

He ran his hands through his hair and pursed his lips as he thought. The damnable thing about airplanes was there were very few places to commit murder, or even mere disabling and hiding of an inert body, in secret, out of plane view. *Oh, nice pun, Tate. Corny, but what the hell?*

He pulled his cell phone out, brought up a CIA airplane app, one his company, Cox Software, had created, and called up the layout and specs of the particular airplane they rode on.

Oh, nice, there's a beverage cart dumbwaiter from the galley to the cargo area. Perfect way to dispose of a body. If that bastard out there really is RIOT, he deserves to be in the cargo area with the dogs. And Mal can rest easy. He'll eventually be discovered.

Now all Tate had to do was get to the galley and lure his tail there. Turbulence played into his hand in at least one way—the flight attendants would be buckled into their jump seats and out of Tate's way.

Hmmm . . . If this guy really is following me, he won't be able to resist seeing what I'm up to in the galley.

Tate pushed open the lav door, walked, or rather bounced, to the back business-class area, and spotted his target.

Mal's right. He is watching us.

The guy looked nonchalant, but Tate was experienced enough to know when he was under surveillance.

Tate strode past him, and then, when none of the flight attendants were looking, but Tate was sure the suspected RIOT agent was, ducked into the galley. The galley wasn't much more spacious than the lav. But Tate figured he and the suspected bad guy could fit.

Tate quickly scoped out the dumbwaiter and eyed it,

making visual measurements. *Yeah, that dumbass should be able to fit. But he won't be comfy.*

Tate looked at his watch. He spent exactly three minutes in the galley. And then he did a trick he'd learned from his magician buddy and now fellow spy, Rock Powers. He created an illusion, making it look as if he'd left the galley, while he actually crouched in wait.

He pulled a stylus pen from his pocket. It was the latest model from research and development. Of course it wasn't *just* a pen, a stylus, a laser pointer, a black light, and a flashlight. It was also a syringe with a single dose of a knockout drug that would put a two-hundred-and-fifty-pound man, or a small horse, out for a good twelve hours.

Tate watched as shoes appeared beneath the curtains of the galley. The curtain slid open and the bad guy slid in, right into Tate's waiting syringe. Tate got him with a direct hit to the neck. The guy barely had time to register shock before he crumpled. Tate caught him and stuffed him onto the dumbwaiter as the plane jounced and bounced in the sky, knocking cans and various airplane cooking supplies off shelves.

A tray of airplane-sized liquor bottles fell off a shelf. Tate dodged them just in time. His victim wasn't as lucky. He took several to the head.

That's gotta hurt.

Theoretically, there was room to stuff a six-foot-tall man on the dumbwaiter. But the muscle-bound thug wasn't as limber as Tate needed. *You need to start doing some flexibility and stretching exercises, buddy. For your own health.*

Folding the thug's deadweight into a pretzel in the midst of turbulence as the ground suddenly became air beneath Tate's feet and unsecured items slid off shelves, Tate both cursed the turbulence, and prayed for it to continue.

Tate duct-taped the guy's mouth and trussed him up

into the smallest package he could make. And then in a flash of inspiration, he seized a luggage tag with a code for Scotland, and slapped it on the suspected RIOT operative.

Very nice. With any luck, they'll check him through. The guy will wake up in Scotland, far enough away not to be a problem.

The man's size thirteens were the problem. They kept sticking out and catching as Tate tried to send the dumbwaiter to the cargo area. Finally, Tate pulled them off and stuffed them into a storage cabinet.

He rigged a wedge behind the guy so when the dumbwaiter went into the cargo bin, the thug would roll off and Tate could recall the dumbwaiter.

At last, Tate succeeded in getting the guy's limp deadweight into the space allowed. Tate pushed the button that controlled the dumbwaiter. *"Adios."*

The plane bounced again. Tate dodged a glass coffee carafe, eager to get out of that galley and back to his seat before he was beaned with something more lethal. Like maybe a dull knife or a business-class chafing dish. Besides, he was losing valuable beauty sleep. He had to look his best if he was going to woo a sweet young RIOT thing when he got to England.

The dumbwaiter resurfaced and Tate let out a breath of relief when it returned unoccupied.

He peeked out the curtain. When the aisle was clear and no one was looking, he stepped out and adjusted his glasses as he sauntered toward the larder as if he belonged in the aisle. He picked up a pack of cookies just as a flight attendant looked at him.

"Sir, you'll have to return to your seat. The captain hasn't turned off the FASTEN SEAT BELT sign."

"Sorry." Tate flashed her an apologetic look. "I just woke up and didn't pay any attention." He was going for the absentminded-professor cover. "Head in the clouds."

He laughed again, playing the professor who was amused by his own lame joke. Everyone onboard was literally in the clouds.

The plane took a sudden drop in altitude. Tate grabbed the larder doors and hung on just in time to avoid being thrown against the ceiling.

"I see what you mean," he said dryly. "It's dangerous out here."

Half the passengers looked green. As soon as the plane leveled out, he scrambled to his seat. As he passed Mal, he leaned in and whispered to her. "He won't be bothering us for the duration."

"What did you do to him?" she whispered back.

"Let's just say, he's laying down with dogs. But he'll be fine. And found. Once we land and they unload the plane." He shook his head. "Unless they check his tag and put him through to his final destination—Scotland."

How can Tate be so calm? Mal thought as they deplaned at Heathrow. *Isn't he at all worried the airport staff will discover the bound thug before either MI5 can apprehend him or we get out of the airport?*

But Tate seemed nonplussed and totally relaxed as they wound their way through the terminal. Mal had never been on a mission with him, and while she knew he traveled with ease, this was a side of him she'd never seen. No wonder the Agency thought so highly of him. He was fearless.

He strode with his typical confident Tate walk, eyeing attractive women and smiling at them as they headed for baggage claim.

"Knock it off," she whispered to him.

He arched a brow. "What?"

Next time she'd put more hiss in her whisper. "You're a mild-mannered, nerdy computer science and mathematics professor, remember? Not God's gift to women. Tone down the charm and act like your cover self."

Tate rolled his eyes, but mercifully kept them straight ahead. "You're no fun, Mal."

"Just doing my job. You're not supposed to be any fun, either. Not yet anyway. You're supposed to be low profile, attracting no attention, or as little as possible. So just stop hamming it up and searching for the spotlight and the paparazzi.

"You're not Tate Cox. Keep that in mind."

Since their divorce, Tate had once again regularly made a variety of "most eligible bachelor lists." Because he dated a wide variety of high-profile celebrity women—actresses, singers, and the like—photographers regularly snapped his picture for the tabloids. While he'd been married to boring old, everyday her, the paparazzi had pretty much left them alone. They'd never cared about Mal in the first place. Since their divorce, she'd been invisible to them. And she liked it that way. She was also fierce about keeping Kayla out of the public eye.

The baggage carousel was already in motion when they arrived. Mal pulled her bag off. "Be a sweetie and get a trolley, will you? We're going to need one."

"Wait a minute," Tate said. "Who's popping out of character now? Aren't you supposed to be my assistant?"

"Fine, I'll get the trolley and you get the big, heavy bags." She grinned.

"Damn," he said, as he realized she'd just manipulated him into doing exactly what she wanted.

She swiped her card, unlocked a trolley, and returned to find Tate surrounded by their bags.

"I thought you only checked the one?" He was frowning.

"Oh, I did. But the Agency sent a few extras along."

"How big is the rental car you booked for us?"

"Tiny, minuscule, like all British cars. But relax, I

got us an automatic." She winked and watched as Tate scowled.

He hated automatics, calling them sluggish cows. But what could she do? Dr. Tate Stevens was not an expert at extreme driving. He was a good old American who would have enough trouble driving on the wrong side of the road that he wouldn't want to mess with also having to shift with the wrong hand.

She laughed and leaned in to whisper to him, "What? You were expecting an Aston Martin DB5?"

He shrugged. "I would have rented a sports car."

"But with university budgets being what they are these days, Dr. Stevens, frugality is what counts."

"Damn it, Mal. I can hardly wait to see what accommodations you've booked us in. If you've reserved a youth hostel, I'll have to kill you."

She smiled and shrugged as casually as he had. "Don't be silly. I'm the only one of us young enough to stay in one. You're much too old." Now that was a direct hit and Mal was delighted. She even wiggled her hips and held up her arms, shimmying them in the way the teens and twenty-somethings did. Ah, it felt good to be young.

She picked up the smallest of the bags surrounding them and pointed to the rest of the pile. "Dr. Stevens is a nervous nerd, always helpful and kind. He wouldn't dream of letting his pretty young assistant strain herself by lifting those monstrous bags. Especially when he's sleeping with her."

"Don't push me, Mal."

"Oh, I wouldn't dream of it. All of this is clearly spelled out in your cover-life dossier."

He picked up a bag and tossed it on the trolley, looking as if he'd rather throw it at her. But she merely smiled and held the trolley steady for him, very helpfully, like a good assistant would.

When it was loaded, Tate got behind it and began wheeling it toward the general public access area. "We're meeting our MI5 contact for tea and further instructions."

"Yes, I know," Mal said. And she was looking forward to it. "I picked the café." She led the way.

Even though he was raggedly dressed in tweeds and a cap, Mal spotted her MI5 cover-life counterpart, Sir Herbert Wedgefield, immediately. He stood to greet them as Tate negotiated the trolley through the narrow aisles of the crowded café.

Mal would have loved to hug her old friend Sir Herbert, but as Tate's assistant, she wasn't supposed to know him. And the Brits were so reserved, anyway. Sir Herbert was Britain's version of Andre Leon Talley—stylish and dapper with taste coming out his ears. He'd worked as editor in chief at some of Britain's top fashion magazines before retiring and joining MI5.

Sir Herbert slapped Tate on the back and shook his hand. "So glad you could make it to the conference, Dr. Stevens. How was your trip?"

"Turbulent, I'm afraid." Tate released Sir Herbert's hand.

The MI5 cover-life artist turned to Mal. "And this young lady must be your assistant." He extended his hand.

As Mal took it, she leaned in and whispered to him. "Tweed, really? You are slumming it, Sir Herbert, darling."

He laughed. "And you aren't dressing your age, my dear. But you look lovely all the same."

They all sat and ordered. Mal ordered tea and scones. Tate ordered coffee, black. Speaking in code, Tate informed Sir Herbert of the real problems of their flight. Tate, of course, knew Sir Herbert as well. After all, he'd been at their wedding and was something of a fashion mentor to Mal. She'd originally met Sir Herbert when she was studying at Central Saint Martins College.

Sir Herbert got on his cell, tapped out a text, and smiled. "Yes, we've located your errant piece of baggage and are processing it. It'll be off to our facilities to be decontaminated within minutes. Good job and very ingenious using the dumbwaiter. Used an airplane app, did you?"

"Yes, well, we Americans are known for our innovation." Tate grinned. "And we have the very best apps of any in the world."

"As you can tell, he's not modest," Mal said, rolling her eyes.

"And why should he be? We use Cox Software apps ourselves. We're looking forward to picking the real Tate's brain. If only you could have come to the science festival as yourself, Dr. Stevens. Although I'm afraid most of what you would have to say is over my head and out of my area of expertise, many in GCHQ would love to hear it. But such is the shadowy world we live in."

Though few Americans knew about it—after all, it had never been featured in a Bond movie—GCHQ was the third branch of Britain's intelligence service and worked in conjunction with MI5 and MI6.

"Yes," Mal said. "I'm with you, Herb." Using his familiar name didn't come easily to her, but it was in her brief to use it when others might overhear. "I have no desire to listen to Tate speak." Her tone was barbed.

Sir Herbert laughed and studied Tate. "It is a shame you two didn't work out. You have so much in common."

Mal arched a brow. Her old friend was so obvious and such a romantic for someone who'd remained staunchly single his entire sixty-plus years. "You must mean our love of fashion and the finer things in life?"

"Yes, exactly that," Sir Herbert said in his staid, uppercrust British accent. "Frankly, I'm surprised your boss sent you two off on this trip together."

"Only out of necessity," Tate said. And then explained,

speaking in code once again, of how onerous it was working with the ex.

"Well, I expect things will be brighter and pick up in Cheltenham." Sir Herbert's eyes twinkled. "The science festival will be of particular interest and quite fun for you, I expect, Dr. Stevens. Given your reputation."

He meant Tate's reputation for chasing women.

Mal changed the subject. "What do you have for us?"

"Your car is waiting outside. Inside you'll find instructions to your hotel and for the conference. As well as a list of events and local dignitaries who are eager to meet you." By which, he meant contacts.

He called up something on his phone. "Let me just show you some of the lovely local sights in Cheltenham." He turned his phone around to reveal a picture of the Government Communications Headquarters, GCHQ, building in Benhall, a small civil parish of Cheltenham.

"Wow!" Mal remembered at last to fall back into her young, eager college-assistant self. "I've never seen a Regency spa town before. Awesome."

She'd been many times and loved the place, loved anything Regency, actually. She was a big Jane Austen fan. But she'd also been to Benhall and now the message was clear—she and Tate were to report there for further instructions and briefings.

Tate arched a brow. "I hope I have the wardrobe."

He was asking whether he should go as himself or the good doctor.

"Oh, they're eager to show around such an eminent mathematician."

CHAPTER FIVE

The Government Communications Headquarters in Benhall was something of a modern wonder of architecture. From an aerial view, it looked like one large, round structure. In reality it was three, all built around a central hub. The beauty, as the Brits claimed, was that you were never more than a five-minute walk from any colleague on the campus, facilitating easy communication. Which was the point of the building and the agency.

The entire building was approximately the size of Wembley Stadium and the roof was based on the design of Centre Court, Wimbledon, lots of glass and sunlight for an airy feel. GCHQ featured a central navigation route, the Street, the Brits called it, and all the amenities of a small town or mall—coffee shops, restaurants, a shop, and a gym. Housing over 5,500 employees, it was, in fact, larger than many small English towns.

The many skylights, the aluminum columns, the greenery sitting around, the open seating areas, and the spiral staircases all pleased Mal's sense of design. Tate seemed oblivious to the pleasures of the design.

The moment they entered the building, he removed his glasses, tucked them into his front pocket, shed his jacket and held it over his shoulder with one finger.

They waited until the director's assistant came for

them. "This way, if you please. Lord Witham is expecting you."

They followed the assistant down the Street deep into the building. Tate walked along cheerily. Mal wondered whether she should be leaving a trail of bread crumbs.

At last, their escort showed them to the executive suite and knocked on the door.

"Come in." Basil Heyden, twelfth Earl of Witham, director of GCHQ, grinned as they stepped into his office.

He stood and came around his desk to greet them. "Cox, you devil. Good to see you again." He clapped Tate on the back.

"Witham." Tate nodded. "I don't believe you've met my ex-wife. This is Malene."

Oh, damn that Tate. Introducing her as the ex, rather than in her professional capacity. He was getting back at her for earlier with Sir Herbert. And showing off that he was on a familiar-name basis with a member of the British nobility.

Mal extended her hand to the distinguished, attractive peer before her. "Malene Cox, cover-life department head for the CIA. Pleased to meet you, Lord Witham."

The earl was graying at the temples, but he couldn't have been more than forty-one or -two. She'd look him up later and see if she was right with her guess. She would be, of course. It was her business.

He wore an expensive, custom-tailored suit. Probably from Brioni in London. The Italians were the best tailors. And they outfitted the fictional James Bond, so why not a real-life espionage professional? There was some fun in that, and Mal got the feeling Lord Witham had a sense of humor.

The assistant stood off to the side in the room and closed the door behind him.

"Please be seated." Lord Witham went behind his desk and sat in a plush leather chair.

Word on the Street was that the rank and file had comfortable chairs made from recycled plastic bottles. But of course the chief, and a peer of the realm, wouldn't be expected to have a common chair.

"May I offer you tea?" Lord Witham gestured toward an antique silver tea service nearby.

Mal had almost forgotten the pleasures of tea and the ubiquitous nature of it in Great Britain. "I'd love some."

The assistant poured. "Cream? Sugar?"

Of course, when in England do as the English. She took hers as they did, with milk. "Yes, both, please."

As she stirred her tea, the assistant offered Mal a selection of biscuits. Tate, of course, was not a tea drinker. He preferred the American habit of consuming great quantities of coffee. He was gracious, though, as Lord Witham's assistant handed him a delicate steaming china cup.

Lord Witham laughed. "Cox, I thought you were renowned for your poker face. But it's plain that you'd like something stronger than English tea." He grabbed a bottle of alcohol from a bar behind his desk. "Scotch?"

"And I've heard you're a master at reading involuntary microexpressions. I don't believe I gave myself away to anyone less than one of the world's top experts. But since you mention it . . ."

"How do you take it?"

"Neat." Tate smiled.

Lord Witham poured Tate's drink into an expensive crystal Scotch glass and handed it to him across the desk as Mal nibbled on a shortbread biscuit.

"You may go now, Alfred. Thank you." Lord Witham waited until the assistant had left and the door had firmly closed behind him. "This is a dodgy business, Cox. I can't believe you've gotten yourself tangled up in it."

"I like dodgy. Dodgy's fun. And can I help it if women can't resist falling in love with me?" He laughed.

"Modest, as always, I see." Lord Witham shook his head. "Yes, well, I rather expect your mother wouldn't approve if she knew what you're up to. She's always been protective of her little boy. How is Cousin Lenora these days?"

Mal resisted doing a head thunk. Tate was related to this particular earl? Of course he was. So now she'd inadvertently walked into another one of Tate's complicated, powerful, arrogant family networks.

Here it was again. Tate as American nobility. *Tate the connected to everyone who was anyone.*

Mal silently cursed Emmett for setting her up. *Again.*

Tate's pain-in-the-butt mother, Lenora Cox, came from good old-fashioned money that could be traced back to the Industrial Revolution. Steel and railroad money. And since then, impressive investments that paid off when steel and railroads began to lose their profitability and a good many steel magnates and railroad barons lost their fortunes.

Lenora traced her roots to the *Mayflower* on one side, which qualified her as a member of the Daughters of the American Revolution, and to British nobility in the early twentieth century when her great-grandmother, a wealthy heiress, wed a British earl. So, in fact, Tate was related to British nobility. Mal had looked him up in *Burke's Peerage* before they married. Back when she'd been young and impressed by such things.

Tate was in line, quite far down the line, to a British earldom. Not like he'd ever inherit the title. Mal found it all very irritating. She wished she'd taken the time to gather some intel on Lord Witham so she wouldn't have been blindsided by his hopefully distant family relationship to Tate. She'd probably read about him years ago in

Burke's. But she didn't remember details like that. Too much important information filled her brain.

"Mother's fine. In the dark about what I really do, like always. Busy with her charitable work and relieved that things didn't work out between Nicole and me. She isn't wild about the French.

"Mother has definite biases. She was relieved when I told her I was off on a little private, low-profile vacation to lick my wounds. She did wonder, though, at the coincidence of Mal going off at the same time." He winked at Mal.

Mal rolled her eyes. *If I gave your mother a shock, then this mission has been worth it already.* She forced herself to smile sweetly.

Lord Witham looked amused, but was too polite to ask any further questions. "Mothers don't need to know everything. Mine certainly doesn't." He took a sip of Scotch.

"How is Lady Witham?"

Though she put on a mask of calm serenity and professional courtesy, Mal sat impatiently through the rest of the polite inquiries into family and mutual acquaintances.

"I believe we're boring Ms. Cox," Lord Witham said.

"Not at all. And, please, call me Malene." She smiled at him.

"You're too kind," Lord Witham said.

He'd probably seen right through her, but at least he couldn't fault her manners.

"Down to business, shall we?" Lord Witham pulled a folder from his desk drawer and slid it across for Tate and Mal to inspect. "We've been keeping an eye on Ms. Ramsgate. She arrived last night with her handler. Getting rid of him could prove a problem. Edvid Bagge is one of RIOT's top handlers and a skilled assassin.

"It would seem that Ms. Ramsgate is too valuable a property to let out of their sight. And rightfully so. What she can reveal to us about their operations will be damning indeed."

"Or they don't trust her," Mal added.

Lord Witham maintained his pleasant, understated smile. "It could be purely precautionary. They realize, as well as we do, that she's vulnerable right now, having just lost her father mere months ago.

"RIOT would reason that if we were going to make a move to get to her, now would be the time to do so. And if she had any secret inclinations to run and desert, now is also the time."

Tate frowned. "Bagge is competent. But it's unlikely he's the only one watching her."

"No, assuredly not," Lord Witham said. "We have several other suspects under surveillance as well." He paused. "RIOT is handling this in an understated way. It's quite possibly a trap. They know we're watching them.

"They'd be foolish to walk right into the town where we're headquartered and not realize we'll be keeping a tight watch on them. Which makes this situation even more precarious—what are they up to?" Lord Witham studied Tate. "It's a very real possibility that they're using the Ramsgate woman as a diversion while they try to pinch something from us or find a way to infiltrate."

Tate shrugged. "I understand your concerns. We'll cooperate fully. But it's not like they aren't trying to infiltrate and penetrate GCHQ on a daily basis."

Lord Witham grinned. "You're right about that."

"Whatever they have planned, we have to outsmart them," Tate said. "The directive that supposedly came from Sophia said that I was to wait until she contacted me. But there must be a way to either force her hand or make it easy for her.

"If this is a RIOT double cross, we want to disrupt their plans."

Lord Witham nodded his agreement. "I'd be all for kidnapping the girl, if that's what it takes. But my orders forbid it. For now."

"But you have a plan?" Tate said.

"Naturally. We've put you in the Dashwood House Hotel, in a room a floor below Dr. Ramsgate's. Easy access. Tempting for her, if she really is inclined to be your lover." Lord Witham shot a glance at Mal. "I beg your pardon."

Mal shrugged and smiled. "I'm fully aware of the mission details."

"Good. Malene's room will be next to yours. We can use it as a base if necessary. And of course, we'll have eyes guarding both rooms ready to step in in case of trouble.

"To spice things up and provide our little RIOT friend the opportunity of contacting you, I've arranged to hold a dinner party at my country house, Highfield Park, day after tomorrow. All the select scientific minds have been invited, including both of you, Dr. Ramsgate, and a group of MI5 agents."

A country-house dinner party? Mal tried not to frown. She wished someone would have informed her earlier so she could have prepared and brought the proper clothes. "Excuse me, Lord Witham, will this be a casual event?"

Lord Witham laughed. "Oh, I think not. White tie will do very well and give those academics apoplexy. But they won't be able to resist the invitation, not from a peer and respected member of their scientific community." He sobered. "But the main point is to appeal to the romantic mind of Sophia Ramsgate. Set the mood, so to speak."

He shot a look at Tate again. "And to showcase our boy in the most romantic possible light to keep her girlish illusions, shall we say, ripe."

Mal frowned. "Very good, Lord Witham. Tate knows how to wear a tux. But Dr. Stevens? He's another matter altogether. Dr. Stevens"—she shot Tate a look—"has probably never worn a tux and white tie in his life. He'll be decidedly uncomfortable. And it will be a challenge to keep Tate from giving away his identity."

Lord Witham grinned. "I understand your dilemma, Malene. I'm presenting you with a bit of a professional challenge. But from what Emmett has told me, you're up to any task we throw at you. I'm sure you'll think of something."

She nodded, wishing she had time to go to London and hoping Cheltenham had something suitable. She wasn't supposed to be making Tate irresistible to Sophia. She was supposed to be keeping him from falling in love with her. If Sophia showed up at a fancy dinner party wearing a fabulously sexy gown . . .

Mal would just have to think of something.

Lord Witham continued. "MI5 has assigned Mason as your local contact. He's head of our local intelligence station here in Cheltenham. The locals all know and love him. And anyone who's anyone in the intelligence community fears him enough to leave him alone.

"He'll be acting as your host during your stay. Which shouldn't raise too many eyebrows, considering the community we're in."

"Mason?" Tate frowned. "Have I met him?"

"Don't tell me your eidetic memory is failing you?" Lord Witham laughed. "Seriously, I don't believe you have. But he's a good fellow. Has a sense of humor, which you should appreciate. And he knows the ins and outs of the Dashwood House Hotel and the city better than anyone."

Lord Witham paused. "I don't have to tell you two that since Dr. Ramsgate arrived, this has been a war of who can outdo whom, electronic surveillance and countersurveillancewise.

"Thank goodness for Mason. He knows every secret

passage, back alley, and hiding place in the city, including those of the Dashwood House Hotel. We've had to resort to good old-fashioned, low-tech spying."

"Secret passages?" Mal smiled. "Sounds like fun."

Lord Witham returned her smile. "I hope you still think so when you discover how dusty and dank they can be."

"So once Sophia turns herself over to us?" Tate said. "What's the plan from there? We've turned the details over to MI5, I believe."

Lord Witham frowned ever so slightly. "Yes, our partner. But in this case, since this operation is in our backyard, we've made the arrangements.

"We've decided the direct route is best. You'll drive from here to London. We'll fly you out of Heathrow with Dr. Ramsgate using Malene's credentials.

"You'll have an MI5 escort and bodyguard. Once Dr. Ramsgate is out of British airspace, she's your problem, I'm afraid."

Tate cocked a brow. "Heathrow seems risky and obvious. Why not smuggle her out to France through the Chunnel and disappear from there?"

"We, the CIA, and MI5 thought it best not to get the French involved. The French have been having their own security problems of late, what with the Muslim terrorists and all.

"Your brass and our leadership think that the fewer governments involved, the better and the less opportunity for something to go wrong.

"You know this business, Cox. Anything that can go wrong will. At least half the time or better.

"It's true RIOT will be watching Heathrow and all the major airports. We'll have extra security and be standing by ready to do anything necessary to draw RIOT away from you should it become necessary."

Lord Witham appraised Mal. "Ingenious of your Emmett to send Malene along so we can switch Sophia for her. Too bad we can't use *you* as a decoy, Malene."

Tate looked like he could go for the idea. But there was no way Malene was leaving him alone to lose his heart to a hot, willing young terrorist.

"Yes, isn't it?" She smiled. "But I have my orders to stay with Tate and keep him out of trouble." She winked at Tate. "I'm sure Tate's up to the task."

Lord Witham grinned. "I'm sure he is. In the meantime, my office is completely at your disposal. Mason will call on you at the hotel.

"You've had a long trip. I expect you'd like to rest and freshen up before the conference starts."

"A little rest sounds heavenly." Mal glanced at Tate. "But first, we have a tux to rent."

Tate shook his head. "As Professor Stevens or not, I don't do rental tuxes."

CHAPTER SIX

As Tate and Mal walked out of the GCHQ building, she couldn't help admiring his tall, athletic build while her treasonous heart beat double time. Tate had always had the power to shoot her pulse into the "I'm so hot for you" range. And sadly, that hadn't changed since his betrayal and their divorce. Physical attraction and chemistry were evidently immutable. At least in their case.

Fortunately, Mal generally spent very little time with him. Most of the time he was either on missions or off running his software company. She saw him when he picked Kayla up or dropped her off after one of his custodial visits. And occasionally around the office. Though generally she had enough warning so she could avoid him if she wanted to. Walking beside him now, getting whiffs of his heat-inducing cologne, she wasn't sure how she was going to survive this mission without making the mistake of succumbing to his charms, even if just for lust and old times' sake. Exes sleeping together was so cliché. She made a mental note to avoid it.

It was early June and cool in that damp English way she remembered so well, but the surrounding fields were green and gorgeous. And the sun was out and lighting them so richly it was a photographer's dream. Perfect weather for seeing the town.

Mal nudged Tate as they left the GCHQ building. "Put on your glasses. You're undercover."

He scowled at her, but complied. Bossing him around was just one perk of the job. His cell phone buzzed. He pulled it from his pocket and replied to a text. "University business."

She couldn't decide whether that was code for NCS business or something to do with Cox Software. As often as Tate was off saving the world, she wondered how he had time to manage the multibillion-dollar company. It was a wonder no one had embezzled him blind or made a hostile takeover attempt.

"Software problem?" she said, testing the scenarios. It seemed like an innocuous enough statement even if some enemy agent were listening in.

"Yeah. Nothing a few grad students can't handle." He winked at her.

"With as little attention as you pay to your research budget," she said, staying in character and speaking in code, "you're just lucky no one has siphoned it off."

When he turned his gaze on her, her heart practically stopped. His eyes twinkled with devilment, a lot like they had on the plane when they'd been simulating the mile-high-club scenario. A lot like they had when they'd first been in love. Maybe he just looked at all women like that. With Tate it was hard to tell. Mal made a mental note to make the most of her time with him and make some at least semiscientific observations.

"Not so surprising when you realize everyone's afraid of me. They know I have secret powers, powerful sources, and the expertise to chase them down and get my money back. And take my revenge."

She laughed. "Now you sound like the godfather." But she believed him. He did have the resources and the know-how. "But it's good to know you're protecting our daughter's inheritance," she whispered.

They were out in the fresh air now and headed for their teeny, tiny, low-end rental car. Acting her part, she put some coed bounce into her step, enjoying her role as his assistant and the opportunity to playact being young and a lot less serious.

"You're walking too confidently," she said with a smile. "Dr. Stevens is a nerd, not an athlete."

Tate rolled his eyes. "Nerds can have a cocky walk, too."

"No they can't. By definition."

He rolled his eyes again and fell into an imitation of Indiana Jones as Professor Jones. Or, at least, Dr. Jones's walk without the swagger of Indiana. Darn it all, but Professor Jones still got *I love you*s written on adoring pupils' eyelids. And nerd and all, Mal had the feeling Dr. Tate Stevens was destined for the same.

Tate strolled toward the right side of the car like the seasoned traveler he was.

Mal cleared her throat and nodded toward the left side of the vehicle. "Dr. Stevens doesn't get out much. He's your typical American. Left side and then fumble around and realize your mistake. You're really going to have to go to the Agency's drama school when you get back."

Tate put on the scowl again as he walked to the left side of the car with his key jangling in his hand and she went to the right side like a dutiful passenger.

He did a dramatic head thunk that would have been adorable, funny, even charming if he hadn't been making fun of her and exaggerating.

She held out her hand. "Toss me the key and I'll drive, Dr. Stevens."

He gave her a deadpan look meant to kill and then

grinned. "Over my dead body. And I mean that literally. Switch sides with me."

Her turn to roll her eyes, but she complied, too.

They settled into the car and Tate backed out of the parking spot.

"The A40 will get us to the A4015 and into the heart of town. Our hotel is a classic Regency-era hotel. Thirty-three rooms.

"King George and the cast of *Harry Potter* have all been rumored to stay there. Such a small, intimate place. And it has a carpark, too.

"In such an intimate setting, we should be able to keep a close eye on your target." Mal had been so busy dreaming of the wonderful Regency hotel and its four-poster beds, the promenade and the nearby parks, the shopping, and taking the waters at the spa, she hadn't paid any attention to where Tate was going until she realized that if he intended to pick up the A40, he should have turned the other direction. Since Tate had the innate sense of direction of a homing pigeon, his wrong turn could only be intentional.

She turned to face him. "Wait a minute! Where do you think you're going?"

"I thought a nice drive through the Cotswolds might perk us up before we check into the hotel."

"Seriously, Tate—"

He turned down a suburban street with immaculately kept homes. GCHQ sat on the very edge of civilization, just blocks away from rolling Cotswold countryside. In less than two seconds, they'd be seeing the Cotswolds, all right. Up close and personal.

"We have a tail."

She knew better than to whip around and see whether he was right or just pulling her leg. But she still fought the urge. Instead, she pulled down her visor and looked in the small, cheap mirror. Sure enough, as Tate took a turn down a meandering street, a car followed them.

"Probably just a communications specialist cutting out early and heading home," Mal said.

"He picked us up as we pulled out of the parking lot." Tate was still driving as sedately and calmly as his voice. But his foot was hovering over the accelerator and she recognized his "I'm going into extreme driving mode any minute" look.

"No! No, no, no, no." She shook her head. "Absolutely not. You'll blow your cover. Dr. Stevens is an oblivious American driver. He wouldn't notice a tank if it was about to ram him, let alone spot a discreet tail."

"If I don't, Dr. Tate Stevens and his lovely grad student Mallie will be dead. Such a tragic loss of young life. Our tail has a passenger with a gun. A rifle with a sniper's scope. Take a look for yourself." He shook his head, amused. "And here I thought the Brits outlawed guns."

Just as Mal looked into the bad, blurry optics of the cheap car's visor mirror to check out Tate's story, he hit the accelerator.

Fortunately for Mal's neck, the little car had all the guts of a gnat. It hesitated and thought about maybe moving as Tate cursed and banged the steering wheel.

"If we're assassinated, it will all be your fault for booking us this damned wimpy cover car." He put the pedal to the metal as finally the little sardine can surged forward.

Tate took a sudden left without signaling, heading toward the open fields of Fiddler's Green in the near distance.

Mal reached into her purse and pulled out her trusty pink pistol R & D had designed especially for her. "Don't make me have to use this."

"Wouldn't dream of it." Tate's eyes narrowed. "Ah, shit!"

The road he'd chosen just happened to be a dead-end cul-de-sac. The green was just beyond. But the way was barred by a quaint two-story redbrick home with white garage doors and a lovely bay window. Oh, and a sturdy redbrick fence. The little tin can they were in wouldn't withstand a crash test against any of that brick at more than two miles per hour.

"The British need better signage." Tate grabbed the handbrake.

Oh, no. Mal knew this maneuver all too well and it made her carsick nearly every time. And this wasn't a big, American cul-de-sac with a wonderfully wide circle of paved road where children could play. No, this was really more a dead-end-in-a-driveway affair.

Mal grabbed the edge of her seat. "There's no room!"

"Ye of little faith." Tate spun the wheel around and executed a perfect bootlegger turn. Not a small feat, especially considering he'd done it backward the British way so that he ended up in the left lane. He hit the accelerator and grinned as they sped past their pursuer.

She let out the breath she'd been holding. "Thank goodness for small cars."

Tate shook his head.

"This is so off script," Mal said as she opened her purse to slide the pistol back in.

"Not so fast," Tate said.

Mal glanced in the rearview mirror. Behind them the tail had also executed a turn and was back after them.

"I guess you were right about him being a tail," she said blandly. "Take us out of the burbs and I'll shoot his tire out."

Tate laughed. "Right. At this moment I wish I had Jack Pierce riding shotgun."

Jack was the Agency's top assassin and best shot. He could hit the head of a pin at a thousand yards, or some such remarkable thing. Mal had had the pleasure of dressing him for a mission or two. Jack looked good in anything, but like most assassins, didn't give a rip about his appearance. Very sad. No doubt Jack would make short work of those tires.

Tate took a hard, screeching right. As the car behind them gained on them, he pulled out his own weapon.

Mal gave him a hard stare. "Don't even think about it. You are not shooting and driving."

"Do you have a better idea?"

"They haven't fired at us yet. Just lose them—"

Just then a bee buzzed past Mal's head. Well, something that buzzed like a bee. The bullet whizzed by and out the front window, creating a small hole and several large cracks emanating from it.

"Get down!"

When Mal hesitated, Tate grabbed her head and shoved her out of the line of fire as he began weaving, doing a bit of evasive-action driving. It was a good thing Mal had taken a Dramamine that morning. But by her calculations, it would be wearing off soon.

Tate took the next right nearly on two wheels. If the little car had had any guts, it would have been a perfect two-wheel corner.

Mal peered between the seats behind her at the car in hot pursuit of them. The bad dudes definitely had more horsepower. And Tate would never let her forget it.

Any good spy knows that anything can be used as a weapon. As Tate headed for the green, Mal looked around for something she could use to disable their tail while either she or Tate got off a shot. Not seeing anything readily suitable, she dug into her purse. Nothing there, either. Fortunately, her backpack was in the backseat.

She tipped her seat back and grabbed the bag.

"What are you doing?" Tate said as another bullet whizzed past.

"Looking for something to slow them down." She looked over her shoulder at the new hole. "Great! How are we going to explain two bullet holes?"

Tate had reached Fiddler's Green Lane. He took another hard right that threw her against the door. "The same way we'll explain one. Didn't R and D give you any gizmos?"

"I'm looking. Lip gloss, hand sanitizer, hair brush, cookies—"

"Cookies?" Tate accelerated.

From the way the engine whined, Mal was pretty sure he was pushing the car into redline. "I stole them from the larder on the plane in case we got hungry." She dug back in the bag. "Mints, hair ties, bobby pins—"

Tate took a hard left and suddenly they were off the main road and onto one of those famous Cotswold roads that can really only be compared to a cow path. One lane. One narrow lane, bordered by a hedgerow and a stone fence just beyond. It wasn't paved and it was full of potholes.

The car bounced ominously. Mal nearly lost her stomach as she prayed they didn't meet anyone coming the other way. There was no place to pull off and let another car pass. At least from what she could tell as bushes reached out and scraped the car.

Their pursuer pulled directly behind them, ramming them and sending Mal's plastic pack of mints flying and rattling out of her hand.

Mal screamed.

Tate cursed. "What have you found?"

"Not a rocket launcher, if that's what you're hoping for. R and D doesn't usually give me gizmos. Gadgets are your department." Remembering her change of underwear, Mal unzipped the front pouch of the backpack.

"Wait! These should do it." She pulled out a pair of

pink thong panties and a matching pink bra with a seductive little white bow between the cups.

Tate shot her a sideways look. "I never thought I'd see the day when I wished you wore big old granny panties." He grinned. "But I've never regretted liking big-busted women."

"Shut up," she said. "I'm glad I decided on these and not either the lace or see-through sets." She grabbed her gun again. "Do you have a plan?"

With the hedgerow hemming them in, it was nearly impossible to see too far ahead.

"Get out your phone," Tate said. "Call up the CIA map app Cox designed for them. Get this cow trail on it and show it to me so I know what we're up against."

Mal hoped Tate knew what he was doing. Otherwise they were trapped like rats in a maze. As Mal grabbed her phone, the car behind them suddenly backed off. Mal breathed a small sigh of relief as she called up Tate's app.

"Oh, shit!" Tate said. "Hurry up! He does have a rocket launcher."

Cox Software made fabulous, intuitive apps that loaded quickly. In seconds Mal had the app up and the phone pointed so Tate could glance at it as he drove. Good thing, too, because by her calculations they only had seconds, if that.

"Prepare the lingerie for launch and have your gun ready to shoot the bastards." Tate glanced at the phone and then in the rearview mirror.

"You must be confusing me with someone who has three hands," Mal said as she took aim.

He laughed. "Since when haven't you been able to hold a phone and shoot at the same time?"

"When I'm also not holding a bra and panties." She took the safety off her gun and put it in her lap, ready to grab as soon as she jettisoned her unmentionables.

"On my signal, send the bra flying out the window. Follow it with the panties. Do a little striptease twirl and fling with them, like you really are stripping.

"Personally, I think sending your blouse and sweater out first would add authenticity to the act. We can hope that the thought of you getting naked will really distract them."

"In your dreams, Tate."

"What? It's not like I haven't seen you naked before."

She took a deep breath. "I can't believe you're pimping out the mother of your child."

"I prefer to think of you as the ex-wife, and I will pimp out anyone for the sake of living another day." He glanced in the rearview mirror. "Aim for the shooter. While he's distracted, I'll take out the driver."

"I'm in a better position to shoot." She glanced at her gun. "You keep your eyes on the road."

"Still don't trust my driving?"

"Still value my life." Mal glanced behind her again and pressed the button to lower the window as she maneuvered around, still buckled, into lingerie-tossing position.

The bad dude in the passenger seat had the rocket launcher aimed directly at them.

Next to her, Tate's jaw was set. "Hold the phone, Mal, so I can see it."

"Hold the phone. Do a striptease. Twirl the panties. You don't ask much." She'd inadvertently let her hand with the phone drop slightly. She lifted it to Tate's eyes, hoping she was ambidextrous enough to pull this off. Good thing years of piano lessons had given her the muscle memory to do different things with different hands.

"On three," Tate said.

She took a deep breath.

"One." He glanced in the rearview mirror.

She positioned the bra, calculating the trajectory that

would get it on the passenger window and blind the guy with the rocket launcher.

"Two." Tate glanced at the phone.

Mal took a deep breath and held the bra out the window, twirling her wrist and flipping the bra like a stripper at the pole.

"Three!"

Mal let her pretty, brand-new bra fly. There was a millisecond or so while the bra flew through the air with the greatest of ease where she thought she saw the driver's eyes go wide, like he was getting excited or maybe he was just confused. Stripping while being shot at isn't normal behavior. The bra flapped like a big, round-winged bird and smacked the car straight in the shooter's line of sight.

Mal read lips pretty well and had excellent eyesight. She read the driver's lips. He was cursing like a sailor. Ignoring him, she ignored Tate's order to also twirl the panties, and went for a pantie snap, aiming them for the driver's side.

They hit just above the driver's line of sight. On impact, they looked like they might bounce off or flip over the top of the car. But to her relief, they slid down the window with a shimmy and came to rest directly in front of the driver, where the wind resistance pinned them like a prize from a drunken hookup.

As the driver flipped on his windshield wipers, Mal grabbed her pistol. The panties caught beneath the blade and the bra hooked on for dear life. They flipped back and forth almost comically as the two terrorists shouted and strained to see past them.

"Forget the tires. Aim for his chest, Mal." Tate was holding his gun.

She didn't need Tate playing backup. "You don't think I can do two to the head?"

"There's a blind corner coming up in seconds." There was no fear in Tate's voice.

His confidence was infectious. She took a deep breath and fired at the exact moment that the road curved sharply left. Tate accelerated and took the corner smoothly.

The car behind them slammed into the ancient stone wall at sixty miles per hour or better and burst into flame.

"Nice shot." Tate grinned as he watched the explosion.

"Shots," she corrected. "That was two to the head and two to the windshield."

As flames leaped toward the sky, Tate shook his head. "The dangers of carrying a rocket launcher."

CHAPTER SEVEN

M al motioned to Tate. "Pull over. We have to cover this mess up."

Tate shook his head, but he was smiling as he pulled as far off the cow path as possible. Which was to say, not at all.

Mal was already reaching for her phone as she jumped out of the car.

Tate followed her out. "Calling for help?"

"Calling 999 to report an accident. There are two sets of tire tracks here. We're going to have to explain them."

"And the bullets?" Tate said. "You were using plastic coated?"

Mal took a deep breath and smiled at Tate. "Naturally. R and D has done a great job of making them more accurate than they used to be. There is no metal in them. That fire will completely destroy them and any evidence of the bodies having been shot."

The operator for 999 picked up. Mal went into full acting mode, putting on the emotional distress full force. "Help. Hurry. There's a car on fire!" Her voice trembled on purpose as she mouthed for Tate to hide their weapons. "Where? I don't know where I am exactly. My professor and I just arrived from the States. And, and we were on a drive and we got lost and now we're on this cow trail in the middle of nowhere and there's a car on fire and hurry! Please!" She broke down weeping, very convincingly.

Tate took the phone from her. "Dr. Stevens here. Yes, yes, we're here for the science festival. Yes, out for a drive. Yes, I think there is someone in the car, maybe two some-ones. It exploded just as it came into view as we turned the corner."

Mal could see Tate was trying to act upset, but being shaken was not his thing. He needed work. Fortunately, he could claim he was the competent professor. Tate knew exactly where they were, but he gave them muddled directions as if he was really flustered and had gotten a bit lost. "Yes, yes, this is an international call for us. Sure. We'll stay here until help arrives. Uh-huh. Thank you. Bye."

He hung up, leaned back against the car and beamed at her. "I'd forgotten how much fun hanging with you during a car chase can be. Remember that time in Istanbul?"

Did she! A couple of RIOT terrorists came after them in the market. Tate managed to maneuver them through the market, but the thugs eventually cornered them. Tate could easily have taken them both out, but he gave Mal her shot. "A girl doesn't forget her first kill," she said.

Afterward she and Tate had gone back to the hotel where he'd held her in his arms as she'd sobbed over tak-ing a life. He'd been so loving and supportive then. She'd loved that Tate, the one who let go of the tough-guy spy persona and showed his sensitive side. The process of comforting her had led to a memorable night of passion-ate lovemaking. From the sympathetic look on his face, Tate remembered Istanbul as clearly as she did. That look of sympathy made him handsomer than ever in her eyes, as attractive as he'd been in Istanbul.

"That makes this your—"

"Second." He knew good and well how many kills she had. She wasn't a field agent. She didn't get many killshot opportunities. As the shock began to wear off, she fought the trembles.

Tate pursed his lips like he was considering the news. Without warning he came to her and put his hand on her shoulder, squeezing it reassuringly. "Are you okay?"

She nodded, touched. Damn Tate. He could be a real person when he wanted to be. And when he was, he pulled her heart directly toward him.

"Sure?" His tone was soft.

She nodded again.

"Hey, it's okay to be rattled." He gave her a lopsided smile. "Look on the bright side—this is Britain. You've just earned your double 0."

"I'm not a British agent like Bond." She was grateful to Tate for trying to put her at ease.

"As the senior officer, I'll put you in for a commendation. That was nice work with that bra and panties. You have good aim."

"High praise." She smiled at him. "If your commendation report makes even one tiny mention of the panties—"

He laughed. "Hey, come on. That was genius, a real creative use of intimate apparel. I liked it."

"You would."

"Quick thinking. Nice cover story." He nodded toward the accident. "We'll be the talk and envy of the conference."

"Well, we can't all go around like Bond leaving messes in our wake. That kind of recklessness builds suspicion and blows perfectly decent covers."

The Dashwood House Hotel was a former Georgian manor that had been home to a duke when it was first built in the late 1700s. In the early 1800s the duke sold it. The new owners put it into service as a Regency-style hotel in 1808. It had remained as a hotel for just over two hundred years, still sporting its Regency style and glamour. With thirty-three rooms, it was an intimate setting where guests were destined to run into one another, giving Sophia ample opportunity to bump into Tate.

It had free Wi-Fi, a complimentary off-street carpark, and was within easy walking distance of the racecourse, the Pitville Pump Room, and the town center. Perfect.

Tate signaled to pull into the circular front drive to drop Mal and the luggage off.

"No! Keep going. Drive around back to the carpark. We'll haul the bags in from there." Mal pointed the way.

"You're kidding. I was going to be a gentleman and drop you off—"

She shook her head. "And then have the valet park the car? I don't think so. You're supposed to be an American nerd who's not used to traveling. A fiercely independent, fiscally conservative—some would say a tightwad—American who isn't used to being waited on. No valet parking. No letting bellhops deliver your luggage to your room, not without protest, anyway. And when the bellhop does deliver your bags, no overly generous tips. A pound per bag and that's it. And act self-conscious about it and unsure."

"And I was just starting to enjoy traveling with you." Actually, despite having to make a stop by the car rental place and get a new vehicle, he'd been enjoying being on a mission with her a little too much. So much so that he needed a cold shower and the carefully constructed wall around his heart was in danger of starting to crumble.

Where was Sophia? He wished she'd show up so he could seduce her on the spot and get this mission over with. The adrenaline from a chase always made him horny.

Mal smiled serenely back at him. "I've only just begun, Professor Stevens. Don't forget your cover story.

"I asked MI5 to book the most romantic room available, preferably one with a fireplace. But I can't guarantee a bearskin rug here in England." She laughed. "I also had them book the room next door. So I'll have my own room to disappear to once Sophia makes contact or if I need to be undercover as someone else. In the privacy of the room, you're free to be Tate Cox. Out in public, however . . ."

He resisted rolling his eyes as he parked the car.

She got out and grinned. "Open the boot."

He popped the trunk, tiny as it was. This new rental car was exactly the same as the old one, but in pristine condition. Good thing the Agency had taken out the extra rental insurance.

They each retrieved their luggage and wheeled it to the hotel entrance, which was framed on either side with a pair of ornately topped, sandstone-colored columns that held up the porch roof. Geraniums bloomed in flower boxes above the porch. A well-trimmed boxwood hedge ran along the sidewalk to the edge of the stairs, three steps to be exact. A large door with a glass window covering the upper half greeted them. Very Georgian or Regency or whatever. Tate grudgingly had to acknowledge that if he were a woman, he'd find it romantically promising. He held the door open for Mal and let her in first.

She paused just inside the door, admiring the surroundings, pleased with the atmosphere. "Isn't it wonderful, Tate? Just like something out of a Regency romance!"

Oh, she was good, sounding young again, her expression the epitome of wonder and excitement. His heart did that damn little flip like it had done the first time he laid eyes on her, that horrible flip that sent him head over heels for her. Thoughts of the long-ago trip they'd taken to the Cotswolds came back unbidden. He pushed the memories away.

"If you have time to read romances, I haven't been working you hard enough, Mallie." He looked around the room, acting like a tourist, but in reality doing a spy's assessment, looking for the exits, escape routes, cameras, places to hide, hidden doors to secret passages.

The lobby was lovely—crystal chandeliers, ornate gilded mirrors, a large potted plant of some kind, and an open polished brass staircase.

A very British receptionist checked them in at the front desk and handed them keys, actual keys, not keycards. Tate made a mental note to install his own security devices. Quaint was one thing. An open invitation to be spied on or murdered was another. A lock was too easily picked. Tate could get into almost any room with a standard lock within seconds. Not that a keycard or an electric lock provided much more protection. He whispered as much to Mal.

She gave him one of her "I know" looks. "I may not do much fieldwork, but I do know a thing or two about personal security. I was married to you, after all. I have the Cox Software security app on my phone, for one."

Was it his imagination or was this her version of flirting? His thoughts were cut short by the appearance of a tall, dark Englishman that had caught Mal's eye. Was she openly gaping?

"Dr. Stevens?" The man's eyes shone with friendliness as he extended his hand for a shake. "I've been expecting you. Mason, James Mason."

Mason's eyes may have shone with friendly intent, but next to Tate, Mal went positively goo-goo eyed. Tate wasn't a ladies' man for nothing. He read the signs of attraction as easily as most men read the online news.

Mal's eyes were wide—when the central nervous system becomes aroused, or interested, involuntary visceral muscles of the eyelids produce rounder-than-normal eyes. Having had Mal's rounded eyes aimed at him too many times to count, Tate recognized them immediately.

Damn, he thought, experiencing an involuntary pang of jealousy.

Worse still, Mal was subtly fiddling with her hair, preening. Whether subconscious or not, self-preening gestures signaled sexual interest. And while Tate wasn't in the habit of assessing other men's attractiveness, Mal's reaction to Mason saved him the trouble.

Mal jumped in before Tate could reply. "Being American, I guess this means I have to call you Jimbo, or Jimmy if you prefer."

Mason obviously got the Bond reference. American CIA operatives in Bond movies generally resisted calling Bond James. Mason smiled widely and subtly ran his fingers through his hair.

Ah, shit—mutual preening, mutual attraction. A string of stronger language ran through Tate's mind.

Mal took Jimbo's hand before Tate could. "Mallie, Dr. Stevens's grad student assistant."

"Lucky Dr. Stevens." Mason took Mal's hand in both of his and squeezed them, lingering in the shake too long for casual business interest. "I prefer James. Or simply Mason."

If Mason kissed Mal's hand, Tate was going to have to intervene and punch Mason out just for the fun of it.

Mal laughed. "James it is."

Tate cleared his throat. Mason finally dropped Mal's hand, obviously reluctantly. As Tate extended his and shook hands, he felt Mason sizing him up. Mason with his immaculately tailored designer clothes, his Italian leather shoes, dressed as Tate would normally be dressed, acting comfortable and casual. While Tate was wearing nerd glasses.

"Pleased to finally meet you," Mason said. "Your reputation precedes you. I can hardly wait to hear your opinions on abc conjecture and the proposed Teichmuller Theory."

Tate smiled, recognizing the request for the code verification to prove his identity. "It will be the greatest mathematical achievement of the twenty-first century if anyone can grasp Mochizuki's new mathematical language and verify his proof. I have my thoughts."

"I'll bet you do." Mason was still sizing up Mal, looking like he wanted to gobble her up whole, or ravish her in a decidedly un-Regency, ungentlemanly manner. But he answered with the correct response. "It looks like you're on your way to your room. I was just on my way up, too. I'm in room 203. Mind if I walk up with you?"

"Our pleasure." Mal's smile was too big and too eager for Tate's taste. "Awesome! We're neighbors. I'm in 205. And Tate is in 207."

Yeah, fantastic, Tate thought, wondering why he'd never run into this James Bond impersonator before. Oh, yeah, because this guy was only MI5, not MI6, which meant he worked on local intelligence operations inside Great Britain, not on international issues and assignments. In Tate's opinion that made him a small fish. A small fish with big pretensions and obvious designs on Tate's ex-wife.

Tate was going to put a stop to this instant attraction immediately. There was no way he was going to chance Mal getting involved with a Brit. Tate knew too well how easily Mal was attracted to British men. He wanted Kayla to have a typical American childhood.

Mason grabbed Mal's bag. "Allow me."

The three of them tromped up the stairs to their rooms. The hall was empty so the three of them ducked into Tate's. As promised, the room had a gorgeous fireplace, a four-poster bed, and a romantic Regency décor done in tones of blue and white. Not at all to Tate's modern tastes, but Mal seemed impressed.

"Beautiful," she whispered as she took it in. "Perfect."

Mason closed the door behind them and whipped out his bug-sweeping device. Not to be outdone, and never trusting to anyone else's competence, Tate pulled out his and did a sweep. "All clean," he said in unison with Mason.

Mal simply smiled and took a seat on the settee at the end of Tate's bed. She looked sweet and sexy sitting there with her legs crossed and an amused, happy expression on her face.

Mason sat on the settee next to Mal, leaving Tate to pull over a chair from an antique desk, an uncomfortable chair at that.

"I hear you had a spot of car trouble on the way here." Mason pulled out his cell phone and brought up a picture. He showed it to Mal. "Recognize these two?"

Mal took the phone and studied the photos. "Mug shots? Don't tell me they were ordinary criminals?" She put some pouty disappointment in her tone and gave Mason a flirty little smile. "They had a rocket launcher."

Mason smiled and inched his leg closer to hers. "Boris Avilov and Vadim Galkin, a couple of low-level RIOT operatives."

Mal handed the phone across to Tate.

"Our cover's blown, then?" The look on her face said she was already thinking up a new cover story and a way to save the operation.

Mason shook his head. "No, we don't believe so. If RIOT is trying to lure Tate out, why kill him almost the minute he arrives? It's too elaborate a plan for a simple assassination, and an inelegant one at that. They have to be up to something else.

"We think it's a case of his cover being too good, actually. They really believed he was Dr. Stevens, an obscure mathematician on the verge of discovering a way to crack a one-time pad. We believe they wanted to kill him before he got the chance."

Mal's eyes lit up with the praise. "Wow, wonderful."

"Wonderful?" Tate crossed his arms. "They wanted us dead."

Mal delicately shrugged her shoulders.

Tate took the opportunity to disabuse Mason of any ideas he might be getting of Mal being a delicate, sensitive woman who needed protecting. "Which one was driving?"

"Boris."

"Nice," Tate said, making his tone light. "It's a good thing Mal pelted him with her panties and shot him for good measure."

Mal shot Tate a quick dirty look before shrugging casually for Mason's benefit. "I had to do something. They had a rocket launcher. Tate said he's going to put me in for a commendation and my double O."

"Your second kill?" Rather than being put off, Mason looked more intrigued and impressed with her than ever.

Damn, I shouldn't have mentioned the panties. Mason is probably picturing her without them as we speak.

"Witham said you're a master of the secret passageways of the Cotswolds," Tate said, changing the direction of the conversation and getting the camera off Mal and back on him.

"Yes, certainly." Mason stood. "You know this house was built by a duke in the late 1700s. The duke appreciated a varied diet in all things, including his women, something the duchess did not approve of. A rather provincial attitude in those times when marriages were arranged to preserve, protect, and increase family power and wealth and few were love matches."

Mason strode to a bookcase near the fireplace. "The duke, if not loved, at least respected his wife's wishes. Or maybe just wasn't one for a domestic fight. From all accounts he preferred a happy, quiet household. So he built his houses with a bedroom to consort with his various mistresses, a bedroom as far away from his wife's suite as possible, and with a secret passage to sneak the mistress into the house and back out again, should the need arise."

Mason stared at Mal with that vacant look that told Tate he was thinking about having a clandestine tryst with her in this very room. He turned and fiddled with one of the shelves, flipped a hidden lever, and the bookcase slid back to reveal a concealed door. He pulled a key from his pocket, unlocked the door, and pulled it open. Almost immediately a dank smell enveloped the room.

He held his arms out in a gesture of welcome. "It leads past the kitchen into the gardens in back. Ignoble and insulting to have to exit at the servants' exit, true. But the duke's mistresses, who were always well taken care of and compensated, probably overlooked the insult. Besides, they weren't likely to be caught by the duchess, who was reported to have rather a temper—a hothead, as you Americans would say.

"It's rumored she went after one of the few women she did catch him in bed with with a letter opener sharpened to cutlery standards. The woman got away in the end." He gestured again toward the door and pulled a flashlight from his pocket. "Shall we have a look?"

CHAPTER EIGHT

Witham *wasn't joking,* Mal thought as she followed James with his flashlight pointing the way through the secret passage. It was dank, dark, and rank smelling. Narrow, tight, winding steps, low ceiling, bare brick walls tinged with dampness, but it was still charming and fun in a clandestine, almost childish way. Mal loved it almost as much as she loved pulling Tate's chain. And pulling she was.

Why she was able to was both perplexing and gave her a ridiculously girlish high. It was being back in England where they'd met, back in the Cotswolds where they'd taken their first romantic holiday together. Echoes of the past before Tate had decided his playboy image and the Agency were more important to him than she was. *Before.* If only she could go back to before . . .

And do what? Change Tate into a man he wasn't?

With her thoughts engaged elsewhere instead of on the treacherous stairs, she slipped on a smooth, tiny step and tumbled directly into James. He spun around and took her in his arms, pointing his flashlight beam into Tate's eyes. "Are you all right?"

Their eyes locked. It was dark in the passage so of course his eyes were dilated, but there was more to it than that. He was attracted to her. He smelled like bergamot and grapefruit, leather and pepper, exceptionally spicy, masculine and daring. Spicebomb? Yes, probably. Mal had an eidetic memory when it came to design, fashion, and cologne, and a nose that would have made her an excellent perfume designer. His hands were strong and warm around her waist as he steadied her.

He was a handsome man, with a British accent that was devastatingly sexy. He reminded her of a British Tate. Tate, damn him. She had to get over him. James might be the man for the job. Being sandwiched between two attractive men had already led her to slip; now she hoped she didn't lose her concentration completely and slip up. James held her a moment long enough to show he was interested.

"Is there a problem? We should keep moving," Tate said from behind her in an obviously irritated tone.

No, it wasn't her imagination. Tate was jealous. Confusing, but wasn't it sweet?

James released her. "It's not much farther now." He led them down the passage to a door that opened to a quintessential English garden in full summer bloom, a Regency garden in classic style—small, well-manicured shrubs that made a room of the outdoors, heirloom and old-fashioned roses in pink and white, bright pink satin flower, yellow wallflower, and evening primrose that was not quite ready to bloom for the day.

James opened the door just a crack. They gathered around and peeked out. Scent is a powerful memory inducer, a mental, olfactory scrapbook entry. How would she remember this moment in the years to come? Whose cologne would have the bigger impact on her—James with his Spicebomb or Tate with his adventurous, sexy Versace Oud Noir? Speaking of which, as Professor Stevens he shouldn't be wearing that scent. She made a mental note to tell him so.

James pointed to an escape route through the gardens. "We'll have a car ready at all times just there through the hedgerow. You know the way to the train station." It was a statement, not a question.

They made their way back to Tate's room where James handed Tate a key to the secret passage. "As far as we know, RIOT hasn't discovered this particular secret passage yet. But keep your eyes on it. If they find it, they'll use it."

"What about Sophia? She doesn't know about it, either?" Tate asked as Mal took her seat on the sofa and the two men remained standing.

"No, not yet. Not until we know we can trust her. Maybe not even then. It's an ace up our sleeve.

"She hasn't approached us directly yet. But we've done everything we can to give her access to you. There's another secret passage that runs from the second floor to the third, one obviously unconnected to yours that the servants used to move about. When this place was built servants weren't meant to be seen.

"The house kept clean magically by itself and the fireplaces were self-lighting. Food miraculously appeared out of nowhere and clothes were laid out and arranged by unseen hands, that sort of thing.

"We've gone out of our way to drop hints to her about the passage's existence. She's a sharp girl. I'm sure she's sussed out its location. Let's hope she's savvy enough to keep it from her handlers."

"How does she seem?" Tate asked James. "Confident? Skittish?"

"Reserved. Cautious. Naïve and charmingly girlish with just a touch of the math geek shining through. Young," James said with too much admiration in his voice for Mal's taste.

Mal didn't like the way either man looked as they

thought about Sophia. "Are our rooms connected in any way? Can we move from one to another without having to use the hall?"

James focused on her, giving her a winning, flirtatious smile that made her wonder if he'd taken her question the wrong way, as an invitation to her bedroom. "Unfortunately, no. That's one thing the duke didn't want. We'll have to take our chances."

James outlined the escape plans, gave them their tickets, and talked about disguises.

"We have disguises covered," Mal said, trying not to sound defensive. "Disguises are my area of expertise."

"Tonight at dinner will be our first opportunity to observe Sophia. She arrived two days ago and so far has dined in the hotel restaurant promptly at seven both nights. She has reservations for tonight.

"Tate, of course, will dine alone so he'll be approachable. Malene, may I have the pleasure of your company? Two sets of eyes are better than one," James said.

"I'm looking forward to it." Mal smiled back at him. "Do you think there's much chance Sophia will approach Tate in public?"

"No," James said. "But she may find a way to deliver a message to him. Sending anything electronically or using social media in any way is too risky. Good old-fashioned paper and pen will have to suffice. I wish she'd had some training using a dead drop."

"I assume I have reservations for seven, too?" Tate said.

"Of course."

"Just like you have reservations for two." It took an expert ear to recognize it, but Tate didn't sound happy, though he was obviously using interrogation-resisting techniques to cover it.

James smiled. "I'm sure you're both tired and would

like to rest before dinner. Jet lag can be a bear. I should be going." He made a move toward the door.

"I'll go with you." Mal jumped up. "You can walk me next door. I'd like to check out the other room and make sure it fits our needs. I'd be interested in seeing that other secret passage, too." She turned to Tate. "I'll check on you before dinner."

James walked Mal to her door next door. "It's been a pleasure. I'm looking forward to dinner."

"So am I." Which was completely true. She leaned in and whispered seductively, "The secret passage?"

James nodded. "Just there past the fire alarm, the large gilt-edged, full-length mirror." He leaned in so closely she could see the stubble on his cheek as he whispered back in her ear. "There's a small lever just behind the mirror."

"The mirror looks heavy." If she turned her head just a few inches, she'd be in position for him to kiss her. Despite how attractive he was she was strangely not tempted. She blamed Tate.

"Not for a determined lover." James's breath was nearly as seductive as if he was blowing in her ear. "It's a decoy, made of lightweight materials."

"Subterfuge, like everything here," she said, spinning suddenly and inserting her key in her door. "Meet me downstairs at seven."

"Not at your door?" He pointed to the room next to hers. "I'm just here."

She smiled. "No. Too obvious. I'll make an entrance through the front door."

Tate rested very little. He'd never needed much sleep. He didn't know why he was so damned irritated with Mal and James. James! He had half a mind to start calling Mason Jimbo to get under his skin. Moving in on another spy's ex-wife in the middle of their first mission together since their divorce was ungentlemanly and below the belt. Tate was having a hard enough time dealing with Mal and keeping a professional distance without this new nuance.

He slapped on his cologne and dressed for dinner in an angry frame of mind, rather than the cool, calculated manner he was used to. No one had ever been able to rattle him like Mal did. She messed with his spy mojo. Always had.

He put his fake glasses on and studied his reflection in the mirror on the armoire. Not bad. Not brilliant, as the Brits would say, but not bad. The glasses weren't as much of a handicap as Mal had intended. The almost hopeful thought that Mal was jealous, too, bounced through his mind. He discarded it just as quickly.

He'd managed to put together a fairly smoking outfit from the wardrobe of nerdy clothes she'd packed for him. She could try to foil him, but he'd lived with her long enough to hone his innate sense of fashion. He grabbed a comb and ran it through his hair and was checking his reflection again when there was a rap on the door.

"Tate? Are you in there? Open up?"

Damn. He couldn't believe she was stopping by to check on him. Didn't she have a dinner date?

More rapping. "Tate! I know you're in there."

He was sure she did. She'd probably been listening for his door to open.

"Hurry! Let me in before someone sees me out here and I blow this cover."

"Coming!" He took the fake glasses off and set them on the nightstand.

When he opened the door, it took a second to recognize Mal. She looked stunning and sophisticated and not at all like herself. She was undercover this evening as Mason's date. Because Mason had a reputation as a playboy who only dated beautiful women, she was dressed as a fashionable, sexy English society woman. Mal, who was an expert, carried her undercover persona confidently. She'd always told him the key to carrying off a cover life was to find something to relate to in it.

Her dress was red, curve-hugging, short, with a plunging neckline halfway to her navel. Her shoes were strappy sandals with wickedly high heels. Her lips were a vibrant red and her hair, which had to be a very good wig, was suddenly a deep shade of brown. And so were her eyes. Colored contacts?

While he was assessing her, and getting turned on, she was studying him and shaking her head. "No, no, no. This won't do." She gave him a gentle shove in the chest backward into the room, following him in and shutting the door.

She put her hands on her hips. "You're supposed to be an absentedminded professor, not a *GQ* centerfold."

He smiled. "You like how I look. I'm flattered."

"Don't be. I didn't say I *liked* it. I just called you a shoddy spy. You're supposed to be staying in character, Tate."

"What? I am." He gestured, indicating the clothes he was wearing. "Did you, or did you not, pack these for me?"

She sighed. "I did. And you know very well they're not intended to be worn together like that. Am I going to have to sew tags in all of them like a mom does for a small child so you can match them properly?" She shook her head again. "Take off your jacket. And your shirt." She held out her hands for them and pursed her lips, still studying him.

He hated obeying her commands, but he wanted to rattle her so he stripped off his jacket, handed it to her, and slowly unbuttoned his shirt. "What's that look for?"

"I'm debating whether the pants work or not."

The suggestion gave him a rise she'd certainly see if he dropped his trousers. He arched a brow, shrugged, and reached to unzip his fly, calling her bluff. "Whatever you say."

"I didn't say. Keep your pants on." She tossed his jacket on the bed and rummaged through his unpacked suitcase.

He rarely unpacked while on a mission. Too often he had to take off in a hurry. Though he would gladly leave these rags behind. He slipped his shirt off and was standing there bare-chested and subtly flexing when she spun around.

Her eyes got that soft, rounded look. Yes, she was interested. Lack of chemistry had never been their problem.

They locked gazes.

"I guess I'm stuck being your valet." She held the shirt out for him to slip into.

As he was about to stick his arms in, she pulled his shirt away like a matador teasing a bull.

"Mal, come on. That's just childish." He took a step into her and smelled her perfume, a scent that reminded him of sex.

She took an obvious whiff of him, frowned, and wrinkled her cute little nose. What the hell? He'd just showered.

"You're not wearing the cologne I packed for you." Her face was set.

"If you think I'm going to wear that cheap, old man's stuff you packed, you're crazy."

"Don't exaggerate. I packed you a perfectly appropriate cover cologne." She turned and headed toward the en suite bathroom.

"Oh, come on, Mal. I'm supposed to be attracting a hot young thing." He had to yell over the sound of running water. "I couldn't attract an old crone with that shit you brought."

She returned from the bathroom with a wet washcloth in hand and a determined look on her face. In three steps she was next to him, scrubbing his neck with the wet, soapy cloth in a way he shouldn't have found erotic, but did.

"Give me your wrists." She took them in her warm hands, and washed them, making slow, mesmerizing circles.

His pulse leaped in her hands. If she were as observant as he was she would have seen it. Maybe she did.

She ran the washcloth up his arm, stroking his bicep, which flexed, preening almost involuntarily beneath her touch and going hard along with his cock. She locked eyes with him and slid the cloth across his chest along his breastbone and over his nipples until they stood straight up in the cold air and he was having a hard time breathing normally.

When she finally broke eye contact and leaned in and sniffed his neck, she stood so close her breasts, which threatened to escape from the barely there confines of her dress, brushed across his naked chest. He could only take so much. He lost all control, grabbed her chin and tipped her face up for a kiss. Not a gentle kiss—a deep penetrating, tongue-dancing kiss.

Either she was startled or stunned, but she opened her mouth to him and definitely didn't fight it except to drop the washcloth and brace her hands against his chest. Even then, she was less fighting and more stroking and getting him worked up in the way she'd been so expert at doing when they'd been lovers.

Just at the point he was ready to take her in his arms and take her to bed, she wrenched free suddenly. "That's enough."

Her chest rose and fell rapidly like she was excited. Her face was flushed and her lips moist and tantalizing. She bent, picked up the washcloth and handed it to him. "You have red lipstick on your lips. It's not your shade."

Damn, she was cold. Just like she'd been at the end of their marriage when she refused to listen to his excuses. When she refused to believe that she was the only woman he loved. *Ever.* That his infidelity had all been just business.

As he wiped the evidence of her kiss off, she grabbed the cover cologne and spritzed his neck.

"Wrists."

He held them out while she sprayed them with the expertise of a perfume counter girl. Without another word, she retrieved his shirt and held it out for him. He slid it on. As he buttoned it, she ran her hands over his shoulders, a move that only kept the burn going in him as she smoothed the shirt over his shoulders.

She gave him a tacky jacket that didn't quite coordinate with the shirt and slacks. Handed him a pair of brown socks when black would have gone better and waited for him as he sat and put them on while she set out his shoes.

When he was dressed, she studied him with a fashionista's eyes.

"Stand up."

He stopped fighting her and did as he was told.

She pulled his shirt, loosening the tight tuck of it into his pants, giving him a slightly sloppy look.

"Starting again?" he whispered.

"You still look too put together, damn you. Next time forget to shave, and maybe miss a spot or two when you do. Stay there." She grabbed a tub of hair gel from the bathroom, and returned to rub a dab between her palms and into his hair, massaging his scalp as she worked it in.

Did she have to drive him mad with desire again? She knew how he loved having his hair played with. But she was all business now. She tousled his hair until it looked just unkempt enough, then handed him his fake glasses and waited for him to put them on.

She studied him again until he felt like a carpet sample being scrutinized beneath her discerning eye. Finally, she reached across and swept a lock of hair across his forehead. "That will have to do. Charming. Bumbling. Cute. She won't be able to resist you."

She pivoted and just like that strode to the door. "Behave yourself at dinner and stay in character tonight." She paused. "And remember—I'll be watching you."

CHAPTER NINE

At least Mason had been competent enough to book Tate a table with his back to the wall, an accessible path past it, and a clear view of all the exits. Tate made a mental note of each of them, mapping several quick escape routes. Unfortunately, he also had a perfect view of Mason and Mal's table and had to watch them flirt with each other whether he wanted to or not. Mal had the sexy habit of crossing her legs provocatively and moving her foot. No matter how much Tate tried to avoid it, the motion caught his eye and drew his gaze to her shapely legs.

Tate sipped a passable table wine and ordered an entree of stuffed mushrooms and an appetizer of rump steak, which was sirloin in American. The Brits had everything backward, calling appetizers entrees and entrees appetizers.

Tate hated dining alone. As a consequence, he rarely did. There were always dinner companions to be found. He sat casually, trying to look approachable in case Sophia decided to make an appearance. Mason had sworn she had reservations. But women were known to change their minds.

There's a rule in the espionage business—always assume you're being watched. As Tate scanned the room he noted several other secret agents scattered about from various countries' agencies. There was an Israeli member of Mossad, a CSIC agent from Canada—what were the Canadians doing here? A Russian, even a Korean.

If Tate were paranoid, he might have imagined they were all aware of his operation. Instead, he took it in stride. A festival like this was a magnet for intelligence types. Everyone wanted the latest on scientific and mathematical breakthroughs. From the string theory of today came the weapons of tomorrow.

Across the room from him, Mason was leaning across the table toward Mal, acting as if he was totally enthralled by whatever story she was telling him. It didn't look like an act to Tate. Mason wasn't that good an actor. Mason was a womanizer through and through. He'd get into Mal's pants if he could. Tate made up his mind not to let that happen. For Kayla's sake. Mal deserved better. Mason wouldn't be any more faithful to her than Tate had been. Probably less so.

Tate, at least, had never *meant* to hurt Mal. She just hadn't believed he could compartmentalize his roles and love her and only her, be faithful in his heart, while doing his duty. In less than twenty-four hours of being with Mal on a mission, his sense of having made a mistake in losing her was multiplying.

She sat next to the window. It was June and still light outside. The low evening sun shone through the window, outlining her sexy feminine form. Her dress was a dark shadow against the evening sunlight. Her face radiant as she laughed with Mason.

The waiter brought them a bottle of wine. Mason went through all the formalities—swirling it, tasting, nodding his head that it was acceptable.

Even though there were a few hours of daylight left, the waitstaff was beginning to come around the room and light the candles on the tables. The room was done in

Regency-period wallpaper. Replica, or Tate missed his guess. The genuine stuff would probably be faded and peeling by now. Mal would be able to say for certain.

Mason poured Mal a glass of wine, leaning over to touch her arm as he told her a joke and the two of them raised their glasses in a toast.

"Dr. Stevens, I presume?" A round-bellied, right jolly old man with a bushy moustache smiled down at him. The accent was undeniably British. The man beneath the convincingly real fat suit and moustache was Vail Belanger, the French spy and master of disguise known as l'Artiste.

Belanger was absolutely the last spy Tate needed to run into tonight. The U.S. and the Brits were trying not to involve their ally the French. And he was partially blocking Tate's view of Mal.

Wait. Are Mal and Mason intertwining arms as they drink their toast?

Tate fought down a scowl and looked up at Vail just as he pulled up a chair uninvited.

"Come on, my old friend. Don't you recognize me?"

"Don't get cocky," Tate shot back. "I recognize you easily enough. I'm just not sure who you're supposed to be tonight."

"Now that's just cutting." Vail sat. "And you in that flimsy disguise. What's the matter with you, Tate? Why the bloody hell are you undercover?"

"Probably for the same reasons you are." Tate took a sip of wine. He had to get rid of Vail before Sophia showed up.

"But wouldn't it be smarter to come as yourself? I'm sure you could even get a guest lecturer spot."

"The Agency thinks I should get some undercover experience." Tate snorted. It was true enough. On the other side of the room Mason was holding Mal's hand across the table. Time to get creative and put the brakes on them.

He sure as hell wasn't going to sit by and watch Mal lose her heart to an inferior Brit with a James Bond complex.

Vail launched into a discussion of some of the more interesting scientific theories bouncing around the serious festival lectures, letting slip what the French were particularly interested in. Tate made polite comments and murmurs, but he was concocting a plan to throw cold water on the budding romance across the room. He owed it to his kid to keep her from getting a low-level British spy as a potential stepdaddy, or at least as her mom's boyfriend. Mason was as likely to settle down as the Iranians were to voluntarily give up their nuclear missile program.

"You're distracted," Vail said at last.

Tate grinned. "I've appreciated the company and the intel. You know how I hate to eat alone. But to be honest, I'm on the prowl tonight. You know how that goes."

Vail grinned. "I see. You may look like the mild-mannered professor, but you're still you." He patted his fat belly. "If I weren't in this suit, I'd be looking for action, too." He laughed and slapped the table. "I'll leave you alone in your pursuit."

Tate knew Vail would be watching him closely now to see exactly who Tate was after. Tate cursed to himself. He hated complications.

Vail pushed back from the table.

What the hell? Tate went for broke, hitting on a way to distract both Vail and Mal. "Do me a favor?"

"Anything."

Tate reached into his pocket and pulled out a pen. "See that table by the window with the brunette and the Brit? Drop this in the aisle in front of their table. I'd like to be a fly on their wall."

Vail was good. He didn't turn to look. "Interested in what the local branch of MI5 is up to?"

Tate grinned. "Always. Aren't you?"

Vail smiled and took the pen. "Later, my friend."

Tate watched while pretending not to as Vail walked past Mal's table and dropped the pen unnoticed. The thing about that pen—it wasn't a listening device. It was a new gizmo the Agency had secured from a private vendor. It was filled with a highly slippery substance that was supposed to literally trip up anyone. The idea was to use it when someone was in pursuit. But this seemed like as good a time as any to try it out. That was the great thing about having friends in the Agency's gags and gizmos department. He got to try the new stuff.

Vail was good. When he dropped the pen, neither Mal nor Mason noticed. *Bad spycraft, you two. That pen could be full of poisonous gas.*

Tate hit a tiny controller button on his watch and the pen popped open, oozing superslick gel all over the carpet. Now that was a compound the eggheads at this festival would love.

Tate leaned back in his chair, took a sip of wine, and waited for the fun to begin as he kept one eye out for Sophia and her handlers. Within minutes a waiter appeared carrying a heavy tray and headed straight to Mal's table to deliver the appetizer course.

Wait for it.

Mal was laughing and smiling at Mason, who was totally oblivious to the danger.

One more step.

The waiter hit the gel and slid into the splits. The tray tilted ominously toward Mal in her stunning dress and Mason in his fine dinner jacket.

Tate was enjoying the scene. Until Mason reached up and tipped the tray away from Mal with a lightning-quick move so smooth Mason didn't even take his gaze away from Mal. The tray tipped onto the waiter and then the dominoes began to fall. The waiter took the tray full of food to the chest and tumbled into the table behind him with a crash, sending it falling over.

The male guest at that table jumped back cursing and knocked over a guest who was walking in the next aisle. That guest toppled over into a second table while the flying food hit several more guests. A hostess ran to the rescue of the first waiter, slipped on the actual pen casing and the spilled food and crashed into the table behind Mal's. Which sent those guests flying and another waiter scurrying to the rescue.

By the time the chain reaction came to its conclusion, three tables had toppled, two waiters, one hostess, four guests—two cowering behind chairs and two more behind overturned tables—and numerous dinners had been lost.

Mason calmly looked around the room, took his cloth dinner napkin and spread it over the gel, stood, offered his hand to the fallen hostess and helped her up. Suddenly Mason was the hero of the evening. Tate watched Mason pocket the pen parts that had caused the entire affair.

After helping the other fallen waiters and guests, Mason took Mal's hand and helped her across the mess to the profuse apologies of the restaurant staff.

He graciously waved them off. "Accidents happen. We're fine. We'll have a snack later in our room."

As Mason led Mal past Tate's table, he pointed to a note that had mysteriously appeared on Tate's table during the mayhem and motioned for Tate to join them upstairs.

Tate scooped up the scrap of paper. Scrawled in a feminine hand on it were the words *See you tomorrow. Kisses, Sophia.*

Damn. He'd been so engrossed in the mayhem he'd caused he'd completely missed the drop and a beautiful woman.

He caught up with Mal in his room. Mason was nowhere in sight.

Mal was once again dressed as Mallie and looking adorably delectable, arms crossed as she sat on the bed and frowned. "You couldn't resist using the slippery pen."

How did she know about that?

Tate shrugged and held up the note. "I got results, didn't I? I had to create a distraction to give Sophia the opportunity to contact me. It was clear she wasn't going to act if I didn't do something."

Mal rolled her eyes. "So, naturally, you decided to make a mess at *my* table?"

"That was pure coincidence. You were across the room from me, as far away as possible. I couldn't very well stage something right in front of my table." He grinned. "And I was testing Mason. He has quick reflexes."

Mal didn't look at all convinced of Tate's innocence.

He waved the note again. "And it worked. She made contact. Tomorrow is showtime." He made a point of looking around the room. "Where's your date?"

Mal whipped out her phone and began texting. "I sent him home and slipped back here to become your adoring little grad student flunkie fling again who was simply too tired from traveling to be up for dinner. And truthfully, I'm fighting jet lag. Why aren't you flagging?"

"I'm used to being off schedule," he said.

"Did you see the parade of agents in the dining room? You'd think the intelligence community was having a convention."

Tate was impressed Mal had noticed them all. He sometimes forgot how good she was.

Mal's phone vibrated. "Mason says they'll be ready." Then Mal flipped the phone around so Tate could see it.

A picture of Kayla smiled back at him and his heart melted a bit. His kid was a gorgeous bunch of energy and questions.

"She says to say hi to Daddy." Mal pierced him with a

look. "You should stay in better touch with her. She misses you."

Tate whipped out his phone and texted his daughter a big squishy bear hug and kisses. "Satisfied?"

"I wish you'd think of it on your own." Mal readjusted until she sat cross-legged on the bed.

"I'll try to do better."

"You mean you'll do better. There is no try."

Tate glanced at his watch. Eight-thirty. "What do we do now? It's early to be in for the night."

"Not for a couple who are desperate for each other and ready to cut loose without the prying eyes of faculty and students." She smiled at him.

He didn't like where this was heading. "You're not really planning on spending the night here?"

"I am. I've told you time and again—we must become our cover lives, believe them wholeheartedly if we're going to make them convincing.

"A professor and a grad student who are having a clandestine affair will not spend their first night out sightseeing. They'll be in banging the headboard and anything else they can find. Then collapsing, dead tired with jet lag."

Banging the headboard sounded pretty good to him. He flashed her a wolfish grin with the full intent to make her uneasy.

"Simulate sex, Tate. That's it."

"This is taking things too far, isn't it?"

"Not at all." Mal stared him in the eye and bounced lightly on the bed, which reacted with a rhythmic squeak. "Nice firm mattress. The springs are just noisy enough. We have to make everything about this cover seem authentic. If someone is walking by our room in the hall right now, we want them to believe we're shagging. If we see them at breakfast, they either smile knowingly or look the other way.

"Now—kick off your shoes and let them thump to the floor. Make it sound like you're eager to get out of them."

He eyed her and pulled them off one at a time and let them drop. He raised a brow. "Good enough?"

"Take your jacket off and toss it over the sofa back."

He shook his head. "You really think anyone is going to hear that?"

She shrugged. "No, but the key to a convincing cover is acting it out."

He shrugged back and out of his jacket, tossing it with a flourish over the sofa as she slid off the bed, walked over to him, and took off her shoes, letting them fall to the floor with a thump.

She walked directly in front of him and looped her arms around his neck. "Hold me tight, Tate, and dance me to the bed like we're necking as we go. Knock something over if you have to, stumble over something. We're hot and ready for each other."

With Mal looped around him, looking like she had when they were young, it wasn't hard to imagine being hot for her. He grabbed her and pulled her close so suddenly, quickly, and fervently that she let out a gasp. "How's that?"

She leaned up and whispered in his ear. "Perfect. Now take me to the bed."

Tate was not a stumbling, bumbling lover, but he did know a thing or two about unbridled passion and eagerness. He held her close and took two smooth steps toward the bed before intentionally tripping on a pair of shoes. He kicked them out of the way, one after the other.

"Good," Mal whispered. "Nice touch."

"What will Sophia think if she hears our charade?" Tate couldn't help asking.

"That we're very good at setting up covers."

He spun Mal around, holding her so tightly her breasts pressed into his chest in the most alluring way. He tried to ignore the way they rubbed against him as he manipulated her toward the bed.

At the edge of the bed, he was about to swing her into his arms when she took him by surprise—she bounced up and wrapped her legs around his waist, squeezing him tightly between her toned, shapely thighs, grinning at him, daring him to be turned on.

He squeezed her grabable ass and fell onto the bed on top of her. The bed groaned appropriately beneath them.

"Perfect." Mal sounded breathless. "Now bounce my bones, Tate. And make it convincing."

"The things I do for my country." He ground his pelvis into her as she continued to hold him as tightly as a vise. And then he began moving rhythmically, seductively, slowly at first.

Mal tossed her head back and closed her eyes.

Damn, he'd seen this view of her many times and it never failed to turn him on.

She rocked against him and slowly started to moan.

Damn her. She really wasn't playing fair. He moved more rapidly, bouncing the bed, and her, more forcefully.

"That's it." Her voice was a sensuous rasp. "Give it to me hard, baby."

He bounced her so hard the headboard banged the wall. Again and again.

Mal's gentle moans escalated in intensity and volume as Tate bounced her and tried to hide his desire.

"Come on, Tate. Get into it. Give me some dirty talk or something."

"I'm a cultured professor." If he started talking dirty to her, he was going to come in his pants like a horny teenager. "I don't talk dirty."

She opened one eye and looked at him. "You're a horny geek. That's the cover. At least grunt a little."

"I'll grunt at the fake climax."

She shook her head. "Make it convincing." She glanced at the clock. "How much stamina should a mathematics professor have? We've been at this five minutes."

"I can go all night."

"I'm not talking about you. You're undercover." Still bouncing against him, she glanced at the bedside clock again. "Let's give him a little credit and give ourselves another three minutes of bouncing action." She was starting to breathe hard, which only turned him on more.

"I think it would be authentic if we climax together." She rocked against him. "On my signal." She turned and stared at the clock.

"Clock watching is not sexy during sex," he said dryly, though personally he was glad for the turnoff. "And it's not authentic."

"Who's running this cover?" She kept her gaze fixed.

He bounced her harder, slamming the headboard against the wall with even more force.

"Okay, ratchet it up," she whispered in his ear between escalating moans. "We're heading toward the big crescendo at the finish. One. Two . . . three!"

Her moan broke into the most seductive, satisfied scream he'd heard in a long time. He grunted and froze over her as her screams subsided.

Finally, he fell back and rolled off her onto his back beside her. "Satisfied?"

She pursed her lips as she turned to look at him. "Not really."

He couldn't help himself. He laughed. "What do we do now?"

She smiled as she caught her breath. "We wait ten minutes and do it again."

She was trying to kill him.

* * *

Mal had forgotten how much Tate warmed the bed and how cold sleeping alone was in comparison. Tate slept hot, while she slept not. After a second rousing bout of pretend lovemaking, Mal had padded to the bathroom and gotten ready for bed, saying that since it was their first night in England, the two inexperienced American travelers would be tired. She'd then boldly taken the bed while Tate got ready.

She'd expected him to take the sofa, although that wouldn't be according to their cover. Instead, he'd brushed his teeth, taken off his shirt and pants, and climbed into bed next to her in his underwear on what had traditionally been his side.

It wasn't like she'd never seen his naked chest before. Or slept next to it. It was more that the chemistry that had caused them to marry in the first place hadn't fizzled simply because they'd gotten a divorce. She found herself aching to toss her arm over his chest and pull him to her, to cuddle against him in the cool English night. Truthfully, every part of her was tight and aching with sexual frustration. Tate knew how to make love and turn her on, apparently even when they were only faking it.

The fake lovemaking reminded her, in a good way, of being a teenager caught up in necking and petting. She tried not to think about rubbing her crotch against his obviously erect member. She'd almost climaxed just pressing against him.

It was all that faked moaning. She'd gotten way too far into the role. She'd told Tate to get out of bed, but he'd thrown her words about living the cover back at her and stayed put. Leaving her to sleep fitfully and lightly, punctuated with sexual dreams of him. Was he trying to kill her?

At morning's first light, she bounced out of bed and into the shower. Being off schedule definitely fit the cover life. She was half afraid Tate would get into the cover life a little too much and decide to join her in the shower. She locked the door and took a cold one, trying not to think about him.

When she stepped out of the bathroom, she found Tate sitting up in bed, still shirtless, reading his iPad.

"Anything interesting going on in the world?" she asked.

"I don't know. I'm reading the schedule of festival events."

"Anything strike your fancy?" she asked with a smile.

"The Secrets of Creative People looks good. The School of Hard Sums is a comedy show featuring math. The Hazards of Life—should we be worried about them? Will that hamburger and fries kill you or do you have a greater statistical chance of being hit by a bus as you drive to the fast-food joint? Or what about Stand-up Maths? I'd like to see a guy not divide by zero."

"I'm sure you would. I'm more interested in Designing for Light and Life."

Tate cocked a brow, shook his head, and looked resigned. "What do we have tickets for?"

"We're supposed to be two math geeks in love—which means you win. We have tickets for all the math shows, as well as the serious math lectures, including the one where Sophia is on the panel.

"But don't get your hopes up. The festival doesn't start until tomorrow and our first show is late in the afternoon. With any luck, we'll have our target and be well on our way to a successful exfiltration by then, under the cover of a family emergency calling our love-struck professor home. The Agency will have to scalp our tickets and recoup the losses." She looked Tate over with an appraising eye.

"Tonight we have the party. You need a tux. And it

would be so romantic if Dr. Stevens bought his paramour a new posh frock for the big doings."

Tate rolled his eyes. He hated shopping for women's clothes. Too bad. She was determined to torture him, and pay him back for the possibility she'd have to sit through a comedy about math.

Tate sighed.

"After we spend a happy morning in the Montpellier district—they have the quaintest shops and best selection of evening wear—our clandestine lovebirds will take in the sights." She was looking forward to seeing the spas again and drinking the waters. But the trip down memory lane? Acting young and in love with Tate again? Even if they were both supposed to be someone else? That was a tall order. She hoped she could handle it. If she were truthful she'd admit there had never been anyone who ever came close to Tate for her. If only he could have been faithful . . .

"By 'take in the sights' you mean scout our exfiltration path?"

"Exactly. We'll be hitting the tourist spots Sophia should be visiting." She tossed him a clean T-shirt from his open suitcase. "Shower and get dressed. We'll have breakfast at a romantic café near the Imperial Gardens, then shopping and, finally, we'll take the waters at the spa before getting ready for the party."

Tate rolled his eyes, looking like he was stifling a yawn. "Are you trying to bore me to death?"

She shook her head. "Cheer up—maybe we'll get lucky and RIOT will take another shot at us."

CHAPTER TEN

Just before they headed out of their hotel room, Mal handed Tate his glasses. "Stay in character. And remember, the moment we open this door, we're two people who are madly in love with each other."

"Yeah," Tate said, sounding decidedly unenthusiastic.

"I'm not any more excited about it than you are," Mal lied. She was enjoying being with Tate again and in danger of getting a chink in the armor she'd built around her heart to protect it from Tate.

"I thought you were the one who put this cover story together." Tate slid the glasses on and picked up his jacket.

"At Cover Story's insistence." She didn't want Tate getting the wrong idea. He was the one who'd left her by sleeping with someone else. The last thing she needed was for him to think she was pining after him. Even if she was.

"With Emmett's stipulation that I accompany you, everyone in the Agency agreed this cover story had the highest probability of success. Is it my fault that Sophia resembles me?"

Tate flinched. It was obvious he hated being reminded that Mal was his type, or that he was predictable enough to have a type. The truth was, Tate dated women from many nationalities and races, but he'd always preferred blondes.

Since first seeing Sophia's picture, Mal had wondered what Sophia was up to and why she'd chosen to make herself so closely resemble Tate's ex-wife. If she'd been in Sophia's position, she would have dyed her hair pink, cut it short, pierced her nose, something, anything, to make herself look different from Mal. If Sophia really was in love with Tate, she was taking a terrible gamble that her resemblance to Mal would turn Tate off, not on. Was she playing off the power of young love? Or was she naïve and stupid?

Sophia's choice gave the whole mission a dangerous edge and practically wrote the mission cover story for the Agency. Not to mention the coincidence of this horrid science festival—an event for the whole family, the egghead family—being in the very city where she and Tate had had their first romantic vacation together.

All of these coincidences smacked of RIOT to Mal. But if they were involved, what *was* their game? What did they know about Tate that made them believe Sophia was a morsel he couldn't resist? Was it just the intelligence she could pass on to the Agency? The glory of bringing her in?

There was only one way to find out—go with the mission flow and keep her eyes and ears open. Before embarking, she'd studied Sophia's style and done her best to subtly imitate it and create a character that Sophia could easily assume. Although Sophia worked for a clandestine terrorist organization, as far as the Agency knew, she wasn't a field operative, in short, a spy. Which meant they were dealing with an amateur and someone who wasn't used to going undercover. And, to make matters worse, in all likelihood, there would be little chance to coach her.

The secret to creating a successful cover for anyone was picking one that was close enough to their real personality and skills that they could carry it off.

In the light of creating that character for Sophia, Mal had dressed for the day of sightseeing in short shorts, a crop top that showed off her belly-button ring—Sophia had one—and lacy canvas flats. Seriously, she'd been wondering whether she was getting too old for the ring and now here it was coming in handy.

"Ready?" Tate had his hand on the doorknob.

She threw her purse over her shoulder, strode next to Tate, and snuggled into him like she had in the old days. Wrapping her arm around his waist and resting her head on his shoulder, she smiled coyly up at him, playing this for all it was worth. She'd been dying to see Tate squirm for way too long. But her plan backfired—it felt good to be cuddled next to him and somehow even like it was her rightful place.

He stiffened beneath her touch and was that a scowl on his face? Too bad for him. Emmett had given him an out for this mission, even tried talking him out of attempting it altogether. So he was stuck with her and her cover antics.

"I am now." She made kissy lips at him. "You know you love me, Dr. Stevens. Make the world believe it. *Showtime.*"

Damn Mal. Damn, damn that woman!

It was probably just a crazy quirk of his, but holding hands in public was a declaration of commitment in Tate's mind. As such, he stayed as far away from it as possible. Yes, he knew it was weird. He could bed women, but hold their hands where someone might see? Nope.

There were thousands of paparazzi shots of him with various celebrity women, but in none of them was he holding hands with them. It was just too intimate and constrictive for a playboy like him. The only woman he'd regularly held hands with had been Mal.

Knowing that, Mal tormented him by grabbing his hand and insisting on holding it everywhere they went. He'd forgotten how well her hand fit in his and the characteristic way they looped their thumbs with his cradling hers. He'd forgotten how warm and comforting her hand felt in his and the way she squeezed his hand as a signal to look at something or to show her excitement. The way she offered encouragement with subtle pressure. Worse, he hadn't realized how much he'd missed this simple intimacy with another person.

She held his hand across the table through a chilly full English breakfast at an open-air café along High Street as clouds scudded by and the sun threatened to make an appearance. Made it damn hard to cut his sausages and fork his stewed tomatoes. Mal didn't seem to mind.

She laughed, smiled, cooed, coaxed, and made moony, lovesick goo-goo eyes at him until he could barely take it. "Relax, Dr. Stevens! Why are you so uptight? No one from the university staff is going to see us here." She'd smiled into his eyes and given his hand a quick squeeze and release that reminded him so much of the good days between them, he'd had to grin.

Just like that, he fell into character. What the hell? He could act like he was in love with the buoyant, positive encouraging woman, or maybe he should say, girl, eating breakfast with him and taking in the architecture as if she'd never seen it before, and it was as delectable as a glass of red wine served with a square of deep, dark chocolate after sex.

After breakfast, she led him down a tree-lined street, walking hand in hand with him as she gaped at the sights and bubbled over with delight.

"Can't you just imagine being dressed in a gown and shopping along these streets two hundred years ago?" She paused to peer into a shop window.

"Not the gown part, no."

She laughed again and leaned her head against his arm. "Well, I can. I feel like I'm in a scene from *Pride and Prejudice,* or maybe *Emma.*" She winked at him. "I am playing matchmaker, of a sort."

"The omnipresent signs for the science festival don't seem anachronistic to you?" he said.

She shook her head. "I'm pretending they're from the nineteenth century, too."

They walked down the tree-lined Promenade past the town hall and through the Imperial Gardens, strolling as if they weren't in any hurry. They acted like two tourists out to have a good time.

Tate's senses were on high alert. It may have been his imagination, but he felt someone following them.

"Look at that!" Mal tugged his arm and pulled them to a stop to admire the thousands of bedding plants planted in formal formations. "Take my picture!" She pulled her camera from her purse and handed it to him. "Wait! Not here." She looked around. "There in front of the red flowers. Make sure you get the Promenade in the background behind the flowers."

He humored her and took the photo, lining her up in front of a tree of fragrant, bright red petunias piled into a wire form to look like a real tree. The sun came out, feeling warm on his face and lighting Mal in warm, golden tones. Damn, she looked hot and her jeweled belly button sparkled in the sunlight. As he framed her in the shot, he had a sense of déjà vu. He'd taken Mal's picture here before on a sunny day very much like this one.

He clicked the picture and handed her the phone. She studied it for a second before blowing it up with a touch of her fingers to the phone's screen. "It's a bit blurry. See there?" She pointed to the figure of a man.

Very sharp of her.

"Take another shot." She posed.

He snapped another picture; this time he enlarged it and studied it before handing it back to her. "RIOT scum," he whispered as if he were saying it was a beautiful shot.

"Mason has our back," she whispered in return. "Should we be worried?"

"Only because he'll scare Sophia off." Tate forced himself to keep from scowling. "Just like we suspected, she's under tight watch."

"Yes, well, I was meandering, hoping to give her time to *bump* into us." Mal's purse strap slipped off her shoulder. She tugged it back up. "I have a change of clothes, makeup, and the Agency-issued disguise kit in here. I was hoping I could get rid of them and lighten the load.

"She said today. I came prepared to change places with her. We can hope she'll pick up our clues and meet us at the formal wear shop or somewhere in the shopping district."

She flipped the camera around and snapped a picture of Tate before he knew what she was doing. "You look so cute in those glasses. Kayla's going to love seeing Daddy looking bookish." Before he could protest, she tucked the phone back in her bag and took his hand again.

Daddy. They should still be a family. He missed his kid.

They walked hand in hand through the gardens and into the Montpellier shopping district. She meandered slowly as if browsing and looking for just the right shop. But he was certain she knew exactly where she was headed. He played along, both of them giving Sophia every opportunity to join them.

Mal pulled her phone out again, looked at the screen as if she was following GPS and up at the building in front of them. "Ah, here it is."

The entrance to the small shop in front of them looked like the others lining the flagstone sidewalk—ornate entrance lined with armless statues of women draped in Greek robes and standing on pedestals, fancy white wainscoting above, flower boxes spilling over with ivy and brightly colored assortments of flowers, golden-toned brick second stories, gold lettering with the store name printed on the maroon-painted wood above the entrance. FORMAL WEAR HIRE. So like the Brits not to call it TUX RENTAL.

Mal leaned into him so close he got a whiff of her perfume and whispered to him. "Play nice in here. With any luck, she's hiding in a dressing room waiting to pounce on you."

"In a men's clothing store? She must be a real vixen." He held the door open for Mal.

They were greeted by a matronly woman with short gray hair who reminded Tate of Dame Judi Dench. For just a sec, he imagined he was talking to M. It was a pleasant fantasy.

"May I help you?" the clerk asked. Her name tag said she was Alice. Another fantasy dashed, *unless* she was M in disguise. Fat chance.

Mal took charge. She evidently didn't trust Tate to make the right tux choice. "We've been invited to Lord Witham's dinner party. It's late notice, but it's white tie and Dr. Stevens needs a tux."

"Lord Witham's, is it?" Alice said conversationally. "You're in for a treat, then. The manor is lovely. You're here as part of the science festival, then?"

Mal nodded, beaming with feigned pride. "Dr. Stevens consulted for one of the talks."

"Isn't that lovely." Alice was sizing Tate up with an appraising eye. She walked past racks of tuxes behind the counter and grabbed a tape measure. "I hope you'll be enjoying your stay. Do take in as many of the festivities as possible. There's a lecture or demonstration for every interest. What is your specialty, Dr. Stevens?"

"Math," he said.

"Ah, math. There's a subject I was never much good at past basic sums. You have to have a bit of skill at sums if you're going to work in a shop. Turn around, will you? Let's get your measurements. We'll start with your shoulders. That's the first step."

As Tate turned his back to her, he studied the shop. If Sophia was hiding out there, she wasn't obvious.

Alice stretched the measuring tape across the width of his shoulders. "Nice broad shoulders." She noted the measurements and kept up a merry chatter about town, the tourist sites, and the festival as she bent and measured his inseam.

This was the part he always hated. It was too intimate. He looked straight ahead over the top of her gray head, out the shop window, conscious of escape routes. He didn't see either the RIOT bastard who'd been following them or Sophia.

Alice stood and consulted the list of measurements she'd taken. "May I make some suggestions?"

"Please do," Tate said, knowing Mal must be dying. She'd love to outfit him. He was sure she already had definite ideas about how she'd dress him, probably in something nerdy. If he was lucky, nerd chic. Tate was happy to put himself in Alice's apparently capable hands. He had a much better shot of getting a tux to his tastes with her than with Mal controlling the selection.

It gave him great joy to smile at Mal and give her a subtle shake of his head, warning her to stay undercover.

Alice was already heading to the racks. "Something from our dinner hire selection, I think." She pulled three tuxes from the rack and carried them to a dressing room against the far wall of the shop. "Follow me."

The dressing room doors were curtains that slid on brass rings on a tension bar. Sophia was definitely not hiding in any of the dressing stalls. Tate hated these kinds of cheap dressing rooms. How was a guy supposed to have any privacy? He was used to being followed by paparazzi, corporate spies, and enemy agents. None of them would be above taking a peek. He could never get the damned curtains not to gap at the edges. Mind the gap, the British would say. And he did. Very much.

Alice hung two of the tuxes and held the third out, showcasing it before hanging it up. "I suggest you try this one, the Regent, first." She ran her hand over the coat. "A black tailcoat with barathea trousers flatters almost every physique, but especially an athletic frame." Alice was either flirting or a very good saleswoman who knew how to flatter her clientele and sweet-talk them into parting with as much cash as she could squeeze out of them.

Tate guessed this was the most expensive hire of the bunch. Once he put it on, the others would pale by comparison. But, hell, if he had to rent a tux, he was going to get the best one available.

"Marcella waistcoat and shirt," Alice continued as she stood back and held the curtain to let Tate into the stall. "With a white bow tie, handkerchief, studs, and cuff links it's essential formal wear for any white-tie event.

"It's classic and very *Downton Abbey*. You'll feel like his lordship in it. The women love it."

He stepped in.

Alice pulled the curtains closed with a screech of the rings on the bar. "While you change, I'll get the accessories. You'll want the complete ensemble. Miss, you can have a seat here."

Mal must really be biting her tongue. Tate was enjoying himself more by the minute, even though Sophia was being obstinate about making an appearance. He figured, though, that when she did, it would be dramatic and designed to ensnare him. If she was smart, which he assumed she was, she'd want to ensure he developed an emotional, or at least lusty, attachment to her and complete "lay his life on the line" loyalty.

Tate slipped out his jeans and shirt and into the Regent dinner hire ensemble and admired himself in the mirror. He looked damn good. Not as good as he did in one of the many high-end designer tuxedos he owned, but much better than he'd expected. Much better than Mal probably wanted him to look, less nerdy anyway and more like himself. Alice was right, too. He did feel like lord of the manor. Maybe he should think about buying a manor house.

When he stepped out of the dressing room, Alice was waiting for him with the accessories she'd promised. "Very good, sir. The Regent flatters you, just as I expected." She turned to Mal. "And the young lady agrees?"

From the round shape of Mal's eyes and the lusty look on her face, she definitely did.

Alice cut Mal off before she could answer. "Don't answer yet. Not until we have the full effect. Sir, if you will— your wrists." Alice put a pair of handsome cuff links on him. "Nice."

"Now that I'm dressed like the lord of the manor, I feel like I could use a valet to help me dress." Tate winked at Alice.

Alice was holding a bow tie that wasn't yet tied. "The young lady can help you with that." She waved Mal over as she pulled the starched collar of Tate's white shirt up. "Have either of you ever tied a bow tie? You can always use the pretied ones. They aren't bad, but they lack that subtle touch of class."

Tate smiled at Mal, relishing the way she squirmed as she finally "admitted" she'd never even tried. That was Mallie speaking. Mal was a pro with a bow tie. And so was he. But he was undercover, so he played dumb.

"Well, then. Let me show you both. It'll be easier for

the young lady to tie it than for you to try to tie it yourself." She waved Mal over. "Come. Let me show you."

Mal stepped closer.

Alice handed her the tie. "Wrap it around his neck just over the collar."

Yeah, Mal looked like she wanted to wrap it around his neck all right. And cinch it so tightly that he couldn't breathe. Tate was enjoying himself immensely as Mal fumbled with the tie and adjusted it beneath Alice's appraising eye.

"Pull a little more to that side. Yes, just so." Alice grabbed the ends and started her lesson on tying the perfect bow tie, pausing at each step to let Mal give it a try.

Tate was enjoying himself until a flash from the past came at him from nowhere—Mal learning to tie his ties for him when they were first married. The way her head was bent over the tie and he could see her part, just like the present. The look of determination and excitement she flashed Alice and him as she tackled each step.

He'd learned how to tie all sorts of ties at the tender age of eight. It was expected of a young man from his social class. He'd never needed Mal's help, but his mother had goaded Mal into learning. Mal, not to be outdone by his mother, learned to tie fancy knots and even cravats, a skill that would have come in handy in Regency England, but was pretty much useless in modern-day America.

Why was he thinking about this now? And why was the gentle way she touched his shoulder so damn erotic?

"There, there. You almost have it!" Alice had all the enthusiasm of a cheerleader. "One more move. Ah! Excellent."

Mal stood back to admire her work and clapped. "I did it! I did it!" She leaned forward and brushed Tate's lips with a whisper of a kiss that sent a tremor of desire all the way to his toes. "You look wonderful." Mal grabbed him by the shoulders and turned him so he could get a look at himself in the three-way mirror.

Tate tugged the tails down and preened. "Does this mean I don't have to try on any more monkey suits?"

Mal kissed him again, this time on the cheek. "We'll take it."

Alice measured the trousers for the hem and promised to have the tux delivered to their hotel by five.

"My girl needs a dress," Tate said to Alice when she was done ringing up the transaction.

"There's a lovely little dress shop three doors down. Good prices. I'm sure they'll have something for you, miss."

"Let's hope so." Tate took Mal's hand. "We don't have much time."

He waited until they were out on the sidewalk before he spoke. "No Sophia in the dressing rooms."

"Disappointed?"

"Not at all. A romantic girl like her? I can't see her missing Witham's grand dinner party, can you?"

She squeezed his hand.

"You were great in there," he said. He hadn't meant to compliment her. It just slipped out. "Very convincing."

She shrugged. "I was always good in drama class."

She was lying. It was written all over her face. She'd been remembering the good times of their past, too, and using that to put on a convincing show for Alice and whoever else was watching.

"But you were awful," she said.

"Me? What did I do?"

"Got a very, what's the word I'm looking for—*dapper*? A dapper tux, one that makes you look good and more like yourself." She laughed. "Dapper sounds so old-fashioned."

"I'm supposed to be catching a hot, young woman's eye. You would have put me in something tacky."

"She knows you're undercover. She's not going to hold that against you."

"Isn't she? First impressions are the strongest. I have to make her feel my animal magnetism." He flexed his bicep.

"Right, tiger. You used Alice to punk me. Once you were dressed in that high-end rental, what was poor little professor-struck Mallie supposed to say? That you looked horrible? You hold the power of her grant in your hand."

"Mallie's a fictional character."

"Not when we're in public."

"I can't help it if I outsmarted you. That's the game."

"It's a game, is it? We're supposed to be on the same team, not fighting each other."

"Exactly," he said. "You're supposed to be handsoming me up for my date, not screwing it up for me."

They came to a stop in front of the dress shop Alice had suggested and paused to peer into the display window.

"What do you think?" Tate asked. He saw several possibilities, including a skintight mermaid fit number with a neckline that plunged to the navel.

"Don't get any ideas," Mal said without even looking at him.

Maybe she'd seen his wolfish expression in the window.

"I'm not twenty-three and trying to look it is killing me. I'm looking for something young looking and innocent. Poor little Mallie is still naïve."

"Naïve, hell." Tate stared at her. "She seduced her professor."

"He used his power and position and seduced her, preying on her aspirations and dreams."

"That wasn't in the cover brief." He pulled the shop door open for her.

"It should have been."

* * *

Shopping with Tate was bringing back too many happy memories. Few men shopped with panache. Even though he claimed to hate shopping, Tate was one of them. He had a discerning eye, particularly when it came to dressing women. He knew the female figure like he knew the intricacies of software apps, down to which accessories took an outfit from good to fabulous. Mal didn't have much good to say about her former mother-in-law, but Lenora had imparted her elegant taste to her son.

Even though she loved shopping, in this situation, Mal would have approached getting her dress like running into the market for a loaf of bread—head right to the bread aisle, grab a loaf, and run for the checkout counter. As she entered the shop and quickly scanned the racks, her trained eye immediately fell on a nude A-line princess scoop-neck floor-length chiffon gown with ruffle beading.

Tate leaned in and whispered in her ear, "I see you in a plunging-neck number. Like the one in the window, but with one side of the dress held together at the hips with a single small gold ring. A dress so fabulous and seductive, you'll leave all the male guests wondering whether you're wearing anything at all beneath it."

Tate was either teasing, or hoping she'd have to switch places with Sophia and he was salivating over the fantasy of the twenty-three-year-old RIOT agent in it. Mal had a mission, a mission to prevent Tate from falling for that RIOT vixen. No way in hell was she going to help the adversary out by giving her the opportunity to wear the dress of Tate's wet dreams.

"In your dreams, professor. Besides, you know a dress like that is all smoke and mirrors and tape. Plenty of it to hold all the bits in place and prevent a wardrobe malfunction. Not so sexy when it comes off." She smiled sweetly at him. "Besides, Mallie has a limited collegiate budget that would be stretched at H and M. The gown in the window is out of hers."

A shop clerk greeted them and, just like in the tux hire shop, Mal had to swallow her professional skill and pretend she didn't know a thing about fashion. Fortunately, the shopgirl had good taste. The armful of gowns she picked for Mal to try on included the nude number Mal had already decided on.

Tate was ushered into a chair just outside the dressing room. When Mal stepped out of the dressing room wearing the first gown—a white off-the-shoulder belted Grecian number, Tate was holding one of the damned, ruffled mermaid gowns in hot pink.

Tate, as professor nerd extraordinaire, shook his head. "Looks like a Halloween costume for a sorority party. Try this one on next." As he handed her the monstrosity, he whispered, "You told me to stay in character. I'm not supposed to have a sense of style, just a sense of lecher."

He was testing her patience, pushing her to the max. It took all of her willpower to keep an expression of girlish infatuation and wanting to please on her face as she grabbed the gown and went back to the fitting room to struggle into it.

It had a corset top that laced up the back. The shopgirl had to lace her into it. When the girl was done, Mal took one look at herself in the mirror and frowned.

"It's not as bad as all that. He wants to see a little skin. Let him have his fun and then we'll fix you up with something nice."

Let him have his fun. Right.

She could have fun, too. She strode out of the dressing room, hips thrust forward like a runway model, giggling to stay in character. The dress was too long. She had to hold it up to keep from tripping on it, which ruined her runway walk.

When he saw her, Tate's eyes nearly popped out of his head the way she was popping out of the bodice of the dress. True to his warning, he'd picked a dress that plunged to the top of the mermaid skirt and flared into a ruffle.

She stepped up on the round platform in front of the three-way mirror. "Well?" She held her arms out.

"Spin." He made the motion with his fingers.

She did a slow three-sixty, feeling his gaze on her as he ogled her hips and butt. He was doing a superb job of playing the lovesick professor.

"Fabulous." He jumped out of his chair and came up to her, standing in front of the platform. "Gorgeous." His voice became deep and seductive as he ran his hands over her hips and butt. "It fits like a glove."

And she tingled to her toes. "You're speaking in clichés."

"It's the one, baby." He pulled on the tag that stuck out beneath her armpit. "And it's on clearance."

She cupped the back of his head and pulled him to her until she was close enough to whisper directly in his ear. "I look like something from *My Big Fat Gypsy Wedding* in this. We aren't going to a vicars-and-tarts party. This isn't the one. In the words of Heidi Klum, 'It's out.'"

"Want to bet?" His eyes danced with devilment.

"It's way too long. There's no way a seamstress can alter it in time for the party tonight. Not without paying a mint, which would put it out of range. Sometimes a bargain isn't really a bargain."

"I'll pay."

"No way, professor. I have my pride." She held up her skirt and stepped off the platform. "Wait until you see the next one."

With the help of the salesgirl, Mal changed into the nude number. It fit her like a second skin and kissed her curves in all the right places. The see-through lace in the bodice dipped low, provocatively teasing at revealing more cleavage than it actually did. The fitted waistband made her waist look tiny and the princess skirt had a beautiful drape to it. At a quick glance, she looked like Lady Godiva—naked.

Tate would love this dress. She loved this dress.

"Isn't it bad luck to see the girl in the dress before the party?" she called to Tate from the fitting room.

"That's just weddings," Tate called back. "Now get out here and show me your stuff."

The shopgirl was grinning as she stepped out of the fitting room to talk to Tate. "She looks gorgeous in it, sir. Truly stunning."

"Sorry, prof. I'm not coming out." Mal twirled before the small dressing room mirror. She would have liked a three-way view of it, but not at the expense of Tate seeing her in it. Where was the fun in that?

"Don't make me come in there." His voice was full of tease.

Through the slats of the dressing room door, Mal watched the shopgirl bar the entrance. "No gentlemen allowed, sir."

"I'm no gentleman."

The sexy innuendo in his voice curled Mal's toes. "I have to have this nude princess."

"Nude princess?" Tate tried to peek around the salesgirl. "That's something I'd like to have, too."

"Nude princess *dress*." The light, flirty sound of her own laughter surprised Mal. She hadn't sounded so girlishly happy in years. Not since . . . never mind since. It was since Tate.

Being coy came back to her like second nature. She'd caught Tate by being coquettish the first time around and she wasn't above using that particular weapon again. Especially here in Cheltenham with its sense of stepping into a past era of Regency manners and protocol.

Tate had always had too many women falling at his feet and into his bed. Being rich, handsome, charming, and a spy with an adventurous edge made him irresistible. She'd been smart enough then to realize that Tate wanted to do the chasing. The apparently unattainable drew him in.

When she first met Tate, he literally made her weak in the knees and gave her stomach an attack of butterflies. Right now, right here, pretending to be Mallie, those butterflies were fluttering their wings again. She felt young and free, totally unlike Kayla's mom and the Agency's go-to cover artist. She was just herself, Malene, unencumbered. Tate was a man who was fun to flirt with.

Mal cracked the dressing room door. "I'll take this one." She smiled at Tate. "You'll have to wait for your nude princess." She puckered and kissed the air. "Until tonight."

She addressed the shopgirl. "Please box this up and have it delivered to our hotel."

CHAPTER ELEVEN

Tate took Mal's hand as they left the shop. His simple, casual touch was electric. Megawatts' worth of sexual attraction and power crackled between them. Too much flirting. Too many memories. Mal willed her traitorous trilling heart to stop, but the happy thing wouldn't obey. It wanted to sing and fly and, worst of all, was threatening to let her love flow for Tate again.

She wasn't a seasoned field professional like he was. She wasn't used to hardening her heart to every emotion and its consequence, and this deception was becoming too real. The shell she'd built up since their divorce was rapidly cracking, threatening to expose her tender heart and true feelings to Tate, who'd crushed it so callously before. There was every reason to believe he'd break it again now. He didn't want her love. He wanted to sleep with an enemy operative. He wanted, as he always had, the benefits of the bachelor life and the thrill of his glamorous job without the trappings of a responsibility, namely her and Kayla.

She beat back her fear of losing control with the old mantra: *For a cover to be effective, you have to believe it.* She was simply trying to be authentic. For her country's sake.

The low cloud cover had finally burned off. The sky

was deep blue above and the sun was gaining warmth as they walked up the Promenade toward Imperial Lane. It was June and the foliage around town was deep green.

"To the bus and coach station?" Mal asked Tate. She was almost as afraid to head there as anywhere in town. Why did Sophia have to choose Cheltenham as the place to meet Tate, and in all probability, seduce him? Why couldn't she leave Malene's beautiful, youthful memories of falling headfirst in love alone?

"Finally. We get to do real spy work." He sounded less than enthused.

She wondered if he was feeling the same barrage of emotions and memories as she was.

"A good spy always knows where all the exits are." She squeezed his hand and smiled into his eyes, leaning her head against his arm. He'd always had toned biceps to die for.

"I know where that exit is."

"It's been years. Things change." Her words were all too true—they'd changed. She had to keep reminding herself.

"Things like historically preserved Regency-era towns that brag about their authenticity? Don't let the historical society hear your heresy."

She laughed. He had her there. But she never backed down. "Don't sound so superior—they might. Even a small new detail could make a difference. A new pothole. A fire hydrant where one hadn't been before. A remodeled interior that repositions an exit from the station. Small details, but crucial."

She pulled her hand free from his and wrapped her arm around his waist, tucking her hand familiarly into his back pants pocket and squeezing his tight butt. Tate's butt was still as firm and grabable as it had been when they first met. She spent hours on the elliptical trying to keep hers toned. If she'd surprised him, he didn't show it.

He reciprocated by wrapping his arm around her, pulling her even more tightly against him, possessively, like in the old days. Any other man would have struggled to slide his hot, firm hand into her skintight back jeans pocket. There was simply no room for anything in that pocket besides her, not even a dime. But not Tate. His hand glided in as if greased with belonging and experience. How did he do it?

He cupped her butt and her toes got the curling feeling again and little thrills of pleasure tingled through her.

Touché, Tate.

"Coach travel beneath you these days?" she said.

"I've never liked buses—stinky, noisy, gossipy places."

"Really? You brought me here from London on the bus. And kissed me right in the station."

He shrugged. "I was trying to impress you."

"How sweet. I thought you were trying not to scare me off with your wealth and power."

"Nah, I'd just blown through my allowance—both personal and Agency allowances. The bus was all I could afford."

"Touching."

"I really hate this cover." He paused, cupped her chin, tipped her head up and kissed her lightly on the lips as if they'd never fallen out of love, or whatever it was they'd done.

"Now there's a compliment." She felt breathless.

"As Dusko Popov said, 'Your life as a spy is your cover life.' I used to be lucky."

"You're still lucky. Or, at least, you'll get lucky very soon." But not with her. A thought that made her burble with anger. She wouldn't let this RIOT chit disrupt Kayla's life. Or Tate's, though he hardly deserved her loyalty and protection.

Malene let the implication and innuendo hang in the air as she brushed a lock of hair back from his forehead, lightly skimming his skin with her fingertips.

He involuntarily shuddered.

Take that, she thought. If he was going to torment her with the casual light, loving kisses she liked, she was going to torture him with the kind of innocent touch that turned him on.

She knew Tate's tastes better than anyone. His bitch of a mother was a cold woman who rarely lavished any kind of physical attention on anyone, least of all her son. Show Tate some real, genuine, loving affection and he'd eat out of your hand. She made a note *not* to tell Sophia that.

"Once Sophia gets her hands on you," she added.

As they strolled past the Imperial Gardens, her heart raced. On the way to shopping they'd come through the gardens on the other side. To get to the bus and coach station now, they'd pass Neptune's Fountain on the south side of the municipal offices. And Neptune's Fountain was full of memories, at least for her. She wondered whether Tate remembered. Or was he such a player that he'd forgotten?

Her palms grew sweaty as they walked beneath the white and cream buildings surrounding the fountain terrace. The architecture was so lovely and elegantly part of a period of class and manners. She tried to concentrate on that and enjoy the beauty alone.

But then that damn fountain came into view—Neptune, Roman god of the sea with his flowing beard and corded abs that belonged on the cover of a romance novel, his flowing loincloth covering only what it needed to. Neptune was surrounded by equally powerful sea horses, heads tossed back, whinnying as they tried to escape the bowl of the fountain. Real horses, not fish seahorses. And on either side of Neptune, a messenger blowing a conch shell to announce his highness. Water fanned out in streams behind the sea god and from a pile of rocks in the pond before him. Bright green foliage surrounded the statue. Beside her, Tate hesitated.

"Do you sense that?" he said. "We're still being watched and followed."

"How do you know?" she teased, but the hair stood up on the back of her neck. "Sixth sense?"

"I know." He tightened his grip on her waist in a protective way she'd forgotten.

"Sophia?" Mal asked.

He shrugged. "Maybe."

Mal hesitated. She'd been enjoying her time with Tate and didn't want to let him go, not to that woman anyway. But duty came first. "Should we give her the opportunity to meet you? Dodge into a shop and I could disappear for a moment? I can tuck into a shop alone, for that matter, and leave you here to enjoy the sunshine while I watch your backside in case you run into trouble." She gave his ass a little pinch to emphasize her point.

"Watch it!" He grinned and squeezed her butt through her jeans. "I don't need you watching my backside."

"You never used to mind."

He grinned. "No more shops. She had the perfect opportunity to approach us in one in Montpellier."

"What do you suggest?"

He grinned and pulled her toward the fountain to exactly the place she didn't want to go. That grin meant he was up to something and she was sure she didn't want to find out what.

Even though she tried to dig in her heels, the sidewalk didn't cooperate by providing enough friction to keep her in place. Tate overpowered her, dragging her back to this location of golden memories. Once upon a time, just like in the fairy tales, Tate had first told her he loved her here in the shadow of this fountain. She could still hear his voice breaking with emotion.

I love you. Only, always you, Mal.

He pulled her to the railing that ran around the fountain park and leaned up against it, releasing his hand from her pocket and twirling her so she came to rest between his powerful thighs.

As he looped his arms around her and settled his hands on the small of her back, Mal hesitated, pinning him with her gaze. "You *do* remember this place?"

He didn't flinch or break eye contact. "I said 'I love you' to you here. For the very first time. I was scared as hell."

"You? Scared?" She laughed, touched and skeptical at the same time. "I thought nothing scared big, *bad* you. Particularly women."

"Emotions scare me, Mal. They always have." He was serious now. "I didn't want you to reject me. I'd told a lot of women a lot of things, but never that I loved them. I held that back until I really did, until I found a woman who was worth risking being vulnerable with."

Why was he telling her this now? And in a tone so neutral he may as well have been discussing the weather. He was so damn inscrutable. She silently cursed his spy training that allowed him to so conveniently mask his emotions from her.

She was at a loss—what could she say?

"You looked damn beautiful that day, Mal."

The fountain burbled and cooed behind them.

A lump formed in her throat. "It's a good memory, Tate. We shouldn't lose it just because things didn't work out between us."

"Do you ever regret it?" he asked. Being circumspect wasn't like Tate. His question caught her off guard.

"Regret what? Us?" Sometimes she desperately regretted their breakup, but there was no way she was telling him that. Especially not now.

"Yeah," he said. "Us."

"No, not for a minute. We were young and crazy and desperately, naïvely in love. I wouldn't change a thing—not the fun we had together or the crazy adventures." Or the wild, passionate sex. But she didn't say that aloud, either, even though thinking about it gave her tingles all over. "You brought some great things into my life. Things I wouldn't have if I'd never met you—my job with the Agency. Kayla. I wouldn't trade our little girl for the world. Never."

He studied her. "No, me, either. She's the best thing we did." He smiled very slightly. "Glad to hear you like your job. I did good there, too."

"Most of the time. I like it *most* of the time."

"Only most?" He comically cocked a brow.

What was she supposed to say? That the politics sometimes drove her crazy? And Emmett? That the raises could be better? That going on a mission and having to watch him chase another woman was worse than she imagined? In the mood he was in, he had to be asking her something deeper.

She grinned and smiled back at him. "Except for times like these when I'm in a gorgeous English tourist town trying to hand Kayla's daddy into the dangerous clutches of a wild-card RIOT vixen when I'd rather be sightseeing and shopping." And not fighting the delightful, sensual sensations his warm hands around her waist caused.

He stared back at her with a look she still couldn't read.

"Kayla loves you." Mal took a deep breath, trying to forget that she loved him, too, trying to shove those feelings back into the box where they belonged. Pandora's box, as it was turning out to be. Who knew love was an evil of the world?

Emmett had tricked her into coming here by playing on her motherly instincts. How long would it take her heart to recover after this mission?

"If something happens to you, it will break her heart." Mal swallowed hard. "Don't do that to her."

He was still staring at her with an intense look that made her feel he was reading those damn involuntary micro-expressions that would give away that she was still in love with him. She looked away.

She waved her hand, encompassing the area. "This is your plan? Sit at the fountain and wait for Sophia to brazenly interrupt this cozy conversation?"

"No." He pulled her against him and cupped her face. "This is my plan—make her jealous so she shows herself." He inched his lips closer to hers. "Don't fight me, Mal."

He grabbed the sides of Mal's face as her heart hammered in her ears.

"Play along." His voice was seduction itself. "Let's give Sophia a show."

His lips gently met hers. He kissed her closed mouth at first, sweetly, innocently, and oh, so seductively.

She closed her eyes and inhaled, smelling the cologne she'd spritzed him with before they left the hotel. The intoxicating, pheromone-laced fragrance she should have known not to use.

What was it about tenderness and attention that turned her on so easily? The sounds of the city traffic, the people walking by, and the bursts of the fountain faded away as Tate pushed his lower lip between hers, begging her to suck on it.

What could she do? She was merely a player on a stage of intrigue and espionage, but sucking Tate's lip was

like languorously sucking on decadent dark chocolate—
heavenly.

Just as she was getting into it, Tate teased her, pulling
away until their lips barely met, running his tongue over
his lips and hers until she trembled in his arms.

Damn you, Tate. She couldn't pull away. Not because
he held her too tightly, but because she didn't want to. It
had been too long since anyone had kissed her like this.

He opened his mouth to her. She responded in kind.
When he touched the tip of his tongue to hers, she went
weak in the knees.

She kissed him back, doing a dance with his tongue.
Clasping him to her, losing herself in the feel of him. Time
fell away and she lost track of it, but they must have been
kissing for minutes on end.

At last Tate pulled away. He was blinking rapidly, a sure
sign of emotional engagement. He looked away quickly,
acting as if he was surveying the area.

"No go. It didn't work." His chest was rising and falling rapidly.

He was definitely excited and trying to hide it. She'd
turned him on. She took satisfaction from that fact. His
plan to tease her had backfired.

"Did you expect her to walk up, pry me from you, and
engage in a hen fight on the street?"

Tate grinned and shrugged. "I was hoping."

She gave him a gentle shove in the shoulder.

He glanced at his watch. "We'd better get back. It looks
like I was right—Sophia is going to make her move tonight.
Probably at Witham's party."

CHAPTER TWELVE

Tate dressed himself for dinner. No way he was letting Mal near his tie or his neck. He'd never needed Mal's help getting dressed and now it was the last thing he wanted. Or rather, her touch and attention were the last things he needed. One more feather-light, attentive caress and he'd throw her on the bed and make love to her and damn the mission.

Their afternoon together had been unadulterated hell on his mission focus and emotions. Mal had always had that unsettling effect on him. He lost his sense of reason and logic around her.

He'd chosen his careers, both the software company and the spy biz, over Mal. She deserved more loyalty and attention than he'd ever be able to give her. Or maybe it was fear of getting too close to her and being vulnerable again.

The afternoon they'd spent together had brought everything back—he was still in love with her, no matter how hard he tried to push his feelings beneath the surface. He loved her.

He'd been throwing himself into the company of beautiful women, dangerous missions, and high-stakes business deals to fill the void losing Mal had left in his life. He'd done a damn fine job of it, too, building a fortress around his heart that had been impenetrable until this mission with Mal. Right now RIOT agents were the least of his worries. Even RIOT assassins like Edvid Bagge, Sophia's handler. His feelings for Mal were far more dangerous. Being near her again, he wanted her back. Desperately.

They drove to Highfield Park in silence with more than quiet hanging between them. Sexual tension charged the air and space. Tate had to get her out of his head.

It was only after they cleared the gatehouse and were admitted to the grounds that he spoke. "The idea to switch Sophia out for you to exfiltrate her was a great one in theory. Logistically, if she approaches you tonight, what are you planning? To swap evening gowns with her in the powder room?

"If so, I'd like advance warning so I can carry out the charade without tripping up."

"Yes, that's exactly what I'm planning to do. If she's game. As for advance warning, you'll just have to stay on your toes. We'll be lucky if we get any warning at all. You've had enough experience dating multiple women at once that you should be able to handle the switch." Mal was staring straight ahead at the imposing sixteenth-century building with its Renaissance porch and Queen Elizabeth's coat of arms emblazoned above.

"The coat of arms is a nice touch. I looked up Highfield Park this afternoon. The coat of arms commemorates Elizabeth I's visit here in the fifteen hundreds. So much history around."

And between them. Tate was sure she wasn't just admiring the architecture and picturing historical events that had taken place at Highfield Park. She was remembering their past and the history that would be made here tonight if they got Sophia out safely. She had to be. He sure as hell was. He also couldn't help wondering if the events of the night would put the final nail in the coffin of any chance of a future reconciliation between them.

And damn him. He wanted to give reconciliation a shot. If only Mal would take him back. Unfortunately, he had no idea how to win her forgiveness. Her good opinion once lost . . .

He cleared his throat. "I hope you brought your bag of tricks and disguises." Tate paused. "Sophia isn't you."

Mal turned and stared at him. "No. She isn't. *No one* is, Tate."

Was it his imagination, or had she just read his mind?

She took a deep breath and smiled. But he could see it was forced. She spoke a little too brightly. "Good thing I have my fake noses and beauty marks with me. If you really need a visual cue or sign, I'd be happy to give her a beauty mole.

"Since the Area 51 fiasco, the chief is all for movable moles to signal authenticity. I'll make it a signal—if it's on her left cheek, the coast is clear. On her right if she's being followed."

"No one would notice that?"

She stared at him again. "You know better than anyone how unobservant most people are."

"We're not talking about most people. The room will be full of spies." He pushed the fake glasses up on his nose. The damn things were always falling down.

"And egghead, absentminded professors."

"Great, we'll fool the wrong half of the room." He pulled the car into the circular drive, ready to hand it over to the parking valet.

She put her hand on his arm as he reached to open the door. "Seriously, Tate. There's only one reason I came on the mission and it has nothing to do with love of country.

"Do whatever you have to do with Sophia, but don't lose your heart to her. Don't fall in love with her."

His heart leaped with hope. Maybe she was coming around to see that sometimes a spy had to do despicable things for the job. Maybe this was her way of saying she was sorry? He held her gaze. "Fall in love with her? Why are we even discussing this?"

Mal stared back at him. "You're a sucker for pretty faces and damsels in distress. Always have been. You lose your heart so easily. Just be careful." Mal bit her lower lip, looking vulnerable in a way that made Tate ache to kiss her hard.

"That's a myth, Mal. I've only lost my heart once."

The parking attendant opened Mal's door, cutting off further conversation. Tate got out of the car and came around to her side, handed his key to the valet, and offered Mal a hand out.

That was a mistake. The minute she slid her soft, slender hand into his and clasped her fingers around his, he had the urge to hang on to her, grab her, run, and not let go. Forget the mission and win his wife back. If he could.

As she stepped out of the car he got an eyeful of her slim ankles and three-inch nude stiletto heels that gave him all kinds of ideas he shouldn't have about his ex-wife. Nude. Everything she wore was skin-colored. Damn.

Her dress floated around her ankles and ruffled in the cool summer's breeze. "What a beautiful house! Can you imagine living here?"

He tried to see the house through her eyes. "Yeah, it is. I spent a couple of weeks here one summer when I was a teenager. It's a little drafty, though."

In profile in the lamplight, she was breathtaking. Not a good thing for an ex-spouse to be. Especially not when he was supposed to be charming another woman.

She took his arm. "Try to act impressed, would you? Dr. Stevens isn't a billionaire like you are."

"I'll try to remember that."

They walked arm in arm to the house.

A butler in formal attire let them in and announced them.

Inside the great hall, candles burned brightly from every surface. In the nineteenth century all the burning wax power would have been an excessive show of wealth. Even in the twenty-first century the candlelight made an impression. Leave it to good old Witham to create a romantic atmosphere.

The butler showed them into the Elizabethan-period great hall with its checkerboard floor, great stone fireplace, open truss ceiling, and imposing portraits of Witham's, and therefore Tate's, ancestors wearing everything from ruffs to current dinner jackets.

Mal leaned into him. "That window looks like it's original Elizabethan glass."

He put a finger to her lips. That was another mistake. The feel of her moist lips against his finger sent a shiver of pleasure through him. "Shhh. You're supposed to be a nerdy grad student, not a connoisseur of antiques."

She kissed his finger. "Whatever you say, prof."

Damn, that simple, casual kiss made him go hard.

A host of science-festival dignitaries from the celebrities of the popular public science and math shows to serious scientists surrounded them. In the far corner, Witham mingled with his guests as he worked his way toward Tate and Mal.

"Look! Isn't that the guy from Comedy Maths? I'd like to meet him. I could be a comedian groupie. A sense of humor in a man is so sexy." Mal put a tease in her voice.

Tate turned in the direction of Mal's gaze. "You're with me," he whispered to her. "My adoring grad student. Act the part."

"Only until I turn into Sophia."

"*If* you turn into her."

Something about the way she said Sophia's name sent a ripple of concern through him. He hadn't thought about it before, but what happened when she swapped with Sophia? What if Edvid caught up to her and realized the switch?

Despite being an office lackey, Mal was trained in self-defense. But she lacked field experience. Experience aced classroom training any day. And that worried Tate. He had an overwhelming desire to protect her.

"On second thought, this is a bad idea," he said. "Leave me your dress and head back to the room to wait for me there."

"I love it when you get demanding," she whispered back. "Nothing doing. I'm not missing all the action and excitement. I haven't watched your seduction skills in action in years. I'm looking forward to the entertainment. And I'm not parading naked through this crowd, either."

"What will you do if you switch and Edvid confronts you?"

"Gas him with my poisonous tube of lipstick." She winked at him. "You don't think I came unprepared, do you?" She looked around the hall as they inched closer to Lord Witham. "Cheer up. We're assuming Sophia will present herself here and make the switch. She may have other plans. Now, where is she?"

Witham had worked his way through the crowd and arrived in front of them with Lady Witham on his arm. Tate hadn't seen Cleva in years. She looked good. He restrained himself from saying so as they approached.

Witham made introductions all around in a loud, hearty voice. "So good of you math types to attend our little dinner. I enjoy mingling with the brightest minds in the scientific and mathematics communities. And Cleva indulges me."

"Listen to him! He makes me sound uneducated and

dull. I enjoy the science festival and lectures as much as anyone. Which lectures will you be attending?"

They made the usual bland small talk—the weather, the festival, have you seen the sights? Mal did a plausible job of acting like a nobility-struck grad student who was out of her element. In fact, she was damn cute acting girlish and young.

Not wanting to get crosswise in her crosshairs, Tate acted as bumbling as he could stomach, doing his best impression of the cliché absentminded professor. "What about our target?" Tate whispered to Witham.

"I have it on good authority she'll be here." Witham grinned. "Cleva has seated you side by side at dinner."

As if on cue, the butler announced her. "Dr. Sophia Ramsgate."

Sophia had chosen to dress nearly identically to Mal. She wore a nude-colored dress that was, in reality, a pale shade of pink. It was a one-shoulder affair with one of those skirts whose hem was longer in back and shorter in front, revealing a shapely pair of legs in strappy stiletto heels, also in nude. The skirt was ruffled and a flower made of the sheer material of the dress graced one shoulder. The dress had just a hint of glitter to it, enough to shimmer romantically beneath the candlelight.

Her blond hair was loose and flowed around her shoulders in soft waves. She wore a pale ribbon around her neck tied in a bow as if she were a present. Her lips were the perfect shade of red for a youthful blue-eyed blonde and the only spot of color on her person. Beautiful, bold, kissable lips. Her eyes sought Tate's from across the room and held them as her perfect red lips curled up in a smile meant just for him.

His breath caught. His mouth went dry and his heart raced. In photos, Sophia bore a strong resemblance to Mal. In person, she was Mal's clone.

What the hell was Sophia's game? Did he so obviously have a type?

Witham went forward to greet her. "Dr. Ramsgate, you must allow me to introduce you to another of the great mathematical minds of our day. Dr. Ramsgate, Dr. Tate Stevens."

"Sophia, please call me Sophia." Her barely perceptible English accent was delightful and a lot like Mal's when they'd first met—a combination of an American broadcast English laced with a touch of educated London and middle class to upper crust. Resisting picking up the English accent was futile.

Beneath the bow around her neck, Tate could almost see her pulse leap. It should have been erotic. But he found himself strangely unmoved. Sophia continued holding his gaze, acting as if they were the only two in the room as she extended her hand to Tate.

When he took it, she pulled him close, so close her perfume wafted to him. She wore a heady, sexual scent, one of Mal's favorites, a scent she'd worn when they first met, though he'd forgotten the name of it. Scent is a powerful reminder. He wondered again what she was up to. He'd learned enough from Mal to know that scent was part of cover. If Sophia, or RIOT, had picked this one, there was a reason. Could she really think it would seduce him?

Sophia held his hand a second longer than necessary, enough to show she was interested. And yet she smiled almost shyly. "Pleased to meet you. You're a legend in my community. A rock star."

She was speaking of his spying career. Tate hoped others didn't overhear. Dr. Tate Stevens was a minor professor of mathematics at a small, unknown university who'd only been invited to Lord Witham's party on the recommendation of a friend of a friend.

The way Sophia gushed was both flattering and unnerving. She seemed very young, almost frightened and convincingly like the ingénue she was supposed to be. He assessed her, trying to determine whether he was being set up. "Tate. It's a pleasure." He pulled his hand from hers. "This is my grad student Mallie Green."

Sophia smiled uncertainly at Mal.

Almost instinctively, Tate took Mal's hand and squeezed it. He lied to himself that he was only acting in character. But he knew better.

Mal was pleasantly surprised, stunned really, when Tate took her hand right in front of Sophia and squeezed it reassuringly. She was wary of the girl on sight. Call it womanly instinct, but Mal didn't trust her.

Something smelled fishy and it wasn't just Mal's college signature perfume that Sophia had taken for her own. The eyes she and Tate had felt during the day had been real and Sophia's. She must have seen the dress Mal had purchased for the evening and then copied it, making an outfit just different enough not to be totally embarrassing. It was, however, derivative and designed to catch Tate's eye. What was up with that ribbon around her neck? Mal resisted balling her fist and plastered a fake serene smile on her face, even though it must have been obvious to everyone in the room that Sophia was after poor little Mallie's man.

Very good, Sophia. If you're really onboard with our plan to switch places.

Otherwise it was simply diabolical to show up in an outfit so similar to Mal's.

Mal sized up the competition, literally. Sophia was her height, the same weight, the same dress size, and unless Mal missed her guess, they wore the same shoe size as well. Her shade of blond was identical to Mal's as was the length and cut of her hair. Her eyes a matching shade to Mal's rather unique bright blue. Was Sophia wearing contacts? Is that how she matched her eyes to Mal's? All of this was convenient when they made the switch. A change of makeup, move the ribbon from one neck to the other, and most people would be fooled.

Mal watched Tate with the trained eye of a woman looking for chemistry and electricity. Was there a spark between Tate and Sophia? If there was, she was missing it. And that confused her. Tate should have fallen for Sophia at first sight.

Sophia obviously idolized Tate. The expression in her eyes said as much. But Mal read surprise there, too. Pleasant surprise. Had Sophia *really* been in love with Tate from afar? Was the expression in her eyes merely pleasure that he was as handsome and magnetic in person as on paper or in digital pixels? Or was something else going on?

Sophia had certainly schooled herself in what Tate liked. Tate, for all his sophistication and the exotic, high-profile beauties he was famous for hanging out with, had a soft spot for untainted beauty and wide-open wonder at the world, for women who still had a hint of a rose-colored view of the world. He'd seen too much evil, death, and mayhem not to be cynical and jaded. Maybe that's what drew him to touches of innocence. He wanted to believe it still existed. Sophia was exuding innocent seduction.

There was only one thing to do—switch dresses with her and get her on that plane for the States before she had time to work her bewitching magic on Tate or spend a minute alone with him.

If Mal was honest with herself, she resented Sophia for interrupting whatever it was that was going on between her and Tate. Mal could hardly deny that *something* was. Though maybe it would all evaporate after they left Cheltenham.

A waiter came by with a tray of wine. Mal gladly took a glass of red, hoping to numb her senses and banish the assault to her heart from being around Tate again. Their day together had reawakened feelings she'd thought she'd locked away forever. And now she was supposed to hand him over to another woman for the sake of her country? Again.

The dining room of Highfield Park was done in Elizabethan Revival. Pendant bosses hung from the richly ornamented ceiling. The fireplace was flanked with Italian marble. A lacquered leather screen dating from the early eighteen hundreds and painted with a pastoral country scene sat in front of the fireplace. A Victorian table was set for twenty-four, each of the chairs done in scarlet Utrecht velvet.

Lord and Lady Witham took their seats at the ends of the table. The rest of the guests were directed to seats marked with place cards. Sophia sat next to Tate. Mal across from him. A math comedian next to her with Mason on her other side.

Through five courses Mal had to listen to science small talk and watch Sophia flirt with Tate and whisper secretively in his ear. Sophia was good. She laughed gaily at everything Tate said. She gently touched his sleeve and then his hand as she gestured and talked to him.

Mal hated touchers, the kind of people who intruded into your personal space. She especially hated Sophia touching Tate.

It didn't take any acting skills at all for Mal to fret and pout and vie for Tate's attention like a jealous coed.

Marty, the math comedian next to her, took pity on her. "You're his grad student?" He nodded at Tate who was laughing with Sophia.

"I am."

"Then you must like math. Are you coming to my show?"

"We have tickets. I'm looking forward to it, but I'd really love a little advance taste of the show." She got an evil idea. "What would you say to a mathematics duel with Dr. Stevens?"

That got Tate's attention. He looked over at them. "What?"

"Marty is going to astound us with some amazing feats of math humor. Think you can keep up?" Mal took a bite of the heavenly dessert in front of her.

"I—"

"Don't tell me you're chicken, Dr. Stevens." Marty was grinning boyishly. "A professor like yourself should be up to the challenge."

Mal liked Marty. He had charm and guts. And was on her side.

"Bring it on," Tate said.

Beside him, Sophia tittered delicately. "My money's on Dr. Stevens."

"Anyone have a calculator?" Marty asked the crowd. "Oh, come on, people. Someone has to have a smartphone with a calculator app."

Suddenly twenty-three phones appeared on the table.

"Very good. I knew you were all gaming people." Marty laughed. "The lovely Mallie has asked me to perform a bit of mathematical prestidigitation and humor.

"Lady Witham, if you will, would you be my assistant?"

Lady Witham started to push back from her chair.

"No need to pull you from your dessert. I need you to operate your phone and do some math for us."

Lady Witham smiled. "That I can do."

"Excellent. Pick a four-digit number, enter it in and multiply it by nine."

The guests watched as Lady Witham did the math. "Got it."

"Good." Marty held up his hand. "Don't tell me what it is. First I need to know whether your answer is a four- or five-digit number."

"Five."

Marty nodded, smiling. "Very good. Five-digit numbers are a personal favorite of mine and much more difficult than four.

"Now, if you will, read me the first four digits one at a time. I'll say yes after each digit as your cue to read me the next digit. At the end, I'll give the last digit of your answer."

"Lovely." Lady Witham smiled back at him.

"Begin," Marty said.

"Five."

"Yes."

"Two. Four."

"Wait! Hold on. Did I say yes?"

"Sorry." Lady Witham laughed. "I got carried away. Witham always says I'm too exuberant." She winked naughtily.

"So," Marty said. "Where were we? Five, two, four, and?"

"Six," Lady Witham said.

"One." Marty gave the answer so quickly he practically cut Lady Witham off.

"Lovely! That's exactly right. But how—"

"That's for Dr. Stevens to explain," Marty said.

Mal held her breath. Tate was good with computers and math, but would he know this?

Tate simply cocked a brow. "Too easy. The digits of any multiple of nine add up to nine, you merely added five, two, four, and six for a total of seventeen and realized the last digit had to be one."

"Very good." Marty tipped an imaginary hat to Tate.

"My turn," Tate said. "Give me the volume of a disc with depth *a* and radius *z*."

Marty whipped out his phone. "This needs a visual." He typed out the answer. "PI•Z•Z•A" He nodded to the crowd and took a small bow. "Speaking of food—what do you get when you divide the circumference of a jack-o'-lantern by its diameter?"

"Pumpkin pi."

"I think I need to add you to my show," Marty said.

"And I think the rest of us should adjourn to the salon for an after-dinner drink." Lord Witham stood.

As the guests rose and followed him out, Sophia excused herself to go the restroom. Seizing her chance, Mal followed her.

CHAPTER THIRTEEN

The bathroom was on the first floor behind a massive, intricately carved wooden door. It was obvious the room had started out its life as something else, a sitting room or maybe a coatroom. Sophia dashed in, oblivious to Mal in pursuit of her, revealing her lack of espionage skill.

Mal plowed into the palatial room right behind her—did anyone really need three hundred square feet for a toilet and a sink—and closed the door behind her, leaning against it and studying the woman she was tasked with exfiltrating.

Sophia saw her reflected in the mirror and spun around to face her, her eyes wide. "What are *you* doing here?"

"Isn't it obvious? Helping you." Mal subtly palmed her phone, ready to call for help if Sophia turned on her, and activated a CIA jamming app developed by Cox Software.

Sophia looked around the room nervously. "You're mistaken. I don't need any help."

Mal studied her. The girl was obviously scared, as she should be with RIOT watching her. "Then why did you ask for ours? I know you know who I am."

Mal studied the other woman. "We don't have much time. Lingering in here too long will arouse suspicions and innuendos we'd both rather avoid.

"You said you'd contact us. Given how you're dressed—almost identically to me—I assume you've caught on to our plan for getting you safely out of here. With Tate. Which is what you asked for, right?"

Mal didn't wait for Sophia's answer. "We're going to switch identities, you and me. Here and now. You can act, can't you?" Mal assessed her. "Of course you can. You've been acting all evening." Mal paused.

"You followed Tate and me around all day, didn't you? We gave you ample opportunity to approach us and make the switch earlier today. Why didn't you act on the chance?"

"I was being followed." Sophia glanced at the door. "There was no opportunity."

Mal nodded. Sophia was obviously very bright and caught on quickly. What the girl said made sense, but it could still be a lie. "You understand the cover story? Mallie and Dr. Stevens are having an affair. They're here for a few days to enjoy the science festival.

"Tate will receive an urgent, emergency message from home and the two of you will take off to London immediately, cutting your stay unexpectedly short. From there you'll fly to the States and disappear. After you've been debriefed, of course." Mal paused, giving Sophia a chance to interject. When she didn't, Mal continued.

"You'll take my travel documents and assume my identity. I'll assume yours, lead your handler back to your room after the party, and tuck myself in for the night. Then I'll disappear before morning.

"The main thing is you'll have a ten- to twelve-hour window before RIOT and Bagge realize you're missing. You should be safely in the States by then.

"The only thing left is to switch gowns and shoes right here. Change our hairstyles and our makeup and each walk out of here like we're the other.

"When you approach Tate, he'll 'receive' his message

and excuse the two of you from the party. As you, I'll plead a headache and leave shortly after. Any questions?"

"No."

"Good." Mal reached behind her neck to unclasp her necklace and make the switch.

Sophia shook her head. "I mean it won't work. Not tonight."

"What?"

"I can't. Edvid is watching me."

Mal frowned. "I haven't seen him here. What makes you think—"

"He's good. He's here. Trust me. He doesn't miss anything." She looked genuinely frightened. "We'll have to wait for another opportunity."

She turned her back to Mal. "You'd better leave now. We'll make the switch as soon as it's safe. Not before. Trust me."

Mal frowned. Trust her? Not likely. But Sophia left her no choice. "Soon."

Frustrated, Mal sneaked out. Mal couldn't put her finger on it. Even though Sophia seemed genuine, something wasn't right. She still wondered whether Sophia was trying to pull off a complicated double cross.

Curious to see what Sophia would do next, Mal waited out of sight for Sophia to come out of the bathroom, telling herself it was her duty to make certain Sophia was safe. A few minutes later, Sophia came out and went directly to Lady Witham. Mal was a pretty darned good eavesdropper. Anyone who worked for the CIA was. She listened in from a distance as Sophia pleaded a headache and left the party.

What? Sophia was stealing her headache cover story. No way Mal was losing her now. She followed Sophia out to the driveway where a car picked Sophia up.

Mal flagged the parking valet and asked for her car,

waiting impatiently for the valet to bring it around. She texted Tate—*Sophia has fled. Am in pursuit.*

The valet appeared with her car. Mal hopped in and squealed out after Sophia.

She saw Sophia's car in the distance, heading toward town. There was only one route to Highfield Park from town.

Mal sped down the narrow hedge-lined country road in pursuit, praying she didn't meet any oncoming traffic. Her cell phone buzzed. Probably Tate. She couldn't take her focus off the road so she ignored it.

Sophia raced away from the party like a scared chick out of RIOT. Mal couldn't close the gap. Sophia's car disappeared from sight just as Mal reached the roundabout to A4019. Where would Sophia head and why?

Mal bet on the hotel. She sped through the roundabout, caught the A4019, and headed back to the hotel in the center of town. Sophia had taken a hired car. There was no reason to look for it in the parking lot to see if her guess was right.

Mal read Tate's text. *Mason and I are on it. We'll find her.*

Mal didn't bother to reply. Tate would use one of his apps to track her to the hotel. Mal let herself into the lobby and took the stairs to Tate's room to do a quick change before going to Sophia's room to look for her. Mal was just a little too obvious dressed in a formal gown. She'd draw too much attention as she prowled around.

At the door to the room, she removed the tiny pistol she had strapped to her leg beneath her gown. When dealing with RIOT, never walk into any room unprepared. She held it at ready as she opened the door and flipped on the light.

The bed was open. The sheets were turned back and Sophia lounged naked in a provocative pose. The ribbon around her neck was the only stitch of anything she wore, besides a stunned expression.

"What are *you* doing here?" they said in unison.

Mal closed the door behind her. This was too much. Damn, she hated it when her hunches were right. Sophia had run off to—Tate's bed.

Sophia sat up and pulled the sheets over her up to her chin. Her clothes were laid out on the back of the sofa. Mal stalked across the room, grabbed Sophia's dress and shook it as she held it out to her while aiming the pistol at her at the same time. "Get dressed."

Sophia's eyes went wide and her mouth made a perfect O. But she didn't reach for the dress.

"Scared little girl? Right. What are you trying to pull?" Mal shot her a steely gaze. "Why did you run here?"

"I told Tate at dinner I'd meet him here later."

It was a good thing for Sophia at that moment that she was a valuable asset to the Agency. It was about the only thing that kept Mal from pulling the trigger. If Sophia's story was true, why hadn't Tate mentioned it in his text?

"Did you." Mal didn't believe her.

"What are *you* doing here?" Sophia made no move to grab the dress and get dressed.

Mal had to get her out of here and back to her room before Tate showed up.

"Keeping up my cover. And doing my job—keeping an eye on you." Mal fought to keep her tone even. She kept the gun trained on Sophia.

Sophia continued to stare at her.

Mal sighed. "I hate to tell you, but lying in wait for Tate in bed is *not* the way to his heart. Better to let him do the seducing."

"That's not what I heard—" Sophia cut herself off.

Mal fought to hold her temper in check. "As his ex-wife, I've heard pretty much *everything*." And each exploit grated and stung. "Women have a habit of sneaking into his bed with startling regularity, as if he's a rock god or something."

Mal's laugh was more of a snort, really. "Famous singer. Software billionaire. I guess it's all the same to some women. Finding women in his bed happens so often, it's become a cliché and mundane. In other words, not the smartest move on your part. Not if you're trying to win his heart.

"If you're truly in love with him, as your dossier claims, use a more subtle technique and let him do the chasing. Why do you think none of these brazen women have succeeded in dragging him down the aisle since I divorced him?"

Sophia didn't have an answer.

"A word of friendly advice—let him make the moves. That's the way to reel him in, if that's what you really want." Mal didn't know why she was telling Sophia all this. She had no intention of letting Sophia snag Tate. And she was doing her own share of lying—how could Tate resist such a stunning woman in his bed?

Sophia lifted her chin. "Get out. I want some time alone with Tate. I need to get to know him before I trust him with my life."

"In the biblical sense? That's how you're going to judge his character?" Mal shook her head. "There will be plenty of time to get to know him once we get you safely to the States. For now, this is perfect. We can make the switch here and proceed with the original plan. I'll text Tate—"

"No!"

"What's wrong now? This is the optimal opportunity—"

"No." Sophia paled. "I know Edvid and how he operates. It's too dangerous to switch tonight. I'm risking my life. I won't go until the odds are better."

"We're risking ours, too." Mal took a deep breath. "We'll have to move soon. Our window for success is rapidly shrinking. The longer we stay here, the more scrutiny we draw. Maybe you haven't noticed—the festival is crawling with spies.

"We're going to try this all over again tomorrow. Tate and I will attend your lecture. Afterward, you and I will exchange clothes and identities. Tate will have a car waiting and you two will head off to Heathrow, again because of a family emergency.

"I'll return to your room and fool your handler for as long as I can. Hopefully I can buy you enough time to get on that airplane and back to the States before anyone catches on.

"I hope you realize the inconvenience you've caused. I'm going to have to reschedule your flight." Mal paused and gave Sophia her "hard-ass take no guff" stare. "You should be glad I'm still willing to put my life on the line for you." Mal waved her gun, just because she could. "Now. Get dressed and go back to your room. I'll give Tate your regrets."

"But—"

"No buts."

Sophia scowled at her. She wasn't nearly as alluring wearing that expression. Mal made a mental note to somehow bring it out for Tate to see.

"Turn around while I get dressed," Sophia said with enough anger in her voice to fuel a small volcanic eruption.

"Suddenly shy? How very sweet and innocent of you." Mal laughed again without mirth. "Girl, I'd have to be stupid to turn my back on you. I've seen everything you've got. Now, put your dress on." Mal dropped it at the edge of the bed.

Sophia slid out of bed and dressed hurriedly in an obvious huff, not bothering to put on her shoes or straighten her dress. In fact, she angrily removed the bow around her neck and tossed it away.

Mal kept the gun on Sophia until she was dressed. She showed her the door. As she closed it behind her with a satisfying thud, she noticed Sophia's ribbon lying on the floor.

Mal picked it up and stared at it. What was Sophia really up to hiding out in Tate's bed? Sophia seemed determined to get naked with Tate. Call it womanly intuition again, Mal couldn't put her finger on the reasons, but she had the feeling Sophia's determination had little to do with love and longing. She just didn't have the look of a woman in love. Mal bit her lip and walked to the mirror.

She studied herself a moment. Her plan was a good one—she and Sophia really could pass for each other, especially if they mimicked each other's actions. Mal was convinced she could copycat Sophia's. She just hoped Sophia was the actress and mimic that she was.

Mal stared at the ribbon again, feeling all the betrayal it represented—Tate sleeping with other women in the name of duty. These few days together had made her face facts—no matter how much she tried to deny it, she was still in love with Tate. Always had been.

She made a split-second decision. After his betrayal, Tate had claimed sleeping with other women meant nothing to him. That he was never eager to do it. Mal read him better than anyone. A test of Tate's character and a trial run of the switch were in order. Mal was going to play the role of Sophia tonight. How long could she fool Tate? Long enough to read his instant reaction to finding Sophia naked in his bed was all she needed.

She texted Tate. *Found her. S. is waiting for you in your bed.*

Mal ran the ribbon through her fingers before tying it

around her neck in a perfect imitation of Sophia's bow. She hurriedly restyled her hair, making herself into Sophia, stripped off her clothes, laid them over the sofa, smoothed the sheets, and climbed into bed to wait for Tate.

CHAPTER FOURTEEN

Tate took the stairs to his room, feeling more like a man on his way to his own execution than a man on his way to a round of lovemaking with a beautiful young woman. Sophia wasn't Mal. And Mal was all he'd ever wanted.

How the hell was he going to get out of making love with her? Whatever Mal thought, he wasn't just a shallow playboy looking for his next lay.

He hesitated at the door to his room. Steeling himself, he opened the door. The room was lit softly with candle- and firelight and smelled deliciously of sexy perfume and fire. Sophia lay naked in his bed, wearing only a ribbon around her neck and a seductive look. She lay sprawled across the covers with her breasts budded tight in a spread worthy of *Playboy*.

He hesitated, thinking fast for a way to turn her down and complete the mission without attempting entry. *Damn. Now was the moment of truth.*

She smiled and crooked her finger. "What are you waiting for? Close the door, Tate."

Mal. Her voice caressed his name. As he took off his fake glasses, he wondered how he could ever have mistaken her for Sophia.

Relief and lust hit him at once with a force that nearly

took his breath away. He closed the door and locked it, noticing the sofa table off to the side, out of place. He cocked a brow in question. Was she serious about making love? "Mal."

Mal leaned up on one elbow, still smiling while her breasts bounced enticingly and her skin glowed creamy and delicious in the firelight. "Barricade the door. We don't want any RIOTous interruptions."

"Are we expecting assassins?" He moved the sofa table across the door and loosened his tie.

"We're always expecting the unexpected." Mal slid out of bed, wagging her finger at him. "That's my job." She grabbed him by his tie and pulled him against her naked body.

He ran his hands down her back, massaging and caressing as he went, remembering every smooth, sensuous curve of the body he'd been longing for these past years apart. He grabbed her pert ass and pulled her against him as she untied his bow tie and tossed it away.

She smiled up at him, wrapping herself around him as she brushed his lips with a kiss and slid off his tux jacket. Even though he was fully clothed, it was as erotic as hell having a naked woman pressed against him.

Being naked and pressed up against Tate's starched white shirt was more erogenous than Mal could have imagined possible. Her heart danced. Her nipples budded tightly, even in the heat from the fire she'd lit in the fireplace. But nothing came close to the way Tate's expression had changed when he'd realized it was her in his bed, not Sophia. That switch, the look of love and longing replacing what could only be called dread and hesitation, had curled Mal's toes and sent a wave of intense heat between her legs so powerful she'd had to resist the urge to touch herself then and there. She owed Sophia one for setting up this situation.

She broke the gentle kiss, unbuttoning the buttons at his collar and running her tongue along his neck down to the hollow where she sucked and licked until he shuddered. His fingers dug into her bottom as he pressed her against his obvious erection.

Hold on, Tate. I'll give you the ride of your life. But only after I build you to it.

She unbuttoned his shirt until it fell open, running her tongue down his chest as she pulled the shirt free from his pants.

As he tried to shrug out of it, she sucked his nipple and ran her hands over his firm, flexed bicep, helped him lose his shirt, which fell on the floor with a gentle swish.

She unfastened and unzipped his pants, grabbing his hips and rubbing her breasts against him as he shimmied out of his pants. He was straining to get out of his underwear.

She stuck her finger in the waistband of his pants, teasing him as she smiled up at him. With a sudden tug, she pulled them down and waited for him to kick them off.

He fell out at full, pulsing attention.

As she leaned down to lick him, he caught her beneath the chin and tipped her head up.

"I don't have that much restraint." His voice was deep and raspy with desire. His eyes were round in the candlelight and his lips slightly parted.

She smiled up at him and rubbed against him, enjoying the hard planes of his body and the way his breath caught at her touch. Every part of her was tight and straining for release, yet she loved being in control and denying herself and him. When she was fully standing in front of him, she wrapped her arms around his neck and jumped up, coiling her legs around his waist as he cupped her butt and gasped.

She kissed him again, hard and deep, doing a dance with his tongue. Tate tasted like wine and desire. Like lust and love. Like the Tate she remembered, as he had the first time they'd touched.

She bit his shoulder and slid down him slowly as if she was sliding down a pole, enjoying the way the heat built between her thighs. She slid until her entrance rested against his erection.

"You're not ready," he said.

She shook her head. "I've been ready for years."

With a sudden, swift move that caught her off guard, he swept her to the bed and laid her down. He was inside her in a single, toe-tingling thrust so powerful it was like he'd thrust into her very being.

Tate rocked her as she arched against him and moaned, her cries riding the rhythm of her waves of pleasure. She'd come home. Back to the man she belonged to and with.

Legs still wrapped around him, she arched against him until her pleasure could no longer be restrained. The climax took her breath away. She was gasping as Tate climaxed and collapsed on her, sweaty and wonderful.

Smaller waves washed over her, like the gentle waves of the outgoing tide.

"I love you," he whispered into her neck.

Her heart stopped. "I love you, too."

It was what they always said after sex. Except during those last angry months together when sex had been rare and tepid. She hoped he wasn't repeating his "I love you" by rote because she sure wasn't. She meant every word and always had.

He kissed her shoulder and rolled off her. She cuddled into him, tracing the definition in his chest that shone with the exertion of pleasure. That was so much better than saying *sweat*.

He pulled the covers over them even though it was early June and a fire crackled away in the antique fireplace across the room.

"No one can say we don't know how to create a convincing cover," he said while stroking her hair.

"Is that what that was?" She wanted to think it was much more.

"No, that was ecstasy."

She laughed. "We were always good together."

"What did you do with Sophia?" He pulled her head into the crook of his neck and played with the ribbon around hers.

"Sent her back to her room. Did she really tell you earlier at the dinner that she'd be waiting for you?"

"What? Is this a test? You're going to talk work in bed?" He played idly with her breasts.

"No. Never," she said. "Tate?"

"Yeah?"

"Would you have slept with her?" She lay in his embrace, looking for any sign of lying.

"No. I'm through with all that, Mal."

She believed him. Maybe because she wanted to, or maybe because she'd gotten good at recognizing when he was telling the truth. She put her finger over his lips to silence him. She slid out of bed before he could protest and took his hand, pulling him with her. She grabbed a candle and led him to the bathroom where she set the candle by the sink and turned the water on in an old-fashioned claw-foot tub. Something about the sound of running water had always calmed her.

Sophia had conveniently left a bottle of wine chilling in an ice bucket and two wine goblets handy. Mal handed

Tate the bottle opener. He popped the cork in the wine like the pro he was and poured them each a glass while she bent over to test the water temperature, stopper the tub, and squirt bubble bath in. Tate came up behind her, caressed her bottom and between her legs as heat and desire built again. He set the wine down and grabbed her hips. She gasped as she felt him hard against her again with his chest pressed against her back.

In the next instant, he entered her from behind. She gasped. As the air filled with perfumed steam and the aroma of fine wine, they moved together until they climaxed together. Mal's knees went weak.

She turned around and kissed him, hard. "Still love me?"

"More than ever."

The tub was already halfway full as she stepped in and did a little dance. "Hot, hot, hot!"

"Yes, it is." Tate reached over, turned up the cold water, handed her a glass of wine, grabbed one for himself, and stepped into the water behind her. He pulled her against him and gently cradled her in his lap as he sat in the tub. The water splashed over the sides and some of Mal's wine sloshed into the tub. But it only perfumed the air more.

"Ah!" Tate relaxed against the back of the tub and held his glass up to hers. "To us."

They clinked and Mal leaned back against him. When the tub was full and threatening to flow over the edges, Mal forced herself forward to turn it off. "We have to talk mission details."

"Do we?" Tate said, nibbling her neck.

"Stop it! You'll give me a hickey and drive Sophia so mad with jealousy she'll probably slap me." Mal paused. "The woman's a bitch. She refused to cooperate with the plan."

"Yeah. I gathered," Tate said. "What went wrong?"

Mal related the details of her meeting in the bathroom with Sophia. "I don't trust her. She says she's afraid, which makes sense. But she seems to be stalling." Mal paused. "What did you think of her?"

"She's not you," he said, simply.

Mal took a sip of wine. She wasn't usually a coward, but she hesitated. Being naked made her vulnerable. "You thought I was her for a minute." Mal relaxed against him, trying to play it cool.

He took a deep drink of his wine. "Only because of the damned ribbon around your neck—her ribbon. And only for a fraction of a second. Why were you wearing it? And where and how did you get it?"

"Did it turn you on?" she asked, evading the question.

"No. I got turned on when I realized it was you in the bed, not her."

"Well, then," she said, screwing up her courage. "It's a good thing you weren't the first one to arrive at the room. She was naked in the bed, waiting for you with nothing but that ribbon on."

She felt Tate stiffen in surprise.

Then he laughed. "Was she? And you ran her off, grabbing her by the ribbon before she escaped?"

"That's a better story than the truth. I held a gun on her and politely asked her to leave."

"Politely, huh?" He didn't sound as if he believed her.

"Mallie is possessive of her Dr. Stevens." She downed the rest of her wine and reached over the tub to set her glass on the floor.

He was too tall for the tub. His knees were bent up out of the water. She grabbed his thigh and squeezed, loving the feel of the power of his muscle beneath her grip. Everything about him turned her on.

"She went without a fuss, then?" His voice was filled with humor.

"After I filled her in on the new plan and how things were going to work." She paused. "She tore off her ribbon and threw it on the floor. I thought if she can wrap herself up like a present for you, so can I."

He smiled at her and kissed her lightly on the lips, making her shiver in the hot bathwater.

She paused again, trying to find the right words to express her concern. "The thing is, I got the definite feeling from her that she was more than disappointed about not having her way with you." Mal shook her head, deep in thought. "I can't explain it, but it seemed like she *had* to sleep with you."

"A lot of women feel that way." He wrapped his arm around her.

She splashed him. "That's not what I mean. Not in that way." Mal paused again. "She seemed almost scared when I forced her out. I don't know, Tate. I don't like this. It just seems like there's something more to it. Something we don't know. I hope it doesn't come back to bite us in the butt."

"I hope not, too." Tate slid his hand into the water between her legs and rubbed her just the way she liked.

"Not that again." She spun around to face him, straddling him.

"Oh, yeah. That. And more."

CHAPTER FIFTEEN

Waking up next to Tate felt right and too perfect. Malene had never fallen out of love with Tate. Not for a minute. Oh, sure, she hated him at times. Cursed him. Wondered why he couldn't have been the husband she wanted. But deep down, she loved him. All the rest was simply a cover story that helped her keep going and trying to move on with her life. After all, she was good at cover lives. That was her biz.

But as she woke, wrapped in his arms, there was no sense of awkwardness. No recrimination. And after she'd seen his initial gut reaction to finding "Sophia" in his bed waiting for him, she was beginning to wonder if she *should* believe in him again. If he had changed. Because that look on his face said the last thing he wanted to do was sleep with the RIOT agent, beautiful and young as she was. In that respect, it was good that it had been Mal and not Sophia because that look was a potential mission killer.

But it made Mal incredibly happy. Deep down she believed Tate would have found a way to get out of having sex with Sophia.

Mal smiled. Tate *had* been desperate for sex with her and his enthusiasm genuine. As she leaned up on an elbow to study him, he woke.

"What time is it?" He shielded his eyes from the

sunlight filtering in through the curtains. It came up early this time of year.

"Time to start the day." She brushed a lock of hair off his forehead.

He smiled. "I hope that means a joint shower." He gave her a sexy, sleepy grin.

The thought made her tingle and silenced the urge to talk about what had happened between them last night and that "I love you" he'd spoken. Better to go with the flow.

As she leaned over to stroke his chest and kiss him, someone banged on the door, startling them both.

"Dr. Stevens! Dr. Stevens! I must speak with you. Are you in?"

Sophia!

Tate stared at Mal as a quick look of disappointment flashed across his face. "Coming!" he yelled back to Sophia, motioning for Mal to get into the bathroom and get some clothes on.

She made a dash for it as he rolled out of bed and struggled into a pair of pants. Mal grabbed a robe and slid into the bathroom, closing the door behind her just as Tate removed the barricade and opened the door to the room.

Mal couldn't see a thing, but she pressed her ear to the door, hoping to hear something and cursing Sophia's timing. She was tired of that woman, really tired of her.

Mal strained to hear, but all that got through was worried murmuring. She thought Sophia was crying. RIOT operatives crying? That either meant things were dire, or she was faking it for some reason. Mal wouldn't put anything past Sophia.

Tate said something. A second later, he knocked on the bathroom door. "Mal? Can you come out here? We have a situation."

A situation?

Mal tucked her robe around her, ran her fingers through her hair to tame it, and came out to find Sophia clinging to Tate like a piece of plastic wrap. Tears stood in her eyes and she looked genuinely afraid.

Something had gone very wrong. Mal's gaze darted between the two of them. "What's going on?"

"RIOT's on to her," Tate said. His voice was tight.

"On to her?" She stared hard at Sophia. "Are you sure? How do you know? How did they find out?"

"I'm sure," Sophia said. "I didn't do something they wanted me to do. For now, they think I have. But any minute, they will realize they're mistaken and kill me."

Was it Mal's imagination or did the look Sophia was giving her blame her for Sophia's failure?

"What didn't you do?" Mal asked, wondering why Tate wasn't jumping in with the third degree.

"Endanger Tate." Sophia shot her a look like daggers as she clutched Tate's arm.

What have I done? Mal thought.

From his angle, Tate couldn't see the way Sophia glared at Mal.

"How exactly?" Mal persisted.

"Later. Right now there's no time." Sophia was agitated. She really did look scared.

"We'll interrogate her later," Tate said to Mal. "Call Mason. We have to leave *now*."

"Now? How now do you mean?" Mal's heart sped into wild pounding mode as she grasped to think clearly. She'd been in on her fair share of mission complications, but on the office side, not out in the field.

"As fast as we can," Tate said. "Sophia said they'll be after her any minute, certainly no later than when they expect her for breakfast."

Mal bunched her fist. "The best plan is still to sneak her out as me." She went to her suitcase and grabbed an outfit. "Slight change of cover-story plan, though. Just in case RIOT has noticed the similarity between us"— Mal motioned between her and Sophia—"we shouldn't cause any alarm bells to go off by giving any indication Dr. Stevens and Mallie plan on leaving.

"Dr. Stevens and Mallie will have to look as if they're totally unaware and unconcerned about any danger to Sophia. They're supposed to be sightseeing this morning. They should proceed as planned.

"Once you're out of the hotel, you'll have to watch for tails and take evasive action. I'll arrange for a car to be left for you at a location we'll determine, somewhere close enough you can walk to it, but where RIOT won't be looking. A carpark at one of the other hotels or a shopping mall. From there you'll drive to Heathrow and fly out using my assumed identity.

"Mallie will be dressed casually." Mal tossed a pair of short shorts and a halter top to Sophia. "Put these on. You can change in the bathroom. Leave your clothes for me."

Tate had to give Sophia a hug, a comforting look, and a gentle shove before she got moving and sulkily locked herself in the loo.

Mal grabbed her phone. "I'll have to call CIA Travel and change your reservations. You two are going to have to walk out of here boldly, as if you haven't a care in the world. No fear, not the slightest scent of it. She has to be me." Mal frowned and glanced at the closed bathroom door. "Do you think she's up to it?"

"She has to be. We don't have a choice." Tate grabbed Mal's arm. "What's your role?"

"The same as before—I'll be the decoy—"

"Like hell!" Tate's eyes flashed.

"Don't use your commanding voice on me." Mal tried to act calm. "We're partners. This was always the plan."

"It's too dangerous, especially now." Tate didn't change his tone.

"I have to buy you time."

Tate took a deep breath. "If we act fast enough, we won't need time. We'll need cover. The plan is basically the same, you and Mason will follow us and ride shotgun.

"Use your disguise skills," he said. "Make yourself look like someone else. Sneak out the secret passage and meet Mason out back. Rendezvous with us at the car and follow us out."

His concern was sweet. Touching even. "But—"

"No buts, Mal." He paused. "I promised you long ago that Kayla wouldn't lose her daddy. I'll be damned if I'll take a chance of her losing her mommy. She needs you more than she needs me." He held her gaze.

The look in his eyes and the tenor of his voice gave her a lump in her throat. And something even better—hope.

She must have looked as if she was acquiescing.

He dropped her arm. "Let's move."

Until this mission, Tate had forgotten how amazing Mal was at creating covers and disguises. She'd always had artistic talent and flair with makeup, but early on in her career the CIA sent her to Hollywood to train with top movie makeup artists. She'd come back a true pro. With her talent with disguise, it was amazing she'd ended up in covers, rather than as master of disguise.

As Tate dressed in Dr. Stevens's sightseeing clothes, he watched as Mal stripped naked and put on a lacy thong nude pantie and matching strapless bra. Did she have to torment him with sexy lingerie and the most grabable ass in the country?

If Sophia walked out of the bathroom and caught him hungering over Mal like that, there would be hell to pay.

Emmett would have his head if he botched this mission, especially after insisting on taking it on. Fortunately, Sophia was still banging around in the bathroom like a petulant child.

Mal pulled on a satiny silver embroidered bustier top with ribbon trim that emphasized her hourglass figure and a slim silver belt studded with crystals that made her waist look small enough to span with his hands. She finished the outfit with skintight white cropped skinny jeans and silver wedge sandals, transforming into a sophisticated and gorgeous woman who was definitely no girl. She caught him gawking and salivating and standing at full attention.

He covered with diversion. "Really, Mal? You think you can watch my backside and keep up with me in those shoes?"

She grinned. "I can watch your backside in anything. Besides, I run better in heels. All the lady cops on TV work in them."

"Uh-huh."

Mal pulled an auburn wig cut in a stylish bob out of one of her cases and strode to the mirror to pop it on. She plugged a flatiron and a curling iron in at the vanity and opened her makeup kit to get to work. With a few deft strokes of her makeup brush, she turned into an entirely different person. He had to look twice. If he hadn't known the woman seated at the vanity was Mal, he would have walked right past her on the street.

That was a lie. The woman before him would have turned his head. Mal should have known better. Plain, everyday-looking spies, people no one noticed, played best undercover. It's one reason Tate had never gone undercover before—he was too high-profile and recognizable. It was better to play that to his advantage rather than risk being recognized.

"What is taking that girl so long?" Mal pushed back

from the vanity and strode to the bathroom door and pounded on it.

Mal even walked differently, strode with a walk oozing sensuality and maturity in a way Sophia did not. It was sexy as hell.

"Hurry up in there! We don't have all day." Mal rolled her eyes and crossed her arms.

Tate recognized jealousy and female competitive spirit when he saw it. Clearly, Mal didn't like Sophia. Which warmed his heart and gave him hope.

Tate pulled his shoes on and dialed Mason as Mal held up her hands and gestured, frustrated, like *what can you do?*

Sophia emerged from the bathroom, dressed in Mallie's clothes, which fit her like they'd been tailored specifically for her, with a pout on her lips.

"Finally!" Mal grabbed Sophia and sat her at the vanity. She grabbed a makeup-removing cloth. "I'll do your makeup. When I'm finished, you'll be a dead ringer for Mallie."

Was it Tate's imagination, or had Mal emphasized the word *dead*?

Tate focused on his call with Mason as he filled him in on the new plan. Then he called HQ and explained the new situation to them.

By the time Tate finished his calls, Sophia had been transformed into Mallie. He let out a low whistle, not a catcall, a whistle that let Mal know he was impressed with her work. He went to the vanity and stood behind Sophia, studying her in the mirror.

"You like?" Sophia put a flirt in her voice.

"You're perfect. You look just like Mallie."

"Physical features are one thing," Mal said. "It still remains to be seen whether she can carry this deception off. The trick is to get into character and become Mallie the grad student." She grabbed Sophia's arm. "Get up. I'm going to teach you how to walk like Mallie and put on her mannerisms."

As Mal dragged Sophia to her feet, she snagged Tate's fake glasses and handed them to him. "Put these on."

Mal pulled Sophia to the corner of the room away from both the window and the door. "Watch me walk. Watch me interact with Dr. Stevens. Pay attention. I only have a few minutes to coach you and all of our lives hang on your performance and believability. Ready?"

Sophia nodded.

Mal walked across the room, young and Mallie again. Her walk was sexy in an innocent, youthful way. When she caught Tate's arm and smiled up at him, love, shy and new and possessive, shone in her eyes. She curled into him and then reached up to brush his lips with a tantalizing light kiss that sent a current of pleasure through him. She really was trying to kill him.

Mal dropped Tate's arm and turned to Sophia. "Think you can mimic that?" She stepped aside. "Give it your best shot."

Sophia shrugged and came toward him, imitating Mallie's walk. She was a gorgeous young woman, and she looked so damn much like Mal, but as Tate stood there, playing Professor Stevens, he felt no chemical attraction. Other than the natural appreciation any man feels for a pretty woman. Nothing special or out of the ordinary.

"A little less sway to your walk." Mal was focused on Sophia and wearing the slightest scowl. "You're not playing Marilyn Monroe. Our little Mallie isn't a sexpot." She sounded like she hoped that was true.

Sophia toned down the sway and took his arm, smiling up at him. For a second his breath did catch, but only because of her resemblance to Mal. When Sophia leaned up and brushed his lips with hers, he felt nothing, not even as he got a whiff of Mallie's perfume.

Sophia misinterpreted his expression and bodily reaction, grinning like she'd just won a prize. Mal misinterpreted, too, and frowned. Damn, he was between a rock and a hard mission in this situation. He either succeeded with the mission or with Mal. He'd made that choice before—career over personal life—and had lived to regret it. Was this mission worth his chance with Mal, and a life as a family with Kayla again?

Sometimes Tate felt as if he had everything. And nothing.

"It will have to do." Mal glanced at the clock.

"You'll do fine," Tate whispered to Sophia, and gave her shoulder a reassuring squeeze.

"When will Mason be here?" Mal asked.

"Any minute." Tate stepped away from Sophia and picked up his lightweight jacket.

"Good." Mal smiled but her eyes were hard.

Tate knew her well enough to see she was worried. "We'll pull this off. We always do." He smiled at Mal. "Take the secret passage. Mason will meet you at the outside entrance. From there you'll sneak through the garden and out to the street. Sophia and I will wait in the room and give you time to get in position.

"Mason will have a car waiting for each of us," Tate said. "Sophia and I will act like we're off for a nice drive in the country. You and Mason will follow to cover our asses. Simple."

"Simple doesn't mean easy," Mal said, looking Tate directly in the eye. "Remember your promise."

CHAPTER SIXTEEN

The secret passage was just as dank, musty, and totally unromantic as it had been the day Mason first showed it to them. It didn't improve upon second viewing. And negotiating the narrow winding steps in high-heeled sandals with a white cardigan sweater wrapped around her shoulders while her mind was on Sophia's performance didn't improve Mal's opinion of the passage. Maybe if she'd been an adventurous eight-year-old playing pretend. But everything was at stake now—her life, Tate's life, which hung on Sophia's meager acting skills, and Mal's possible happily-ever-after with Tate. Kayla, that little imp, had been trying to manufacture a reunion her entire five-year-old life, or so it seemed. She'd be so happy to get her daddy back full-time. Well, as full-time as Tate ever was.

Mal slipped and caught herself with a hand against the rough grain of the wall. She wielded her key-chain flashlight and negotiated the steps more carefully. She'd watched Tate sail out of the room with a giggling Sophia on his arm and then scrubbed the room of anything that would give them away to RIOT before leaving. She'd latched the door to the secret passage carefully and locked it behind her. Her thoughts were as dark as the passageway as she made her way toward the exit and Mason, looking over her shoulder from time to time as if she expected RIOT to be on her tail already.

When she reached the exit, the door lock was stuck. *Remind Mason to get some graphite on this lock.* She swore to herself until she finally got the key to turn. *Why do little things always go wrong when I'm in a hurry?*

She had just minutes to get out of the building, meet Mason, and get in position to cover Tate when he and Sophia left the hotel. The plan was that she and Mason would tail them, keeping watch for any enemy tails and taking any out.

Mal turned the handle and the door stuck. *Damn, damn, damn! Bloody door!* How easy it was to slip into Britspeak.

She took a deep breath and sighed. *This must be another RIOT plot to foil us.*

She didn't remember Mason having this trouble when he showed them the secret route the day they arrived.

There was nothing for it. She was going to have to use her brute strength, meager as it was, and either knock the door loose or break it down. She hoped that door wasn't as dirty as the rest of the passage or it was curtains for her pretty white sweater.

She aimed her shoulder at it and gave it a good ram. *Ouch! That stung.*

The door remained unsympathetic to her pain and stubbornly closed. She rubbed her newly aching shoulder. *Great, it can join my bruised foot. A matching set.*

She eyed the door, ran her flashlight over it looking for weak spots, drew a bead on the most likely spot with her shoulder and threw herself at the door again, wishing for the first time in her life that she'd been born stocky like her brother. The door shuddered, groaned, and gave way. She tumbled out, right into Mason's open arms, ending up bracing herself against his hard chest.

"Now that's the kind of enthusiastic greeting I like—women simply falling into my arms from out of nowhere." His eyes danced and he was smiling.

"And here I thought you were expecting me." She looked over her shoulder at the door. "There must be a trick to that beast. Did I have to say 'open sesame' or something?"

"Now that you mention it, it is a bit of a beast. Oh, you soiled your sweater." He gave her shoulder a gentle brush. "Nothing but a bit of dust." He swatted at her shoulder again while she tried not to wince. He studied his work and smiled. "There you go! All gone and back to rights and snowy white." His gaze bounced to the door again. "She can be cranky. You have to know how to coax the old girl."

"You might have mentioned it."

"And missed out on having you in my arms?"

She pulled out of his embrace and dusted herself off, resisting the urge to look pointedly around for RIOT creeps. "Do we have company?"

"Not yet." Mason shut and locked the door. "But we mustn't linger near doorways. You never can tell with RIOT agents. They show up uninvited at the most inconvenient times." Mason offered her his arm and led her through a beautiful, fragrant, traditional English garden full of pink roses, lavender, hostas, and lilies as if they were merely out for a stroll and in no rush at all to get into position to play bodyguard to Tate and his charge.

"Shouldn't we hurry?" she asked him when her subtle efforts to move faster failed.

"We have plenty of time. Tate knows the route. If we miss him, we'll catch up to him well before he reaches the car."

"What if someone else *doesn't* miss him?" she asked.

Mason grinned. "Don't worry about Tate."

There wasn't anything more beautiful than a dewy

English garden on a sunny June morning. Gunfire and blood would absolutely ruin its ambience.

At the edge of the garden, near a lush patch of magenta daylilies, Mason hesitated. "Into the hedgerow with you." He gave her a gentle shove and followed her into the bushes.

There was a locked gate buried within. Mason unlocked it and pushed it open, extending his arm. "After you."

"How gentlemanly. First out of the hedgerow will take the first bullet."

He laughed. "And I'll be forever sorry, wondering what could have been." He sounded almost serious.

But he was a playboy from the same mold as Tate. A woman couldn't trust what he said.

"I'm sure you'll get over it."

He smiled, held her back, and took a look around. "The alley is clear."

She stepped out with Mason following her. He took the lead and led them to a carpark just up the street. Another of those tiny British cars waited for them. It looked suitably unimpressive.

"I hope that thing's turbocharged," she said.

"Better—it has wings."

She stared at him, wanting to believe him. He was so very much like Bond come to life that it seemed almost possible. She laughed. "Shut up!"

"Almost had you." He beeped the car.

There was a second where they both held their breath, almost expecting it to explode and burst into flame. The moment passed. He pulled out a mirror and wanded the car, looking for bombs in the undercarriage.

"You'd think I'd be less gullible than the average girl on the street." Mal watched the proceedings. "In my defense, I've seen some pretty fantastical stuff."

"Really?" He tucked his folding mirror on a stick away. "Like what?"

"You said that with such a straight face. Do you really expect me to easily spill top secret intel?" She laughed.

"A spy can try." He walked to the passenger side of the car and opened the door.

She shook her head and held out her hand for the keys. "No way I'm riding shotgun again. I'm much better at driving than playing sniper."

He hesitated.

She tilted her head, gave him a serious look, and waved at him with her palm up, urging him to toss the keys to her. "Come on. I work for the Agency, and better yet, I was married to Tate. I've taken more than my share of driving classes. I had to keep up somehow."

He made a point of sighing, and followed it with a laugh. "You win." He threw the keys to her. "I'll give you directions."

"Fine by me. As long as you aren't a backseat driver."

"I have no intention of being in the backseat."

She smiled at him and slid into the driver's seat. "Where to?"

"I know a cozy little spot where we can watch the hotel entrance."

Danger and threat had always given Tate a rush. But now as he walked down the steps toward the lobby with Sophia clutching his arm and giggling and gushing about sightseeing, he sensed the gravity of what his job required. And the consequences of failure and mistakes.

He mentally cursed Emmett again for sending Mal on this mission, but not in the same spirit he'd had at the outset. Now he was genuinely worried about her. Everything hinged on Sophia keeping her cool and doing at least a passable imitation of Mallie.

Tate was not an exfiltration expert, but he'd heard stories from his colleagues who were and asked for tips before he left on this mission. Fellow spies were much easier to exfiltrate than everyday citizens. They knew tradecraft and how to keep their cool under pressure and danger of being found out. They knew how to maintain a cover. Everyday people got too nervous and easily slipped up. Even an innocent comment that was off cover could blow things.

The experts had coached him that it was best to give your target a cover that was as close to their real lives as possible and get them to memorize every detail of their cover life. Looking like Mal and being a mathematics grad student was a brilliant cover for Sophia. Tate gave Mal and the Agency credit for that.

Working for RIOT, Sophia fell in between spy and average citizen. There had been no time to have her memorize the details of her cover story. Fortunately, they were exfiltrating her from an ally country who would help. But RIOT would be looking for her under every moss-covered English rock. And unless Tate missed his guess, RIOT had double agents working in every aspect of British society. One small slipup once they noticed Sophia was missing and the whole thing could go down the tank. He and Sophia could both end up dead. And Mal and Mason, too.

The thought of Mal being shot bothered him most. And of Kayla being left orphaned to be fought over by both of their mothers. He'd never admit this to Mal, but in a custody battle between their two mothers, he hoped hers won. His mom, Lenora, was a force to be reckoned with. She had more money and more influence and power. She'd been good for Tate and forged him into the man he was. But she was cold. Tate's little girl deserved open love and affection. His former mother-in-law overflowed with love for Kayla.

Sophia just had to keep up the act until they were out of Cheltenham. Then it should be smooth sailing until they reached Heathrow. There would be a lot of pressure to hold her head there. Once they cleared security and were on the plane and out of British airspace, everything would be fine. Mission accomplished.

He patted Sophia's hand where it clutched his arm. She flashed him an adoring smile full of hero worship and faith.

How much information did RIOT have on him? What caused this girl to fall in love with him simply from his files and photos?

They turned the final corner of the steps into the lobby.

"You're doing fantastic," he whispered to her. "I think you have Mallie's walk down perfectly."

Even smiling she looked frightened and who could blame her? If RIOT had caught on to what was going on, they could end her life with a sniper bullet as they came around the corner and took the last half flight of stairs into the lobby. He had to encourage her and keep her confidence up. "You're doing great. Keep it up through the lobby. Once we're out on the street, it should be smooth sailing."

Mercifully, the lobby was empty. The front desk clerk looked up and smiled at them. "Dr. Stevens. Miss Green. Off to see the sights and enjoy the festival?"

"That we are," Tate answered.

Sophia smiled shyly, a little too shyly, and nodded.

"First day is always exciting," the clerk said. "Enjoy yourselves."

"We will. Thank you." Tate led Sophia to the door. "See? That wasn't so bad. You fooled him."

But it was false praise just to bolster her. The desk clerk should have been just about the easiest person on the planet to fool, right above a complete stranger. From even a slight distance, Sophia's general similarity to Mal, Mal's clothes, and her expert makeup job should have fooled her own mother. For a second, at least.

Once they were out of the hotel, their chances of meeting anyone familiar dramatically decreased. Tate's heart raced as he strolled, propelling Sophia along, toward the door. He hoped like hell RIOT didn't come charging down the stairs with guns blazing and that Mason and Mal had disabled any potential threats outside the hotel.

They crossed the lobby without a problem. Tate held the door open for Sophia. And they were out in the fresh English air with the sun shining down on them. Tate took a deep breath, ready to heave a sigh of relief just as Vail Belanger turned up the walk and waved to him.

Damn. Of all the bad luck and timing.

Tate whispered to Sophia out of the side of his mouth, "That fat man is a fake. A French spy who's already suspicious about why I'm here. He knows Mal well enough to recognize her. And he knows she's my ex. Let me do the talking. Especially if he mistakes you for her. Pretend you've lost your voice if you have to."

Mal cruised past Dashwood House with Mason playing lookout.

"No one idly lounging around. No known terrorists. No one depositing backpacks," Mason said. "Pull over there."

He directed Mal to a secluded spot with a clear view of the hotel entrance.

"How convenient this prime spot is open," Mal said, casually as she parked the car, tongue-in-cheek.

"Yes, very."

"You couldn't have parked here in the first place? It was hardly worth burning the petrol from starting the car to go such a short distance and I would have enjoyed the walk."

"Two problems with that—I prefer having a little armor between me and people who might like to kill me and, more importantly, this spot wasn't open when I arrived." He smiled devilishly, letting Mal know a tow truck had probably done his dirty work for him.

"The power of MI5," she said.

"Now for the boring part of surveillance. We watch and wait."

"Tate has impeccable timing. He'll be out any minute." She hoped.

Mason had gone silent and was staring at something. "Fucker," he whispered beneath his breath.

Mal followed his line of sight. A white man—average height, average build, light brown hair—was walking down the street. He wore a gray hoodie and jeans like a tourist and looked about as nonthreatening as a person could—

She squinted, studying him, trying to see what Mason did. And then it hit her. "Asymmetrical gait. Right-side stride is shorter." The hair stood up on the back of her neck.

Another pedestrian passed him and the guy did an upper-body shift, protecting his right side. The pedestrian turned and disappeared into a small café. Fortunately, it was early and the street was deserted except for Mr. Average.

"Upper-body shift." Mason reached for the door, gaze glued on Mr. Average, body poised for flight.

The guy stepped up on the curb and made a quick circular movement with his hand, a clear indicator he had a gun. A gun carries its weight in the grip, rather than the barrel. As a consequence, it's unbalanced and shifts easily in a pocket when the shooter goes up stairs or steps up on a curb. Tate had taught her that. Handguns were illegal in Britain, which meant—

"Strike three!" Mason slid out of the car and walked casually, trailing Average, gun drawn in his jacket pocket.

Mal reached for her purse and pulled out her pink

pistol, which intentionally looked almost like a toy. She silently cursed as she grabbed her keys, wondering what to do next.

She shook her head. In all probability, Average was Sophia's handler, Edvid Bagge, badass RIOT assassin. Mal looked up Bagge's profile on her cell phone and made a visual ID. Yes, definitely Bagge. *Damn.*

Average walked casually toward a gap between buildings, acting as if he had no idea he was being followed. Mal saw it all playing before her eyes as if in slow motion. Bagge was leading Mason into a trap. It was the old box-canyon trick.

Mal slid out of the car and took off after them, praying no one else came along. The last thing they needed was a witness to blow their cover and the mission.

Bagge ducked into the shade in the gap and waited. It all happened so quickly, there was no time to yell a warning. As Mason came even with the gap, gun drawn, Bagge took aim at Mason's chest. Mal removed the safety and took aim with her handgun, initiating the laser sight.

Just as Bagge was about to squeeze the trigger, he looked down and saw the red laser bead aimed at his heart. The bastard grinned. Mal had no choice. She squeezed the trigger.

Bagge clutched his chest. His knees buckled, and with a crazy grin still on his face, he fell to the ground.

The pink pistol had a silencer and very little kick. Mal couldn't believe she'd actually shot.

Mason ran to Bagge. By the time Mal reached them, Bagge was foaming at the mouth.

"Suicide pill," Mason said with disgust, his gun aimed at Bagge's temple. "He won't tell us anything." He glanced at Mal. "Nice shot. One threat down. Next time go for the head."

She was shaking. "I'm not an assassin. I aim for what I

think I can hit—the largest target." She stared at Bagge, shaken even though he was a piece of scum who'd killed more than his share of friendly agents.

Mason put his arm around her. "Don't take it so hard. He killed himself."

She nodded, trying to believe Mason was right. "What do we do with him now?" she said, trying to sound dispassionate and professional.

"You, in your pristine white jeans, need to step aside while I pull him out of sight and call Witham to get rid of him before someone finds him."

Being exposed and leaving Tate uncovered was making Mal jumpy, especially given how real the threat was. RIOT killers traveled in packs. She glanced over her shoulder at the street just in time to see the French spy Vail Belanger, dressed in a fat suit, appear around the corner headed toward Dashwood House.

"Tate's in more trouble." She pointed to Belanger. "That fake fat man could blow our whole mission. Let's hope Sophia really can act."

CHAPTER SEVENTEEN

D r. Stevens, I presume?" Vail Belanger cocked a brow as if asking a question and laughed, shaking his fat-suit belly and running his gaze over every curvaceous inch of Sophia with a lusty, curious twinkle in his eyes. The way he studied Sophia, it was obvious he recognized her, and yet he didn't. He sensed something was off.

Damn him, Tate thought, enjoying Vail's confusion while cursing the Frenchman for playing spy games with him and slowing his escape.

"We meet again," Vail prompted in his very British accent.

"Indeed we do. Nice of you to remember me. I'm not a scientist of the highest record. Just a small cog who helped with a paper that's being presented later today." Tate had to let Vail know he was still undercover. As an ally, he should respect it and keep his nose out of Tate's spy business.

Then again, the rule to trust no one was always in full effect. Tate decided it was best to continue running with the cover ruse and let Vail think what he would. He wondered whether Belanger had recognized Mal the night before as the subject of Tate's practical joke.

Tate purposely waited until Belanger cleared his throat and stared pointedly at Sophia.

"Where are my manners?" Tate smiled at Sophia. "This is my graduate student assistant, Mallie Green. She helped with the research on my paper." Now it was dicey. Tate had no idea who Belanger was supposed to be. "Pardon me. I know we were introduced, but your name has slipped my mind."

Belanger was still studying Sophia with that look that said he was trying to place her, that he wasn't quite sure she was Mal. "Dr. Thomas Bell. I'm here purely as a tourist looking to take in some of the popular demonstrations and shows."

Following instructions, Sophia didn't speak. She merely nodded and smiled.

Belanger leaned in and whispered into Tate's ear. "Working with the ex? What are you up to?"

Tate grinned. "That's only for those with a need to know, old boy." He slapped Belanger on the back. "Now if you'll excuse us, we're off to do some sightseeing. Enjoy the festival!" He took Sophia's hand and led her down the front steps and onto the sidewalk, leaving Belanger to stare after them.

When they were out of earshot, Tate whispered to Sophia. "Perfect job back there. He thought you were Mal." Tate laughed. "He'll be chewing on that one for a while." He squeezed her hand and, feeling Belanger watching them, impulsively kissed her breezily on the lips to give him even more to speculate over.

Tate felt no zing in that kiss, even as Sophia pressed up against him and kissed him back with passion and a gentle flutter of her tongue. When he pulled away her eyes were round and wide and her skin flushed.

She looked at him coyly, almost shyly from beneath her thick lashes, doing almost a Princess Di impersonation. The princess had always used that look to full effect. Sophia had mastered it perfectly, so expertly Tate wondered whether she'd practiced it. It should have knocked him to his knees, but it didn't. Chemistry was a fickle thing, he decided.

"Tell me about your ex-wife—do you get along?" She continued to use the Princess Di look on him.

Interesting topic to bring up after he'd just kissed her. Kiss a woman and bring out what's really on her mind? Jealousy was a vicious monster.

What a tangled web deception and the spy business wove. He decided it was best to stick to conventional wisdom about the two of them since only he and Mal knew things had changed.

"Sure." He grinned at Sophia. "As long as we stay away from each other and keep things superficial. Then we're great."

"But you're here together?" Her eyes were still wide and lovely. "Sleeping in the same room."

"Only out of necessity." He hesitated and decided to go for broke. "And a weird quirk of fate. Your natural resemblance to her is uncanny. Which gave the exfiltration experts at the agency the brilliant idea of using her identity to sneak you out."

Sophia's brow furrowed. Somehow she managed to still look lovely and fresh. "And my resemblance to her is a bad thing?" Her tone was half flirt, half worried question.

"I never said Mal isn't gorgeous. A guy would have to be blind not to notice her. I married her, after all. Not to sound like an arrogant ass, but women find my money attractive. I can have my pick.

"Unfortunately, Mal's personality didn't match her beautiful hide. Or at least, didn't mesh with mine." He had to convince Sophia he was crazy for *her*.

"That I look like her, especially now, made up like her, doesn't bother you, then?" Sophia asked.

"No," he said, completely serious. "On the contrary.

Maybe I'm just a guy who has a type, but I find you very sexy."

She smiled at him. "That's what I like to hear."

"Let's blow this place." He squeezed her hand again, reassuring her. "We have a car to find and a plane to catch."

Mal felt very much the spy as she watched Tate handle Belanger on the steps of Dashwood House, with her pulse roaring in her ears.

"How are they doing?" Mason asked as he finished hiding Bagge's body in a flower bed for his crew to find later.

Hiding a body in an English flower bed made Mal feel like part of an Agatha Christie novel. As she'd predicted, it ruined the ambience and made her look at flower beds warily. She hoped Witham's people arrived before the gardener or he was going to be in for a terrible scare.

Mal turned over her shoulder and cupped her hand around her mouth to direct her words to Mason. "They seem to have managed. They've just left Belanger looking stunned and puzzled. Are you finished there? Or am I going to have to tail them myself?"

Mason dusted off his hands. "Just finished now."

Mal turned back and peeked out of the gap between buildings just in time to watch Tate kiss the RIOT witch on the sidewalk. There's blood-boiling jealousy, murderous jealousy, and then there's soul-killing jealousy. In that instant, Mal felt all three, but not in equal measure. Lucky for Tate that murderous jealousy came in a distant last and Belanger looked merely bemused as he watched that kiss from his perch on the Dashwood steps.

Tate is playing the part of the cover. Doing what he has to do to exfiltrate the girl.

That's what the logical, confident part of her believed. But the other part, the part that had been worn down and given up on her marriage kept whispering at her to close up her heart and forget Tate. He hadn't changed his play-boy ways and never would. That he was enjoying that kiss way too much and looking too adoringly at Sophia.

"If looks could kill," Mason said as he came up beside her.

I'm that obvious?

Mal tried to control her scowl. "We have a daughter together. I don't ever want that woman anywhere near her. Do you see the way she's looking at him?"

Mason took her arm. "I do. The tart! She's very convincing. Either she really is in love with him as she claims, or she's a better actress than we give her credit for."

Mal wasn't about to give her credit for anything. "Falling in love with a man because of his picture and exploits is falling in love with a fantasy. Let's hope Tate can live up to that fantasy until we deliver her safely to our expert debriefers."

"Do you doubt him?" Mason asked.

"Not for a minute." She laughed. "And that's the conundrum. Even if Tate manages not to lose his heart to her, I have a horrible feeling about this.

"Once we learn everything we can from her, Sophia is going to have to disappear. Which means she'll have to let go of Tate and the fantasy dream she's created of him or risk her life."

"That should solve your problem," Mason said as they waited for Tate and Sophia to get a comfortable distance ahead of them before stepping out of the shade to tail them.

"Yes, you'd think. But what are the odds Sophia isn't going to go all *Fatal Attraction* on us? She's young and idealistic enough to think love will conquer all and that she's invincible. If she didn't, she'd never try to escape from RIOT in the first place. If that's what she's really doing."

"The spy biz has made you cynical," Mason said.

"Maybe our little RIOT wench has repented and is simply desperate."

Mal looked at Mason and shook her head. "You aren't helping.

"I have this horrible feeling she isn't going to go quietly. She may look all innocent and lovely. She certainly knows how to play men. Around women, or at least me, she's perfectly vicious, as you'd expect from RIOT." She sighed and forced a smile. "I think they've got a decent lead on us. Where is their car?"

"The Beachwood Shopping Centre carpark. It's just up High Street and an easy jaunt onto the A40 to Oxford and London from there. It's a busy place. Lots of people coming and going. We should be able to blend in and sneak out without much problem." Mason held his hand out to indicate she go first out of their hiding spot.

"Do you think there are any more of him?" As they stepped into the sunshine and headed toward the sidewalk, she pointed over her shoulder indicating Bagge.

"I hope not."

"You really need to work on your reassuring skills."

Mason laughed. "We Brits like to be understated."

"Uh-huh." Mal put on her rearview sunglasses with their stylish frames, large lenses, and fine optics that allowed her to see clearly behind her and around corners. They were handy for more than spy purposes. They also hid her scowl as she was forced to endure watching Tate and Sophia hold hands as they strolled along ahead of her like two lovebirds, imitating the way she and Tate had gone around town the day before. "Are we going to pick up the car?"

"No. That one's a red herring in case anyone was following us. I have an identical one waiting for us at the carpark."

She gave him her deadpan you-have-to-be-kidding look. "We had a car to drive two blocks?"

"We might have needed it." He smiled. "Nice that we didn't. Now it's a perfect morning for a stroll. It's much easier to tail them on foot. We'd be conspicuous driving along at strolling speed."

"Yes, we would."

"Besides, I know how much you love to shop. You'll love winding through Debenhams."

"When you put it that way."

There are few things more torturous in life than having to watch another woman hit on your man, even if he is your ex. Mal should have enjoyed their stroll along High Street on such a gorgeous morning, but her thoughts were dark and she saw shadows and spooks at every corner. The shadows may have been figurative, but the spooks were real enough. Cheltenham was crawling with spies, both friend, or as friendly as they got, and foe. With so many espionage types on the street, it was hard to tell whether they were being followed or not.

Mal was glad for one thing—Beachwood Shopping Centre was the opposite direction from the Montpellier shopping district and Neptune's Fountain that she'd visited yesterday with Tate. None of her memories would be ruined.

You'd think holding hands would be a simple task, but as Tate walked toward High Street holding hands with Sophia, it felt awkward, like their hands were wrestling even though they were still. He and Mal always held hands in a certain way with his thumb looped over hers. It was disconcerting to be with a Mal double and have it feel odd and off.

Sophia looked calm enough, but her hand trembled slightly in his. "There are spies everywhere."

"The festival is known for them. Everyone is trying to recruit the scientists to their cause. No one wants to be left out. Don't worry. Most of them mind their own business. They have their own agendas and are too busy to worry about us."

"By now they will know I'm gone. Edvid is thorough. He's following us. He has to be. If he catches us—"

"He won't. Trust me." Tate was fully aware of Mason and Mal tailing him at the accepted distance. They were good. If he hadn't known they were there, he might have missed them. It seemed as if Sophia had. He decided it would be better not to mention them.

Debenhams came into view. He led Sophia toward it. "Time for some shopping."

"Good. I love shopping." Sophia's smile was radiant. "What are you going to buy me?"

"Oh, that's the way it works, is it?" Tate held the door open for her. "I buy for you."

"You are the billionaire and I am your girlfriend." She flashed him that flirtatious look again, the one that should have made him follow her anywhere, but didn't.

"Sorry to disappoint. Today it's just quick window-shopping as we escape."

Mal and Mason followed Tate and Sophia through Debenhams, trailing at a respectable distance. Shopping was usually a huge part of Mal's job. If not for the danger of RIOT chasing them, Mal would have loved to linger over the fashion and shopping treasures in the department store.

Instead, she and Mason followed Tate and Sophia into the mall. Tate gave Mal a scare when he and Sophia ducked into a little boutique.

"Evasive action," Mason whispered to Mal. "There's a middle-aged man that might be following them. If I'm concerned about him, I'm sure Tate is." Mason subtly pointed the suspected tail out. "Let's keep an eye on him."

Mal was forced to linger on a bench outside the store

while Mason watched the suspect. Mal held her breath while the man paused outside the shop entrance. The last thing they needed was an incident.

Just as Mason approached the man, he wandered off. Mason came back beside her. "Clear." He texted Tate the same.

A minute later, Tate emerged with Sophia, who wore a brand-new silver Claudia Bradby necklace around her delicate neck. One that would have fit perfectly in Mal's collection. Claudia Bradby was a favorite designer of the princess. Mal imagined that Tate had bought it to keep up the cover of a couple in love out for a shopping trip, but still . . .

"They're on the move." Mason tucked his phone into his pocket as Tate and Sophia left the store.

They followed Tate as he wove through the mall with Sophia hanging on him. Then, just when Mal was barely hanging on to her professional demeanor, Tate ducked into an exit to the carpark.

Mason nodded to Mal. They headed for another exit.

"I hate parking garages," Mal whispered in Mason's ear. "Nothing good ever happens in parking garages. They're the modern-day version of a haunted house or a scary basement—gray, dismal, plenty of places for killers to hide. No smart heroine should enter one unprepared." She pulled her pink gun from her purse and took off the safety.

Mason pulled a pistol from his pocket, eyed hers and shook his head. "Pink? The CIA should really get you a more impressive gun."

"What are you talking about? This one was specially designed for me," she said.

They slunk around, covering Tate as he arrived at another decidedly unimpressive vehicle.

"Really?" Mal shook her head. "MI5 should spring for sexier rental vehicles."

"It's more impressive than it looks."

"Sure it is." Mal grinned at Mason. "I bet it's even electric, gets fifty miles per gallon, and has a V-one engine."

"V-one?" Mason looked confused. "Are you insulting our horsepower?"

She cocked a brow and gave him a deadpan look.

Mason laughed.

Tate helped her into the vehicle.

Mason pointed to a car that was identical to the one they'd ditched near the Dashwood. "Our chariot awaits."

Mal shook her head again. "I hope that one comes with extras." She eyed it skeptically. "It doesn't look big enough to house a rocket launcher."

Mason shrugged. "It has a rather decent speaker system and factory-installed air."

"That's what I thought." Mal slid into the driver's side of the little silver car and revved her engine. "Not exactly an Aston Martin DB5."

"Not everyone can be Bond. That's movie stuff." He grinned at her. "Go easy on the engine. Don't want to overtorque it."

Mal sighed. "British cars."

Mason laughed again. "Save your road rage for RIOT."

Mal arched a brow. "What are you talking about? I'm in complete control."

"A woman in denial." Mason shot her a look full of disappointment. "You aren't over him. I really don't have a chance in hell with you, do I?"

Mal looked him directly in the eye. "What do you mean?"

"You know what I mean. You're still in love with Tate."

Tate slid into the driver's seat, eager to get the hell out of the parking garage. He hated parking garages. They were ideal hiding places for assassins, snipers, and murderers of all varieties. With RIOT on their tail, he was even less eager to linger in one. He slid the keys into the ignition. As he started the car, Sophia covered his hand with hers and stopped him.

"That was fun." She bit her lip and smiled, playing idly with the silver strand around her neck. "I'll always cherish this."

Tate forced a smile, thinking how that little shopping excursion had been anything *but* fun. Keeping a watch for RIOT. Always on guard and ready to defend Sophia. Looking for the escape route in each shopping department. Sabotaging any chances at a reunion with Mal with every flirtation he faked with Sophia. Pretending to be in love with Sophia and humoring her with Mal watching—excruciating torture. Ducking into that boutique to lose a suspicious tail. Buying Sophia a necklace he knew Mal would love to keep from looking suspicious and taking no joy from the purchase. Visions of Mal in that lovely silver necklace and nothing else gave him a rise.

Sophia leaned forward, dropped the necklace from her fingers, and moved her lips to within inches of his as she grabbed the shoulders of his shirt and bunched them in her hands.

What the hell?

"You're much more handsome and *sexy* in person. Only part of your magnetism and charm comes through in your photos."

"And here I thought I was photogenic."

She halved the tiny distance between their lips. "You are. But you're better in person. The camera can't capture heroism. Not every man would risk his life for a stranger."

"For a woman as beautiful as you? Take it from me—most men would."

"I love you, Tate Cox." Her words were a breathy whisper. "You're my hero."

She released the lever on his seat, throwing it back into the full reclining position, sending him as flat on his back as the seat allowed. He didn't know how the hell she did it, the woman was as agile as an acrobat, but she maneuvered over the console between them, past the steering wheel, straddling him with a move so smooth he hadn't seen it coming. Before he could move, she was giving him a lap dance and removing her blouse, revealing a transparent lacy bra and fully budded breasts.

"Make love to me, Tate," she whispered in his ear. "Don't make me beg. Just love me." She kissed him furiously as she reached for his zipper and moaned, rubbing against him.

"What in the world is she *doing*?" Mal shut off the car engine and glared at Sophia on top of Tate.

"If you don't know that, you need a lesson in the birds and the bees. I'd be happy to oblige." Mason flashed her a charming, roguish look.

"I know what she's doing—but in the parking garage of all places? With RIOT after her?" Mal bit her lip. "It feels like a setup. I don't like it. Not at all." For a variety of reasons.

Mal grabbed her cell phone.

"Who are you going to call?"

"Tate. I'm not going to sit here and watch this."

Mason cocked a brow. "You can close your eyes. I'll do the watching."

"Men! Shut up. This is a public carpark. What if a little kid gets an eyeful of that?" She shook her head. "Plus, in the throes of passion, Tate will be a sitting duck. And the last thing we need is an arrest for public indecency."

"I don't see any police."

A motion in the corner of her eye caught Mal's attention.

Mason saw it, too. They both swiveled toward it at the same time.

"A camera, bloody hell," Mason said.

Mal hit Tate's cell number as she started the ignition. "Pick up, pick up, pick up!" From Mal's vantage point all she could see was the whale hump of Sophia's perfect butt in the air. Someone with a telephoto lens and a better camera angle would have a picture-perfect shot.

She watched as Tate apparently pushed Sophia to the side, at least judging from the way her butt slid out of view.

"Yes," Tate said, too dazedly for Mal's tastes.

"Smile. You're on *Candid Camera.* And not the friendly version." Mal tried to keep her voice neutral. "There's a photographer filming your escapade on your left toward the exit. Get out of here. Now!"

CHAPTER EIGHTEEN

Tate struggled to release himself from beneath Sophia's hot body, grabbing her wrist and holding it firmly as he stared into her eyes, trying to keep his anger at bay. What had she done? "We have company. And they're shooting us—with a lens. Time to roll."

He scooted her into her seat flat on that pretty little ass of hers, put his seat back in the full and upright position, and peeled out of the parking spot toward the exit, keeping his eye on the rearview mirror to see who came after him. "Put your blouse on." He was ready to make a U-turn if he had to. Or ram an unfriendly vehicle out of his way.

Fortunately it was early still and the garage was nearly empty.

Mal and Mason pulled out leisurely in pursuit. There was no point in them blowing their cover. They knew where he was headed and knew he'd wait for them to catch up. He also knew they were trying to intercept any RIOT agents.

Tate was cursing silently, hoping this was just paparazzi who'd gotten a tip that he was here at the festival. Then again, that meant his cover was blown. No, there really wasn't a good scenario.

The problem with carparks are the exit gates. He could have blown through it, but he didn't need the cops on his tail, too. Fortunately, there wasn't a line. He scanned his credit card as Mal and Mason pulled up behind him. Damn delays. In an instant, he was out of the garage and heading toward the A40 and Oxford and London.

He felt jumpy and hyped up like he'd had too much coffee. Adrenaline rushes did that to him. Usually he reveled in the rush. Today he was too worried about Mal. Both of Kayla's parents should never be out on a mission at the same time.

They drove to the A40, going as much above the speed limit as Tate could get away with without drawing attention or running over any tourists. Beside him Sophia looked pale and frightened. And she didn't look like she was faking it.

"Who was that back at the garage? One of your RIOT buddies?" His jaw ticked, a dead giveaway he was angry. Damn involuntary microexpressions.

Sophia was pale and her eyes were wide when she looked at him. "I don't know. *Really*. You have to believe me." She gently touched his arm.

He wanted to, but he'd seen enough double agents in his life not to take anything at face value. There was nothing in her demeanor or muscle movements to indicate she was lying. That didn't mean she wasn't. Sociopaths lied with more ease than they told the truth and he hadn't ruled out that she was one.

He glanced in the rearview mirror, looking for a tail besides Mal and Mason. "I'd like to believe you've been straight with me."

"It's a straight shot from here to Oxford on the A40." Mason had his gun ready, but he looked and sounded calm. "We appear to have lost our photographer friend."

Mal was happy to be driving, even on the wrong side of the road. It kept her mind off other matters, like the way

Sophia kept touching Tate in the car ahead of them. "What do you think her game is?"

"You don't think she's genuine?" Mason laughed, clearly egging her on.

"You know the answer to that one." Mal frowned. "I'm worried about that photographer. Either RIOT's up to something, something we can't figure out, or the paparazzo's caught on that Dr. Stevens is Tate. Neither one is good. And why isn't anyone following us? What does RIOT have up their sleeve? Either way, by now they must have noticed Bagge and Sophia are missing.

"The way Sophia pounced on Tate in the carpark, it's as if she was giving them time to catch up to us."

"Pessimist. Maybe we got away clean."

"No." Mal didn't believe that for a second and she didn't think Mason did, either. "The thing with the photographer is evidence to the contrary."

Just outside Oxford, Mason's cell buzzed. He picked it up. "Mason. Yes. Right. I see."

His side of the conversation was cryptic, but not encouraging. She couldn't hear the other side. When he hung up, he looked grim. "Change of plans. Heathrow's out. Someone killed a security officer there this morning and stole his credentials. MI5 was just notified after a janitor found the body in a broom closet. Bad business. We fear RIOT has infiltrated the security screening. Until we know more, it's not safe to take Sophia out through Heathrow."

"Damn."

"Yes, bloody hell. It is bad news," Mason agreed. "Do you have a plan B?"

"I always have a plan B. I just need a few minutes to think one up. That's why I was sent on this mission. I'm good on the fly. I'll need a place to pull over and rearrange our travel plans."

"Oxford has motorway services."

"Excellent. Text Tate and tell him to pull over there." Mal glanced in her rearview mirror. "We just picked up a tail."

Mason casually glanced in his passenger side mirror. "It would appear so."

"Better warn Tate about that, too." Mal eased off the accelerator, closing the gap between the tail and them, giving Tate time to escape. "This is your territory," Mal said to Mason as he texted. "Got any ideas on how to lose them?"

"The motorway services at Oxford are large and busy. With a little creativity, we should be able to lose them there." Mason's cell phone buzzed. "Tate says let's meet up in the food court. Give him time to get a coffee at Starbucks before we rendezvous."

"Coffee? In the middle of a chase, Tate thinks he needs a coffee?"

"Even spies need coffee breaks. Nothing like a shot of espresso to get the juices flowing. Better that than a double burger with cheese like he could get at Burger King. Tasty, but those can weigh you down on the run."

Mal lifted a brow. "So much for British atmosphere. It's like I never left home. Don't you Brits have your own coffee and fast-food franchises?"

"We have Dixie Chicken."

"You mean an imitation that combines McDonald's and KFC? Right. Imitation is the sincerest form of flattery." She laughed.

"We Brits are very accommodating. We cater to our New World guests. I forgot to mention that motorway services has a KFC, Krispy Kreme, and Papa John's Pizza, too."

"All the comforts of home." Mal rolled her eyes and glanced in the rearview mirror again. Their tail was still on their tail. "I could go for tea and a scone."

"Starbucks has those."

"Great. And I left my Starbucks gold card at home. No free tea refills for me."

Ahead of them, Tate whipped into the motorway services' petrol line without signaling. Mal whipped into the parking lot and found a spot where she and Mason could keep an eye on them as they filled up. If there had been any doubt about the tail, there was none now. He pulled in and found a spot between Mal and Mason and Tate and Sophia.

"He doesn't seem in any big hurry to kill us." Mal shut off the car and tucked the keys into her purse. "A shot to the gas tank, a nice explosion, and he'd be done. Why does RIOT need him *and* a plot to apprehend Sophia at Heathrow?"

Mason shrugged. "Plan B."

"Or he's just following to make sure Tate and Sophia get to Heathrow where RIOT can snatch and torture them to see how much damage has been done before they kill them. He's a herder."

"He could try to grab them now," Mason said.

"If that's his intent, I say we don't let him." Mal reached behind her and grabbed her large woven tote that contained her cover goodies and iPad. "Watch my back."

"Gladly." Mason grabbed Mal's arm as she reached for the door handle. "I have an idea. You dress as Mallie. I imitate Tate. I say we draw our tail off here while Tate and Sophia escape disguised in new covers."

Mal did not want to leave Tate alone with Sophia. She could not, *would* not do so. "I'm under orders not to leave them alone. My boss is highly suspicious of Sophia's motives and has thought all along this may be a trap. But I like your plan. I have a variation that should work."

"Of course." Mason dropped her arm.

Sophia studied him with her professional eye. Mason

was about the same height, weight, and build as Tate. Hair about the same color. That was where the similarity ended. It was more than she often had to work with.

"I love it when a woman stares at me with intensity and an appraising eye."

"Get over yourself, Mason. I'm trying to figure out how to turn you into Tate." She paused. "I think we'll need a hat and a pair of sunglasses."

He laughed. "There's a WHSmith inside. They might have something."

Mal paused. "Since Heathrow's out, I assume so are the other airports in England. We'll have to fool RIOT somehow. They'll expect us to try Wales, maybe even Scotland. I'm thinking we take evasive action and book half a dozen options with the goal of sending RIOT on a wild-goose chase. We'll split up. But I have to stay with Tate and Sophia.

"RIOT won't be looking for a threesome. Do you have any female agents who can impersonate Sophia?"

Mason shrugged. "I'm sure we can scare up somebody. We have an excellent female impersonator who should be able to do the job."

Mal arched a brow. "Seriously?"

Mason laughed. "Come on, don't be like that. If men can impersonate Marilyn Monroe with authenticity, they can impersonate you and your evil twin. Besides, he's an excellent shot and has a black belt. He's also lethal with his hands. RIOT won't be expecting a man to take them on. Imagine their surprise when they jump Sophia and learn she's grown a pair." He paused. "They know Sophia's shortcomings. My guy will have none of those."

"By shortcomings, I hope you don't mean estrogen and two X chromosomes?"

"Not at all. I mean what scares her won't scare my

man. Her private fears aren't his. And need I repeat—he can kill with his bare hands. That will take them by surprise."

Mal took a deep breath. There was something vaguely upsetting about being played by a guy that hit at the heart of her feminine insecurities. But she was no bigot. "Good point. Get him on the horn and get ready to head for Scotland with him on the Caledonia Sleeper. I'll book you two a romantic private sleeping compartment."

"That's taking things a little far," Mason said, but his tone was teasing.

"It was your suggestion." Mal paused. "Too bad we don't have time to wait for him to join us here. This is my plan—we confuse our tail here and get him to head out after you toward London. At first, he won't have a clue we're on to RIOT's plan to capture Sophia and Tate at Heathrow.

"In London, you'll duck out to the train station, meet Mallie/Sophia's double, and head for Scotland. I'll contact Sir Herbert and make sure he has the proper costumes and covers ready for you. And us.

"In the meantime, I'm going to get back into my Mallie costume here. I'll make it look like I take off with you. As you suggested, we'll change Tate and Sophia into you and me. They'll head to Reading to catch a train to Liverpool and from there a ferry to Belfast and fly out from there. I'd prefer to go to Dublin. It's closer, but that would mean involving a country outside of Great Britain and we want to keep things as uncomplicated as possible. The fewer countries involved, the better."

"I'm going to be losing your company? I'm crushed," Mason said, with his eye on the tail who was still sitting in his car watching Sophia and Tate as Tate hung up the petrol pump.

She smiled sweetly at Mason. "I'm sure you'll get over it. After all, you'll have my double to keep you company."

"Touché." Mason laughed with her. "If you ever tire of waiting for Tate, promise you'll ring me?"

"Cross my heart." She reached for the door again.

Mason stopped her once more. "MI5 will insist on sending an agent to cover you on the train and ferry. Work him into your plan."

Mal nodded. "Let's go shopping."

Mason rolled his eyes. "What is it with women? Terrorists on their tails and they have time for retail therapy."

Mal left Mason in the food court to keep on eye on things while she went to WHSmith and bought a touristy cap with a British flag on it and a cheap pair of aviator sunglasses. She "ran" into Tate and Sophia at the coffee shop where Tate was, indeed, getting the largest iced mocha available.

Mal ordered her tea and scones, the small vanilla ones she loved. As she waited, pretending not to know him, she unobtrusively slipped him the hat and glasses and whispered instructions. "Make a show of buying a matching set of these and put them on. Then give these to Mason. We're going to play a shell game. Be prepared to meet me at Mason's car. From there we're heading to Reading to catch a train. Give me a few to make the reservations. Tell Sophia to meet me in the loo. We're going to switch identities."

The barista called Tate's order. He picked up his coffee and a Frappuccino for Sophia. Laughing and acting as if his life was in no particular danger, he leaned in and said something to Sophia. A quick pout formed on her full lips. A second later she headed toward the public loos.

Mal stashed her scones in her tote and headed for the loo, too. She caught up with Sophia as Sophia was reapplying her lipstick and primping before the mirror. Mal hated that girl as she pulled her makeup compact from her bag and, rather than powder her nose, swept Sophia for bugs and tracking devices.

When Sophia came up clean, Mal couldn't decide whether to be relieved or upset. "You and I need to swap identities. I'll need your clothes."

Sophia ran her gaze over Mal in an insulting way. "No."

"No?" Mal gave her nose a quick powder and slid her compact back into her bag, resisting the urge to get her pink gun out. She hoped she didn't have to use force. But her killer pink poisonous lipstick was still awfully tempting. "Do you want to escape from RIOT or not?"

"Yes, but only with Tate. He's the *only* one I trust."

Though Sophia looked genuinely scared, Mal had no sympathy for her. "We're on the same team."

Sophia stared directly at Mal. "Are we? I think you're still in love with him and will do anything to sabotage me because I love him and he wants me."

The arrogant little bitch. Mal took a deep breath. "We're being followed. We have to lose whoever's chasing us." She briefly outlined her plan. "Both couples are switching identities. You'll still be with Tate, but as me."

Sophia blotted her lipstick and tossed the tissue in the trash. Reluctantly, Sophia walked to a stall. The two exchanged clothes over the stall wall. When they were changed, Mal transferred her wig to Sophia and remade each of them in the other's image. When she was finished, Mal held out her hand. "I need your jewelry, too."

Sophia gave Mal her watch, earrings, and bracelets.

"The necklace."

Sophia hesitated.

"Do you have a death wish?" Mal barely kept her exasperation out of her voice. "*Every* detail, no matter how minute, must be convincing."

Sophia shrugged and tucked the necklace beneath Mal's

bustier. She turned and walked out the door before Mal could stop her.

Cursing, Mal did another bug and tracker sweep of herself. There had to be some way RIOT was tracking Sophia. Mal came up clean. There was nothing to do but go on with the show. She reached into her bag of tricks and pulled out a cheap, long silver-colored necklace and tossed it on, hoping Mr. Tail didn't have an eye for fashion as she cursed Sophia.

When Mal strutted out of the loo and into the food court, Mason and Tate had already exchanged clothes and were each wearing their caps and sunglasses. At least some things were going according to plan.

Mal as Mallie walked up behind Mason as Tate where he sat at a table and ran her fingers through his hair. When he looked up and back at her, she leaned down and kissed him upside down. Kissed him as if he was Tate, to be exact, full tongue, full-throttle passion. Mason deserved a little something for his trouble.

He was grinning like an idiot when she broke away. "Tease," he said.

"Convincing actress." She gave him another light kiss on the lips. "Do you have Tate's keys?"

Mason nodded and grabbed the remains of Tate's iced mocha.

"Let's go." She took his arm when he stood.

"Dressed as a college girl you are incredibly hot."

"Thank you, baby." She cuddled into Mason.

"What's the plan once we get to the car? Are you going to teleport into Tate's?"

"I wish." She laughed, trying to make it appear as if they were having fun and totally unaware they were in danger. "I'm going to use a trick of magic—inattentional blindness—to my advantage. But I'm relying on you to be convincing.

"In my bag, I have an inflatable doll and a blond wig."

"You travel with an inflatable doll?" Mason said.

She shrugged and grinned. "Don't get any lewd ideas. I travel with several. Assassins never leave home without their weapons. I never leave home without mine. Inflatable people are flat and easy to pack. And they serve all kinds of purposes.

"Once I climb into the car, I'm going to inflate her and put her wig on. Your task is to talk to her like she's real and not let your tail get close enough to realize she's not. Although she's very lifelike."

"Anatomically correct, I hope."

Mal laughed. "And stacked. You'll love her."

"That still doesn't explain how you're getting out of the car."

"Tate is going to create a distraction and I'm going to climb out of the car and join him before we even leave the lot."

"Sounds tricky," Mason said. "Let's get to it."

"Just make sure we hook our tail first." Mal smiled at him as she took his arm and they made their way to the car.

Their tail, who'd been watching them as he ate a doughnut, casually got up and followed them before heading to his car.

This was where things got tricky. Mal had coordinated efforts like these, even trained people on the methods for using dummies to escape tight situations. But she hadn't performed one in the field. The timing had to be perfect.

Fortunately, Tate had been driving so that it was reasonable for Mal as Mallie to get into the passenger seat. She pretended to buckle her seat belt and then bent as if to get something from her purse. Her heart thumped wildly as she pulled Inflatable Annie from her bag, unfolded her, and positioned her in the seat. Mal pulled her own hair back into a tight ponytail, put on a baseball cap, and pulled a different T-shirt over her blouse.

She texted Tate. *Now.*

In response to her text, a car alarm went off. Everyone in the lot turned to look.

"Our tail's distracted," Mason said. "Now."

Mal hit the button on the self-inflating dummy. Within seconds, she inflated into a three-dimensional woman. Mal slapped a wig on her.

"Tate's moving into position. He'll be blocking our follower's view in three, two, one—now!"

Mal slid out of the car. "Take care. And treat my girl nice."

"I'll buy her dinner before I make any moves," Mason said.

She grinned back at him and was out and just another tourist walking into the food court, with her heart pounding.

Mason took off with the tail after him and his inflatable friend. Mal dashed through the food court to Tate's waiting car. She slid into the backseat.

Tate wasted no time pulling out. "Nice work."

"Everyone should have an Inflatable Annie."

"There are a lot of lonely men who'd agree with you." Tate consulted his GPS and pulled out of the services area tailing the tail tailing Mason.

Mal tried to get a good view of Mason's car to see how authentic Annie looked. Pretty good. Convincing. From this distance and angle, she easily passed for a real woman, especially if you expected her to be one. She'd be great to use in the carpool-only lanes back home.

Mal glanced at the tail following Mason. The driver reached for something.

"Damn! He's got a gun." With one hand on the wheel, Tate reached for his.

Before Tate could get it out, a bullet shattered the back window of Mason's car. Inflatable Annie slumped forward, losing air. And Sophia let out a bloodcurdling scream.

CHAPTER NINETEEN

Tate cursed to himself as the tail's car accelerated. Tate took aim just as the tail backed off. "What the hell?" Tate frowned. "RIOT wants *me* alive."

"Lucky for Mason," Mal said.

Damn if Tate was going to take any chance of the RIOT bastard changing his mind and catching up to either of them. He fired, taking out the tail's left rear tire. The tire collapsed onto its wheel, grinding and squealing on the pavement as the driver fought to maintain control.

The tail lost the fight. The vehicle veered off the road ahead of them and crashed into a rock wall, crumpling like the crap car it was. The driver slumped forward over the steering wheel, unconscious.

"Nice work," Mal said, reaching for her cell phone.

"Thank you." Tate was shaken and more grateful than he could express that Mal had insisted on coming along with Sophia and him. He was right—it was too damn dangerous for her to pretend to be Sophia. If she'd tried to lead RIOT on a rabbit chase, she'd have been a dead bunny. He swallowed hard, pushing away the image of telling Kayla her mommy was dead and he was to blame. He could never have forgiven himself.

Sophia grabbed Tate's arm with urgency as they rapidly approached the wreckage. "Stop!"

"You want to stop and help him?" Tate had just a few seconds to make up his mind.

"I want to make sure he's dead." Her voice was as warm and cuddly as acid. "If he isn't, he'll never give up and we won't be safe."

Tate drove past, in no mood to be delayed and questioned or show fake concern for the assassin's hide. He'd be damned if he'd commit a covert murder in front of an audience, either. Especially for a woman who was causing him so much trouble.

He glanced in the rearview mirror. Cars were already pulling over. Innocent people rushed over to help, cell phones to their ears. A crowd was forming and gawking. Traffic slowing. Tate was glad to be ahead of it. Morbid curiosity was hell and a damned nuisance.

In the backseat, Mal was texting. "I'm contacting MI5. They'll pick him up and deal with the mess. If they can get through that crowd. Emergency services will be arriving any minute. If they hurry, they can intercept them."

Tate accelerated. "Let's hope MI5 gets him and he squeals. Has Britain outlawed waterboarding?"

Sophia dropped her hand from his arm. She was still pale and shaking. "I could be dead."

Mal leaned forward in the backseat and poked her head between them. "You mean *I* could be dead. I was the one who was actually in that car for a time impersonating you. If I hadn't had Inflatable Annie, I'd be getting a posthumous star on the Agency wall." Mal frowned. "Poor Annie. She was a good inflatable. She didn't deserve to go like that."

Sophia stared straight ahead, not bothering to thank Mal. It was clear she viewed Mal as the competition and despised her for it. Being in the spy biz was a thankless job.

Mal switched topics. "Why did RIOT go to all the

trouble to take out a guard at Heathrow if they were planning to kill Sophia just outside Oxford?"

"We must have gotten it the wrong way around," Tate said. He'd been wondering the same thing. "Heathrow was the backup plan. Dual redundancy in case we managed to slip through the assassin's sights."

"What is their game?" Mal said, still leaning forward. "They're up to more than meets the eye. We just can't see it." She pounded the seat beside her.

"Whatever it is, it's clear Sophia is now expendable. Maybe even a liability." Tate glanced at Sophia as she clenched her hands tightly in her lap. "Is it because you ran and they know you betrayed them? Then why not kill you in the parking garage?"

Sophia stared in her lap. "I don't know."

It wasn't easy reading Sophia while driving, looking for the involuntary microexpressions that signaled she was lying. He didn't see any evidence in her body language or expression. But he wasn't convinced.

"And how did they catch on to us so quickly?" Mal asked.

"I don't know!" Sophia buried her head in her hands.

Tate rubbed her shoulder. "It's okay. You're fine. We're going to get you out of England and to the States where you'll be safe."

Mal's cell rang. She glanced at it. "It's Mason." She picked up. "Are you okay? Good." She paused, listening as Tate strained to overhear. "Yes. Yes, very sad." Mal laughed. "Me, too. Poor thing. I agree. No, you're spot on. Take the train. Yeah, you, too. Bye."

"What's up?" Tate asked, not liking the flirty tone Mal had taken with the British agent. "How's Mason?"

"Calm and unflappable as always. Amused and mourning the loss of Annie. I think he was falling for her in the short time he knew her. He has a thing for blondes. He said she was the perfect woman—gorgeous and totally able to keep a secret." She laughed again. "If he hadn't been teasing I'd have to hold his chauvinism against him."

Tate wasn't amused. "How is he going to deal with the shooting? Is MI5 planning to fake Sophia's death?"

"No. He spoke to his bosses. They think it's too dangerous with too much potential for something to go wrong. They don't know how deeply RIOT has infiltrated. Do they have people in the coroner's office? Someone there who could definitely ID any body they try to pass off as not Sophia?

"How do they explain Mason being in that car? What would his cover be? Trying to hide reality from the press all to fool RIOT, who may not be fooled anyway, will involve too many people. And the moment RIOT realizes you weren't with Sophia, they'll know something's up."

Tate frowned. Mal and MI5 were right, but he'd feel a whole lot better if RIOT believed Sophia was dead. "What do they suggest?"

"They're not going to mention it. Mason is going to impersonate you as Dr. Stevens. He'll take the train to Scotland with his cross-dressing fellow agent dressed like Sophia, hoping to lead RIOT astray while we escape through Ireland.

"With any luck, it will take a while for RIOT to realize Sophia's still alive and go looking for her. That will buy us some time. In the meantime, we proceed to Reading as if nothing has happened."

Mal's cell pinged. "Ah, a text from Sir Herbert. Our new covers will be waiting for us. When we get to town, I'll give you directions to the drop site."

In Reading, Mal directed Tate to a parking spot a couple of blocks away from the historic Reading train station. "We're to leave the car here. MI5 will take care of it. After we pick up the cover change drop, there's a nearby coffee shop where we can change and dump our current clothes. Then it's off to the train station and Liverpool."

Mal reached for the door handle. "I'll retrieve the drop. Cover me."

"Just a second." Tate stopped her. He surveyed the area and took out his gun. "All clear. Be careful."

He kept his eyes on Mal as she walked across the sidewalk and retrieved a duffel bag from beneath a clump of bushes.

"You watch her like you're still in love with her."

He nearly jumped at the sound of Sophia's voice beside him. "Do I? Sorry. I'm not. I was just reminiscing. We met in England. It was a good time. We were very much in love before things went sour."

"I didn't think hardened spies were sentimental."

"You thought wrong." He didn't take his eyes off Mal. He was lying, on all counts. "Does it bother you?"

"No, it's sexy and sweet." Sophia cuddled into him.

Mal hurried across the sidewalk and hopped back in the car. Was it Tate's imagination or did she look a touch guilty? Damn, that didn't bode well for him. Nor did the look on her face as she glanced at Sophia.

Mal swept a lock of hair out of her eyes. "Let's see what Sir Herbert has left for us. I gave him our measurements so I'm not worried about fit." She looked up at Tate. "Oh, come on, you two. Stop looking at me like that. Sir Herbert has exquisite taste. I can't tell you how lucky you are to come to his personal attention and be dressed by him. It's an absolute honor."

Tate thought she protested too much, or at the very least was overselling, which put him on his guard. And he wished Sophia would stop clinging to him like ivy sucking the life out of its host tree.

Mal pulled a pair of jeans, a hoodie, and a women's T-shirt out of the bag. "Sophia, this has your name on it.

Look at these fabulous flats he sent for you." She handed them over the front seat.

Sophia took them cautiously. "Who am I supposed to be?" She looked less than impressed with her costume.

"My baby sister." Mal spoke with all the superiority of a bossy big sis, looking as if she was going to enjoy her role.

Tate had another bad feeling about this.

"What?" Mal said when she caught him staring at her. "It's an obvious choice. Sophia and I can easily pass for sisters. I'm older, so I'm the big sis. That also allows me to issue orders covertly." She grinned and turned her attention back to rifling through the bag. "I didn't want too much scrutiny on this trip. We're going to have to look and act like everyday American tourists." Mal turned to Sophia. "Think you can handle that?"

Sophia gave an almost imperceptible shrug of her shoulders. "I don't want to be your sister."

"In all honesty, I'm not so wild about being related to *you,* either, so we're even," Mal said. "As a rule, I try to stay out of Tate's love life and far away from the women he's dating." She glanced at Tate. "But I was assigned to this mission to bring you back to the States alive. And that's what I'm going to do. I'm the expert here, not you. You can either follow my orders and do as I say, or get out of this car right now and take your chances."

"Ah, family!" Tate couldn't resist. "Isn't it wonderful? I can hardly wait for Christmas."

Sophia scowled. "Fine." Even angry, she was stunning. But Mal was even sexier, especially when she took control like that.

"Great! Glad you see it my way. You'll be the sister who's been living abroad here in England for the last year. That will explain your *slight* British accent and your familiarity with the country. I'll be the American sister who's come to visit you—"

"And Tate will be my American boyfriend who's come to visit me," Sophia said with a triumphant smile. "You may be the big sister, but you get to be the third wheel."

Tate should have been amused and flattered to have Sophia fighting for his affections. Instead, he was worried about her addictive personality. She was too clingy and oddly more concerned about being with him than staying alive. Something was off about that. He could hardly wait to get her to the States and out of his hair.

"You might change your mind when you see what Sir Herbert has for Tate." Mal pulled out a pair of women's jeans in a size that looked like something from the big and tall women's shop, along with a padded butt insert with a front fly, a padded bra, a pair of silicone inserts, a frilly lavender embellished T-shirt, and a pair of men's size twelve lilac crochet women's slip-on shoes that looked like a Toms knockoff.

"Don't try to pass this off on Sir Herbert." Tate fairly exploded. "This is *your* doing. It's why I've never let you arrange my cover life and for good reason—"

"You've never had a cover life before."

"This is payback." He studied Mal and was convinced of two things—she was acting as if this really was payback and revenge, but he was sure it wasn't, and she was doing everything in her power to keep Sophia and him apart. He knew that was part of her mission. He also realized Mal was trying to make it look as if she and he were still on the outs so Sophia wouldn't abort the mission.

"What are you talking about? Just because our marriage ended on a sour note and I was a tiny bit peeved that you aced me out of designing the alien costumes for Rock Powers's show doesn't mean I'd take revenge." Her eyes flashed.

Okay, maybe she was still pissed about that.

"I'm going to kill you, Mal," he said, playing along.

She smiled sweetly and laughed. "Tate, Tate, Tate, you're overreacting. You'll hurt Sir Herbert's feelings if he ever finds out about your reaction to his clever plan."

"I don't give a rat's ass about Sir Herbert's feelings."

"Well, you should. He's gone out on a limb for us and worked overtime readying these new covers. Do you think covers grow on trees? This took thought, planning, emergency covert shopping, budget, and careful consideration—"

"Dressing me as a woman took careful consideration?" He snorted. He'd bet Sir Herbert had had lots of fun thinking up this cover and finding a way to humiliate him. Sir Herbert had never been overly fond of Tate. He thought Mal had married beneath her. Tell that to Lenora. His mother would be furious.

"I thought we were supposed to blend in and not draw attention to ourselves. What about a six-foot-three woman who's a man in drag won't draw attention?"

"RIOT won't be expecting us to be obvious. They definitely won't be looking for three women traveling together. A man in our company is a dead giveaway."

Sophia winced.

"Sorry," Mal said. "Bad choice of words. You'll just have to channel Lenora. Act like her and you'll scare away anyone who even thinks of approaching us."

There was a certain warped logic to the plan, but Tate still didn't like it. "I'm not an undercover expert. You've always told me the best covers, those easiest to maintain, are those closest to your true self. Those are the covers you choose for amateurs. I'm not woman material."

"Channel your inner female side, Tate, and you'll do fine."

"Who says I have a female side?"

Mal kept smiling. "Then think of all those tall, leggy

models you've dated and act like one of them. Confidence! That's what sells a cover.

"You always said you love a good challenge. Sir Herbert's thrown down the gauntlet. Rise to the challenge." Mal looked around nervously. "We're wasting time bickering. It is what it is. Both of you will have to deal with it."

Tate gave up. "Okay, so I'm a woman—what's my story?"

"You're the middle sister." Mal sounded way too gleeful about that.

"I'm the middle sister?" Tate looked between Mal and Sophia. "I look nothing like you two."

"You look like Dad, darling." Mal laughed.

"Hey, I'm older than you are and I have seniority in the field. I should be the older sister."

Mal shook her head. "Poor baby, only child. Can't stand the thought of being the overlooked, invisible one in the family?"

"I hardly think I'm going to be overlooked. I tower over you two."

Mal ignored him. "Being in the middle will be good for you. Teach you empathy and how to get along.

"And don't worry about looking like dear old dad. When I'm done with you, people will swear they see the family resemblance in all of us."

She pointed to a dive of a pub. "That's where we'll change. Sir Herbert says it's a safe house. We can use the back room."

Sophia was giving Mal the evil eye. It was a gorgeous, sultry eye, but cracking with rage nonetheless. She opened her mouth to speak.

Mal held up a hand to silence any opposition. "Let's get everything on the table. I've booked us regular fares.

Sorry, Tate, no first class. Too much scrutiny and individual attention."

Tate couldn't resist rolling his eyes. Sophia smiled her sympathy at him. In truth, Tate was enjoying the sparring with Mal. It was almost sexy.

"It's a three-and-a-half-hour ride from Reading to Liverpool. From there we catch the overnight ferry to Belfast where we board a flight to the States. Simple plan. The devil's in the details.

"MI5 has assigned another agent to play bodyguard to us on the train. A man. He'll make contact and give us a code so we know he's legit. If anyone else is watching us, they aren't a friend. Any questions?"

"Yeah." Tate held up the shoes Mal had given him. "Do you have these in teal?"

Mal led Tate and Sophia into the little dive of a pub.

Tate's taking things better than I expected, Mal thought as she did subtle recon, looking for threats. She thought he'd caught on that she was trying to pick a fight with him to keep Sophia from being horribly unhappy and realizing there was something going on between them.

Mal was also keeping an eye on Tate to see whether he succumbed to Sophia's numerous charms and just how far he would go for the mission. She had to admit that if he was still willing to be unfaithful for the sake of the job, that was a deal breaker, no matter how much she loved him. If she was going to seriously consider getting back with Tate, she had to know he would remain true.

A hardened old bartender was wiping down the bar counter when they entered. He looked up. Mal mimed the signal Sir Herbert had given her. The crusty old guy hitched his thumb toward a room in the back and shoved a key across the counter to Mal. "Second door on the right.

Be quick about it. The afternoon rush starts in less than an hour."

Mal nodded and led her charges into the back. She unlocked the door, which opened into a storeroom that was surprisingly tidy and fairly clean. But the lighting was terrible. "It'll have to do." She made a face. "Not exactly what I was expecting."

She slid the duffel off her shoulder and doled out their cover stories. "Read these and commit them to memory." She dug into the bag for their wardrobes, which she'd stuffed back into the duffel before leaving the car. "After we're in costume, you each can read your cover story while I make up the other one. Then we'll destroy the dossiers before we leave here. Let's get changed."

"I don't get a separate dressing room?" Tate set his cover story down and stared at her.

"Shy?" She grinned at him. "Why do you need a separate room? You're just one of the girls now. Get used to it."

Looking her in the eye, he stripped his shirt off and ran his eyes over Sophia's form. "On second thought, dressing with the girls has its perks. When do you take your shirts off?"

Mal held back a curse. The man really was too sexy for his shirt. And flirting with Sophia, which she knew he had to do. But it didn't mean she liked it.

Sophia lit up under Tate's flattering appraisal.

Mal studied Tate's chest. "The good news is that you've never had a particularly hairy chest." She pursed her lips.

"Don't get any ideas. I shaved it yesterday."

"A touch-up is in order." She reached for her bag and the razor she'd asked for.

Tate lunged forward, grabbed her by the wrist, and shook his head. "If you think I'm letting you near me with a razor, think again."

She handed it to him along with a tube of shaving cream. "Do the honors yourself, then."

"Here?"

"There's a utility sink in the corner. Or I could pluck for you. Sadly, I forgot to ask for wax. Next stop, maybe."

She and Sophia watched him shave. When he was finished, he ran his hands over his chest, looking for spots he'd missed, most probably. Why was it so erotic watching him?

He tossed the razor into the sink and flexed his pecs. "Have I missed anything?"

Mal let her gaze travel over him. "You're good."

"Good." He unzipped his pants, slowly as if he was doing a tantalizing striptease and was about to reveal a very erect show of interest.

Beside Mal, Sophia was practically drooling.

Zip, one metal tooth at a time. How did he do it so slowly? Make every notch build the anticipation. Her eyes were riveted on his crotch. Beside her, Sophia was breathing heavily. Another metal tooth fell away. And another. This was way sexier than the rip-away pants male strippers used and the quick jerk that revealed all. At least her pulse thought so. And Tate knew it.

Just when Mal was hot and frustrated enough, in all ways, to tell him to get on with the show because they were wasting time, the fly fell open, revealing a manly bulge of the most tantalizing sort. Mal balled her fists and caught a glimpse of Sophia from the corner of her eye. Sophia's eyes were wide and round with lust. *Damn her.*

Zipper unzipped, Tate shimmied out of his pants, revealing lean hips, taut, muscled thighs, and an enticing, firm ass just made for pinching and grabbing. He smiled, looking a little too triumphant, as if issuing a dare. "Not a shy bone in my body."

Mal eyed his bulging crotch and arched one brow.

"That was quite a show. If you're expecting a tip, too bad. Much as I'd like to stuff something down your briefs, I don't have any ones on me." She shook her head and leveled her gaze at his crotch, hardening her voice as she pointed. "*That* has to go."

His eyes went wide. Had he gone slightly, too? Now this was finally fun.

"At the very least disappear from sight." Mal shoved his fake butt and hips into his arms. "This has crotch control. Female impersonators use them all the time. Just make sure you tuck your boy under." She paused and smiled wider. "Let me know if you need any help. I'd be happy to tape it under for you."

"I bet you would."

Sophia was still gawking as if she'd never seen a well-hung man before. Maybe she hadn't. Mal liked to think the RIOT bastards Sophia worked with were not hung like real men should be. Even still, Mal didn't like her drooling over Tate like she wanted to get a piece of him. And Tate certainly didn't need the boost to his already inflated ego.

Mal grabbed Sophia by the shoulders and spun her around so her back was to Tate. "Give the boy his privacy." Mal stuffed Sophia's change of clothes into her arms and picked up her own clothes.

She changed into them quickly, not willing to give Sophia the satisfaction of sizing up the competition. Behind her, she heard the rustle of clothes and Tate's quiet cursing.

"Need help back there?" Mal asked.

"I'm fine."

Sure he was. Mal adjusted her T-shirt, slipped on her shoes and jacket, and turned around to see Tate, dressed in ladies' jeans, struggling to hook his bra. He'd gotten the fake hips and butt combo on beneath his jeans and they looked good, giving him subtle hips. All evidence of his manhood was gone.

"Honestly, Tate! There goes your reputation as a ladies' man. You'd think you'd know how to dress a woman."

He paused and gave her a death glare that turned into a wickedly charming grin. "My skill is *un*dressing women." His eyes danced with flirtation. His voice oozed innuendo and promise. He'd always been able to turn the sex appeal on at will. His mercurial nature was part of his appeal. "In a pinch, I'm pretty damn good at dressing them. Dressing myself in women's clothing? Not my particular talent. For obvious reasons." He made a muscle.

"You mean there's something Tate the great can't do? Poor baby. Let me help you." She walked to him, spun the bra around, resisting the urge to flick his nipples, waited while he stuck his arms through the straps, and fastened the bra behind his back. The straps hung loose and flopped over his shoulders. She shook her head. "Neophyte." She cinched the straps tight and slapped him on his toned back, indicating the task was done.

"Let's take a look." She walked around to the front of him and studied his silicone cleavage with a critical eye.

"Hey! Stop gawking at the girls." With two fingers he motioned between his eyes and hers. "Eyes up here. Women!" He shook his head. "When are you going to get your mind out of the gutter and respect us guys?"

Mal grinned. "Excellent! You're getting into the role already." She continued studying his breasts. "This is only professional interest.

"I told Sir Herbert you shouldn't be more than a B cup, but would he listen? A C is just too much for your frame." And a little too hot for the cover she'd envisioned for him. "I'm not going to push you too far out of character. We have to make this as believable as we can, given the circumstances.

"Be thankful for small mercies. No femme fatale in killer heels for you. There's no time to train you to walk in them. Your cover is you're a bit of a tomboy, a former girl jock, the lean athletic type. Skinny, no bust, like most supermodels. It takes a certain kind of woman to carry off a chest." She shook her head. "You're lopsided."

She stuck her hand into his bra.

Tate had her by the wrist so quickly she didn't see it coming. "Keep your hands off the goods."

"Oh, shut up. You can't feel this anyway."

"Octopus. Anything to get your hands on me." He grinned. "Being a woman is awful. I'm not even in public and already you're feeling me up."

She rolled her eyes.

"Just practicing defending myself against unwanted advances. Now that I'm a woman I have to be on my guard."

"Let go of my wrist, stand still, and let me rearrange your falsies, will you? You can't go around lopsided."

He arched a brow and dropped her wrist so she could work.

"These are nice." She gave his falsies a squeeze. "They feel surprisingly lifelike. Authentic in case you bump up against anyone or some guy tries to get a feel of you. And the fake nipples are a good touch."

"And in a permanent state of nonarousal."

"You don't want to bud up if some guy looks at you, do you?" Mal was enjoying herself. "I can talk to R and D about making a working pair for next time." She handed him the frilly T-shirt. "Put this on."

Tate stared her down and pulled it over his head. "If some guy looks at me, or tries to get his hands on this piece of meat, he's going to get a fist to the mouth."

"Sounds like you have fending off unwanted advances under control. But what are you worried about? You won't even feel it. Same thing if someone pinches your butt." She twirled her finger, signaling him to spin around. "Let me take a look at it."

He grinned. "Pervert." He turned his profile to her and Sophia, who was remaining surprisingly mute. "Do these jeans make my fake butt look big?"

"They keep you from being top-heavy," Mal said, eyeing him critically. "Why is it that female impersonators never have fat in all the wrong places like we real girls do? You have an irritatingly nice figure, Tate."

He ran his hands over his hips. "I really do, don't I?"

Mal shook her head. "What do you think, Sophia?"

"I like him better as a man."

"I'm still a man, sweetheart. Believe me."

Sophia practically melted under the grin he gave her.

"I'm never going to look like a woman," he added.

"You will when I'm finished with you." Mal pulled a blond wig from the bag of disguises Sir Herbert had sent. "See? You're going to be blond like us. Take a seat over there so I can get to work."

She turned her eye on Sophia. "After I'm done with Tate, I'm going to change your makeup subtly to give you a slightly different look. And give you a new hairstyle."

She reached into Sir Herbert's magic bag again and pulled out the gleaming pair of precision scissors she'd asked for. "Snip, snip."

"No!" Sophia grabbed her long, blond locks and shook her head.

Tate put his hands on her shoulders to comfort her. "Trust Mal. She's a pro."

"Not my hair!" Sophia's eyes flashed defiance. "Why doesn't *she* change *hers*?"

Mal wasn't impressed. The woman protested too much and was probably playing on Tate's sympathies again to win him over.

Mal had had enough. "I'm not the one RIOT is looking for. All I have to do is change back into myself, revert back to my age-appropriate style, and I'm golden. Suddenly our similarity is less striking. No one will mistake me for a twentysomething kid.

"You, however, are the one they'll be combing the country for. They know what you look like, and probably how vain you are about your hair. I could put you in a wig, but a cut will be more comfortable, more realistic looking, and won't fall off at the worst possible moment.

"Not to mention safer. RIOT obviously hasn't given you any self-defense training. Long hair, especially in a ponytail or braid, provides a perfect grip for a kidnapper or assassin. You're going to have to disappear for good. You can't go around looking like yourself. That's part of the sacrifice you have to make to escape from RIOT. It's now or later. And now is better for all of us.

"I promise I'm not going to ugly you up. Given your bone structure and thick hair, you'll look stunning in a current, trendy bob. You'll love it. I promise."

Mal felt like a stylist on a makeover show trying to talk sense into a woman who's never cut her hair.

Tate led Sophia to a chair. "Better take care of her first."

Mal handed her a mirror. "You can watch me work, but we have to hurry. Time is running out and we have a train to catch."

Fifteen minutes later, she'd given Sophia a fresh, youthful bob and redone her makeup to emphasize her cheekbones and lips rather than her beautiful eyes. The shift in emphasis was enough to make her look like another person.

Tate took Sophia's hand, looking ridiculous as a man from the neck up and woman from the neck down. "You look beautiful."

Sophia offered him a shaky smile.

"You're next, mister." Mal guided him into a chair, put his wig on, and got to work. "You." She pointed to Sophia. "Memorize your story."

Tate's hair was no problem. The wig was high quality and prestyled. His makeup was another matter. She spun him around in the chair to face her and crouched as she worked.

It wasn't until she was applying his makeup, touching his face, scrutinizing him, and trying to avoid looking him in the eye that she realized what intimate work applying makeup was.

Covering his beard shadow on both his face and chest was problematic without making him look like he was wearing stage makeup. It took her ten minutes of hard work until she was satisfied. Then it was on to his eyes, which were lovely and full of emotion she was working hard to avoid.

"Hold still while I apply your mascara," she said to him. "Not that you need it. You've always had lashes most women would kill for. It's so unfair."

"They're coming in handy now."

"Yeah." She finished wielding the mascara wand and got out her gloss. "And fine, full lips, too."

"Can I help it if I was born beautiful?" he said.

"I thought you were ruggedly handsome. That's what you used to brag to me, anyway."

"True. And beautiful, two in one."

Finally, she brushed his full, sensuous lips with gloss, trying not to think about kissing them. When she finished, she stood back and studied her work with an artist's eye, looking for flaws and giveaways.

Sophia stared, too. From the way she was looking at Tate, Mal would lay odds she was thinking the same thing Mal was—Tate was a sexy woman. How in the world did he ooze sex appeal no matter what gender he was?

Mal handed Tate a mirror.

He took it and studied himself, turning side to side to admire his profile from each side and peacocking into the mirror. "Huh. I really am a ruggedly handsome woman."

"Hate to quibble, but *I'm* a really talented artist. Whatever looks you have are thanks to me."

Tate made an air kiss into the mirror. "And here I thought I had pedigree, great genes, and good old mom and dad to thank."

Mal wasn't about to play to his vanity. She took the mirror from him. "And an Adam's apple that gives you away." She grabbed a scarf and tied it around his neck. "You absolutely have to wear this. No matter how hot you get."

"This scarf that could be used to strangle me?" He cocked a brow. "It's more dangerous than a ponytail."

"Okay, if someone tries to strangle you, I give you permission to remove it." She looked at his arms. "Too hairy. They have to be shaved."

Tate sighed. "I'll do it. But I won't like it."

"No one said you had to." Mal glanced at her watch and handed a lady's sports watch to Tate. "Your accessory. It has the usual watch spy features.

"Give me five to do my makeup and hair."

Mal changed her identity while Tate clogged the sink with his arm hair and Sophia flirted with him, laughing and speaking in hushed tones.

When Mal was finished, she destroyed the cover story dossiers and stuffed all their original clothes into a dustbin she'd been instructed to use. Just before she tossed the duffel in, she pulled out a paperback copy of *War and Peace*.

"Some light *reading* for you." She handed it to Tate.

"Thanks, but if I want to read, I'll read on my phone or my tablet."

"But neither of those are both a bulletproof plate and a revolver." She showed him the trigger. "Take the book, Tate. The last thing you want is to get into a situation where you wish you'd taken the book-gun. Use it wisely." She took a deep breath, wondering, not for the first time, whether these new covers were going to be the death of her career and her biggest professional failure.

She handed Tate his new purse. He winced and took it, holding it all wrong, more like a computer case than a handbag.

"No, no, no!" Mal handed Sophia the new cover purse. "Show him how it's done."

Sophia modeled hers. Tate shrugged and mimicked her.

"Good enough," Mal said. She was sure Tate was messing with her. He knew how women held purses. He was just pulling her chain.

"Your purses are filled with everything you need for the new cover, including ID, passports, the right shade of lipstick and gloss for your coloring, a comb and enough items so you'll have a feel for what your cover is. Everything a purse should have to be authentic."

"Mine weighs a ton," Tate said, shaking his head. "Why do women carry so much crap around?"

Mal ignored his complaint and took a breath. "It's time to roll. Do you think you can walk like a woman, Tate?"

CHAPTER TWENTY

N ot like that." Mal stopped with her hand on the door-knob and gave Tate a look meant to upbraid. "You're sashaying and swaying your hips too much. Stop trying to walk like Marilyn Monroe. Remember the cover story—you're an athletic woman. One who walks a lot like a guy. We're keeping it simple and playing to our strengths."

"I'll say it again—playing a girl is not my strength." Tate was staring at her like he really did want to kill her. Or kiss her. Either way it was a little disconcerting having another woman, a crazily sexy woman, look at her like that and have her body react.

"Your voice! I almost forgot. Feeling rushed is messing with my mojo."

Tate shrugged. "That's fieldwork for you. Get used to it."

"Stop talking like that."

"I'm telling it like it is."

"No, I mean in that masculine tone of voice." Mal took a deep breath and fished the duffel out of the dustbin. When she turned it upside down, she came up empty.

"What are you looking for?" Tate asked.

"Sir Herbert promised to send a voice modulator for you. Husky female voices are one thing. Bass voices another. It will give you, and by association, us, away." She shook the bag out. Nothing. "It's not here. You're going to have to wing it." With more frustration than she intended, she stuffed the duffel back into the bin. She'd originally been worried about Sophia carrying off the cover. Now Tate was the bigger problem.

He pitched his voice into a grating falsetto. "This is the best I can do."

She frowned and pointed her finger at him like she did at Kayla when she was misbehaving. "Don't mock me. Don't you dare. I can make you a real soprano with no trouble at all."

"Good luck with that." He gave her a smug grin. "My boys are tucked safely away in this crotch-control garment you gave me."

"Look, just make your voice *slightly* higher. And softer. With a touch of hoarseness thrown in." She demonstrated as she was speaking. "Mix up your word choice to have a more feminine pattern."

"Like this?" Tate said.

Damn, he affected a sensual, throaty voice, just the kind of low, slightly feminine tone men claimed drove them crazy. Mal was going to have to face facts—Tate was almost as hot as a woman as he was as a man.

"Better. Keep working on it." The last thing she wanted was to encourage him. He'd get cocky. And a cock was the last thing he needed right now.

Mal glanced at Sophia. She'd done way too good a job on her. Sophia was more beautiful and sensual than ever. *Maybe I should bob my hair,* Mal thought.

"Sophia, unless you want people to think you're a lesbian—which would be fine by me if Tate weren't supposed to be your sister—stop making eyes at him. Remember the cover story, people. And if in doubt, let me do the talking." She tapped her head. "I have the whole thing committed to memory.

"A quick quiz before we go. Sophia—what's your name?" Mal asked.

"Sonia Bell." She made a pretty pout. "Because it sounds similar to Sophia and has the same cadence. Easy for me."

"Right. It'll catch your ear automatically." Mal took a deep breath. "I'm Lena, because it's close to Malene." She looked at Tate. "Tate?"

"Just call me Kate."

"Great." A movement from Sophia caught Mal's attention. She was stuffing a cell phone into her new purse. Mal reached out and snatched it away. "No! What are you doing?"

"I need my phone."

"Where did this come from? Have you had it on you all along?" She swung on Tate. "You didn't get rid of the phone?"

"I thought I had."

Sophia smiled prettily. "I may have smuggled it back."

Mal whipped back to Sophia, brandishing the phone. "Cell phones are like carrying around a tracking device." Mal made thin eyes at her. "Is this how RIOT's been tracking us?"

"I'm no idiot." Sophia made angry eyes back at her. "I know that. I'm a mathematical prodigy. I disabled its tracking capabilities."

Mal didn't trust her. "So you say." Mal took a deep breath and buried it in the dustbin. "Open the purse."

Sophia gave her a look of hate, but complied. Mal rummaged through it. Nothing was added that she could tell. She held out her hand. "If you have any other electronic devices—iPods, anything—or any other items that were not part of what I provided in this storage room, now is the time to hand them over." She waited. "Don't make me do a body cavity search."

"Don't listen to her," Tate said in a sexy tone. "I get to do all body searches."

Sophia smiled at him and handed over an iPod shuffle. "That's it. Really. Not that I wouldn't love a pat-down from you."

"Do a sweep, Tate," Mal said.

"All clear," Tate said when he finished.

"For the duration, you're not to carry any electronic devices. No borrowing, renting, stealing, or buying any. Got it?"

Sophia shrugged, which Mal took as affirmation.

With very little faith that Sophia and Tate could pull the cover off, Mal led them out of the pub.

The walk to the train station took only minutes. The station itself was a mixture of old and new. Part old historic light-colored sandstone brick building with hanging baskets full of bright pink and white petunias dotting the building. Part new and wanting to be newer. There were plans in the works for something completely modern. Signs announced the expansion ideas.

Mal led her "sisters" into the station, consulted the timetables, and led them to their gate. "Just play it cool. Our train will be here in less than half an hour." They took their seats on a bench and waited for their boarding call.

Mal also waited for their contact. She was jumpy, feeling the pressure of the stares Tate got. He really did attract attention—a lot of male attention, which was a downright insult to both her and Sophia. Why had she made Tate into such a sexpot? She decided charisma and sex appeal had no gender. She hated being blindsided by the revelation too late to do anything about it, but there it was. If she'd anticipated this complication, she would have done things differently, like made Tate into an old hag, their grandmother or something. Darn, and she'd tried so hard not to overdo it. Now there was nothing for it, but to deal with it. That didn't stop her from elbowing Tate. "Tone it down."

"What? I can't help it if men find me attractive." He grinned. "You know, I get hit on by guys all the time, even when I'm my normal self."

"Ever considered you're putting out the wrong kind of signals?" She couldn't help jibing him.

He shrugged. "You're just jealous that I'm upstaging you."

"Am not. They're staring at you because you're a six-foot-three-inch woman."

"Yeah, a big hunk of burning love."

"You know, those guys who hit on you when you're you, they only want you for your money."

Tate laughed, deeply.

"Stop that." Mal shook her head. "You're drawing attention. And please, learn to titter daintily, like a real girl."

"Now I have to learn a new laugh." He shook his head. "Sorry, babe, but laughing is involuntary and automatic. This is the laugh you get."

Mal narrowed her eyes and glared at him.

"That guy in the gray slacks over there is staring at me."

Mal glanced past the man in question. "Let's hope he's not RIOT."

As if the fellow had heard them, he got up and walked past them, dropping the front page of his newspaper as he did. "Pardon me. I lost my grip."

Aha! Mel felt vindicated. He was MI5 and that was the initiation of the signal she'd been expecting. Mal leaned over, picked up the paper and handed it back facedown as she'd been instructed. "Hold on tightly. There isn't another one until tomorrow."

He smiled. "Thank you." He winked at Tate. "Hope to see *you* on the train. Have a nice day." He walked off.

Tate raised a brow. "See what I mean? I'm irresistible."

"Right. That was our signal and you know it," Mal said, relieved that Tate was not more attractive than she and Sophia. "That was our contact, not some guy trying to hit on you, Kate." She rolled her eyes. "Memorize his face. He'll be keeping tabs on us."

"No problem. He'll be looking for us on the train, wanting to hook up with me." Tate winked at Sophia. "Don't you worry, either."

Tate was teasing again, which meant he'd eased into his role as a woman and was accepting it. Maybe things would work out after all. "Absolutely no hooking up," she replied with a smile, knowing Tate was pulling her chain for fun.

A few minutes later, a train arrived in the station. Mal experienced a moment of panic as a stream of passengers detrained and walked past them. She felt like she had a target etched on her forehead. Inflatable Annie's untimely death had really spooked her.

Any good assassin could have killed them with ease and no one would notice until the crowd cleared. Next to her Tate seemed unconcerned, but she knew him well enough to recognize it as an act.

After the crowd thinned, they received their boarding call and stood to file along with another crowd toward the train. Tate was doing better with his walk and keeping quiet. Sophia looked nervous. Their contact was right behind them.

And then, out of nowhere, some old man came up behind Tate and pinched his fake silicone butt. Tate kept walking, totally unaware he'd been harassed.

Mal sprang into action. "Hey! Back off, old man. Hands off my sister."

The old guy and Tate both looked startled. The old guy slunk away through the crowd.

Mal upbraided Tate. "Pay attention! I thought you said if anyone touched you you'd take a swing at him. That old man just gave your butt a bruising pinch and you didn't even react. Not that I advocate a right hook, but a cold stare can be effective. Especially on an old man like him."

"Huh." Tate shrugged. "I didn't feel a thing." Tate climbed aboard the train, shaking his enhanced booty.

"Stop wiggling your butt. And next time, act like you did feel something," Mal said.

"Fine. Next time I'll slap the offender's face. Will that make you happy?"

"Watch your vocal tone. You're giving yourself away." Mal was getting a headache.

Tate found a pair of empty seats facing each other. He plopped into one. Sophia plopped in next to him, practically in his lap. Mal took the seat opposite.

Their contact came up beside them and hesitated. "Is this seat occupied?"

"It's all yours," Mal said. "Help yourself."

They exchanged a few more pleasantries, with Tate as Kate joining in and providing the proper parts of the code verification. Their contact passed the exam.

And the set was complete—two American spies, a member of British intelligence, and the asset they were trying to spring from RIOT's death grip.

"Lash." Their contact extended his hand.

"Lena," Mal said, carrying on the charade. "And these are my sisters—Kate and Sonia." She indicated each.

"Pleased to meet you lovely ladies," Lash said. "Where are you headed?"

"We're taking the train all the way to Liverpool. We're on vacation. We have to see the home of the Beatles."

"Fans of the boys from Liverpool. Excellent. I'm going to Liverpool, too."

All should have been well, but Mal was worried about

Sophia. She looked on edge and nervous and kept grabbing Tate's hand.

Mal shook her head subtly at her. When that didn't work, she cleared her throat. And again, loudly. Sophia ignored her, forcing Mal to lean forward and admonish her. "You're supposed to be sisters, not lovers."

Good grief! Did Sophia have no shame and no fear for her cover?

"Sisters can hold hands for support." Sophia shot her a defiant look. "There's nothing wrong with it." She looked at Tate, appealing to him and appeared to tighten her grip on him. "Holding his hand gives me comfort. I'm risking everything to do this."

She's risking something, Mal thought cynically. Right now, it was a thrashing from Mal.

"Lay off her, Lena." Tate gave her a warning look as he spoke in his husky woman's voice. "She's right. It's fine. We're a close family. My baby's scared." He tucked Sophia in against his shoulder. "Let me take care of little sis." He kissed the top of Sophia's head.

Next to Mal, Lash, the British agent was trying not to laugh. "Ah, family. Can't live with them. Can't kill them."

This was going to be a long ride.

This mission is going to kill me, Tate thought. *Or at the very least, kill my defunct marriage and stop its rise from the ashes of divorce.*

He didn't like taking Sophia's side, but he was up against orders. He had to bring her in.

His cell phone buzzed. He pulled it from his jeans pocket, wishing women carried their phones in shirt pockets like men do. Much more convenient that way. He glanced at the screen. "I have to take this."

Mal pointed toward her neck. He got the message— talk like a girl.

He put on the husky female voice. "I'll just take this in the lav." He pried Sophia's hand from his and walked down the aisle to the restrooms. Fortunately, they were single-occupancy, unisex units. He wasn't in the mood to give anyone a scare in the toilets, least of all himself.

He swung in and locked the door behind him. "Cox here. What's up, chief?"

"We have a problem, Tate."

"All right." As Tate settled in to deal with mission complications, his reflection in the mirror startled him. He was used to being uncomfortable in these women's clothes, but still not used to looking like a woman. And not a half bad-looking woman, either. A little on the tall side. He reminded himself a bit of his second cousin Amy. She was a tall, broad-shouldered woman, too.

"Hit me with it. And if I start talking in a woman's voice, just ignore it, sir."

"I know all about your cover, Tate," the chief said with a hint of amusement in his voice. "How is it being the fairer sex?"

Tate primped in front of the mirror. Was his mascara smudging? "Harder than it looks. I'm having to fend the men off. And it takes forever to get ready to go anywhere."

"Every cover has its hardships." Tate imagined the chief saying it with a straight face.

Not my usual cover, Tate thought. Then he remembered his playboy cover had cost him the love of his life. "What's the nature of the problem?"

Tate hoped the assassin hadn't gotten away and warned RIOT. Or that RIOT was already on to NCS's deception and the fact that Sophia wasn't dead, just poor old Inflatable Annie.

The chief cleared his throat. It wasn't like him to be nervous or pussyfoot around. "It's a personal problem as much as an Agency problem. Which is why I'm approaching you before Malene."

Shit. A bunch of random, and frightening, scenarios bounced around Tate's head, foremost, his gorgeous child. "Has something happened to Kayla?" His heart pounded.

"Kayla's fine."

He took a deep breath, letting relief in. Nothing was as bad as Kayla being in trouble. "My mother? Has she finally discovered Dad was a spy and so am I?"

"Lenora's as deceived as ever."

"Not something to do with Cox Software?"

"It affects Cox. In fact, it appears it's as much targeted at Cox as it is at the Agency and you. Once I give you the details, you'll need to contact Brad and brief him on damage control."

"Not another hostile takeover attempt?"

"Tate, can we stop playing twenty questions?"

"RIOT isn't trying to buy me out and humiliate me using a shell corporation again, are they?" Tate was tired enough of the usual corporate foes any company faced—corporate raiders and offers from bigger techie fish trying to absorb his company. Even though he didn't devote as much time as he should have to the business, he had no intention of selling. Cox Software provided his spy cover and he'd never give that up.

But Cox Software faced an additional threat from RIOT head Archibald Random, who made a play for Tate's company at least once a year. Random was maniacally genius and his attempts were getting more sophisticated, inventive, and covert. Harder to block.

"Yes," the chief said. "RIOT is trying to ruin you and take Cox Software down at the same time."

Tate cursed beneath his breath. This was almost as bad as Kayla being in trouble.

"They're taking a new approach," the chief said.

"We've exploited your reputation as a playboy for our purposes for years." Emmett sounded as if he was carefully weighing his words. "It now appears RIOT has, too."

For the moment, Tate wondered whether yet another woman had stepped forward claiming to be pregnant with his baby. He'd never gotten a woman besides Mal pregnant, but there was a certain type of woman who'd even use her baby to extort money from him. "Don't tell me there's a RIOT bitch claiming she's having my baby?"

"Worse."

"Worse?" What the hell could be worse? Unless his cover was blown. Sophia—

Emmett cleared his throat. "It looks like our worst fears have been realized. RIOT has double-crossed us using Sophia. We're still not sure whether she's a willing accomplice or was duped into it." There was a pregnant pause.

Odd as it was, Tate felt a sense of relief. If Sophia was in league with RIOT, he didn't owe her a thing romantically. He could tell her to go to hell with a clear conscience. Just bring her in and let the Agency deal with her. This latest wrinkle absolved him of any obligation to sleep with her. A year from now *she* wouldn't be able to blackmail him with a baby. *Small mercies,* he thought. Who'd have guessed he'd be relieved not to have to sleep with a beautiful woman?

Then he thought of Mal and almost smiled. The odds of rekindling a marriage and getting his family back were improving every minute.

"I'm sending you a news story that's making the Twitter rounds," the chief said, interrupting Tate's thoughts. "It's already been posted on one of Britain's major gossip rag's online site. The hard-copy version has gone to press. It's too late to stop it, though we tried with MI5's cooperation. It'll be on the newsstands by the time you reach Liverpool.

"I've sent you an encrypted message with the full story, complete with pictures." Emmett paused.

Tate swore beneath his breath and braced himself—what could RIOT be up to? He switched his phone so he could view the message.

"Of you in bed with Sophia," the chief finished with the panache and showmanship of a stage actor.

The message came up. Tate read the headline. "Eligible International Playboy Tate Cox Beds a Sexy International Terrorist—"

He clenched his fist and pounded the wall. "What the hell?" His conscience was clear. "I *haven't* slept with Sophia."

He scrolled down and took a look at the picture, frowning as his heart raced. There he was in bed with a beautiful blonde straddling him. The shot was taken from above. The bastards must have been hiding in the room above.

The photo could have been lewd. Instead, it was almost artistic the way the lighting fell, highlighting her naked shoulders and slim, shapely legs. The way her blond hair fell over her gorgeous breasts, the fullness of them exposed. The nipples only alluringly alluded to. Her head was tossed back. Her eyes closed. Her lips gently parted. The look on her face was pure ecstasy. It was clear from her expression she was in love with the man she was screwing. Tate grew hard just looking at it. Any red-blooded hetero male would be hard-pressed not to.

"That's not a terrorist." He had a hard time speaking with rage coursing through him. His privacy had been violated. If he ever caught those bastard photographers—

Then again, the look on her face made life seem right and hopeful. He'd have to order a copy of this picture to frame and hang in his bedroom.

"That's Mal." Tate somehow got the words out.

"Mal?" It was hard to tell whether the chief was surprised or not. "You're sure?"

"I know my own wife."

"Ex-wife," the chief corrected.

Somehow that stung.

"You were supposed to be seducing Sophia." Emmett's voice was neutral, without its signature hint of amusement.

"Yeah. But Mal and I—" Mal and he were what?

Tate cursed and banged the wall again. "What do we do now? Sophia, Mal, and Lash the MI5 agent are sitting together in the coach compartment. Do you think Sophia has any real information to give us?"

The chief hedged. "Debriefing her could still prove valuable to us."

"You still want me to bring Sophia in?"

"Yes," the chief said. "What is your take on her involvement?"

Tate frowned, thinking through the various scenarios. "You heard about Inflatable Annie's deflation?"

"Yes. My condolences. She was state-of-the art."

"Yeah," Tate said. "After that Sophia became scared to the point of panic. Thinking it all through, I believe she was under orders to sleep with me so RIOT could get that shot of us in bed together and use it to ruin me personally and professionally, both with Cox Software and the Agency.

"After that, she was expendable. They tried to take her out. It's just a matter of time until they realize their mistake.

"I'll bring her in. She might be willing to cooperate in exchange for her safety, same as before."

There was silence on the chief's part for a minute. "Are you up to the task?"

"I'm always up to the task."

"The question is—how do we plan this?" the chief

said. "It will be almost impossible to keep the news story from Sophia."

"Yeah, and when she sees it she'll know it's not her."

"She doesn't have much bargaining power now," Tate said. "Not if she wants to live."

The chief was thoughtfully quiet. "You're right about that. And the Brits will certainly still be onboard. Present her with her options." The chief paused. "We still have to snuff the brush fire the story caused. We can't have the head of Cox Software associated with a known terrorist."

"Absolutely not." Tate's thoughts were rambling. "Is RIOT really going public now by claiming Sophia as one of their terrorists?" Tate asked.

"No, hell no. And it's not as if we'd let them if they tried. But they have Sophia dead to rights on being associated with half a dozen known groups. No doubt she did work with them on RIOT's behalf.

"Stop evading the issue, Tate. What are we going to do about this photo of you and Mal?"

"She's going to be livid. And really embarrassed."

"That goes without saying."

Tate took a deep breath and made a snap decision. "We tell the truth—that's me in bed with my ex-wife."

"Lenora will be fit to be tied when she hears the news."

"I can deal with Mom."

"But what about Mal?" the chief said. "Can you deal with her? The gossip press and the entertainment mags will have a field day with this—Tate Cox and his ex reuniting."

"I didn't say anything about reuniting."

"You look exceptionally reunited in that picture."

Tate rolled his eyes. "Maybe it's just a one-night stand, a hookup."

"Is it?" the chief said.

Tate almost ran his fingers through his hair. It was a nervous gesture. He stopped himself just in time from ruining his hairdo. Being a woman really was a pain. "Hell, I don't know, Emmett."

"Word will get out that you two were staying in the same hotel room, playing at fake identities and were seen lovey-dovey all over Cheltenham. That won't look like a hookup. You two can break up later if that's what you want. But for now, you're back together. Get Cox's publicity department on it right away."

How was Tate going to tell Mal?

CHAPTER TWENTY-ONE

M al was looking out at the English countryside rolling by when Tate came back from the bathroom.
He'd been gone longer than she expected, and frankly,
she'd been getting worried. All sorts of scenarios had
flashed through her mind. Like RIOT taking him out in the
bathroom.

He flashed her an apologetic, sexy smile. She was just
about to tell him to cut it out and act like a lady—wait. Was
there a hint of hesitation and apprehension in his manner?
That was so out of character for the unflappable Tate that it
sent a wave of apprehension through her.

"Everything okay?" she asked as he hovered in the aisle.

"Just peachy." He spoke in the sultry, husky female
voice he'd manufactured.

A man a row over looked up, obviously searching for
the source of the sultriness. He found it in Tate and ran
his gaze over him.

While Mal was grateful Tate was staying in character,
they didn't need the scrutiny of horny onlookers. Maybe
Tate was right—she should have made him into someone
who didn't draw any attention. The problem with Tate was
that she could dress him in sackcloth and toss a paper bag
over his head and he'd still ooze sex appeal.

"Can I have a word, sis?" Tate arched a brow.

"Sure."

"In private." He took Mal's arm and pulled her to her feet before she could protest, shooting Lash a look that told him to keep an eye on Sophia.

Tate pulled Mal into a loo and closed the door behind them.

For a moment, Mal was keenly aware of the train clacking rhythmically along the rails. The sound was so normal. So reassuring. "What's this all about?"

Tate wrapped his arms around her and pulled her into him. The next thing she knew, his lips came down on hers. He kissed her deeply, urgently, insistently, smudging both their lipstick jobs and taking her breath away.

Before she could protest, his hands were up beneath her T-shirt and he was lifting it over her head. But let's face it—she wasn't going to protest. Unless he dropped the shirt onto the floor. He set it by the sink.

Then his hand was on her jeans, button-front jeans. With one tug he pulled them open and was unzipping the fly on his own. What had brought this on? Hopefully not imminent death. There was nothing like a threat to give Tate a hard-on. They'd had some of their best sex while in dangerous situations.

She helped him pull his jeans down and was confronted with the impediment of his crotch-reducing garment.

"Damn, I should have gotten rid of this before getting turned on."

She felt for him. Being bent back like that had to hurt, especially when he was erect. She pulled the garment down and he popped out like he was spring-loaded. He sighed with a mixture of relief and lust.

While she went wet at the sight of that beautiful erect, pulsing member, he pulled down her panties and pulled her to him.

"What do you call having sex in a train bathroom?" She kissed him lightly and sucked his lower lip, taking the rest of his lipstick right off. Vanilla. Nice. "It's not the mile-high club."

"Call it whatever you like." He bent at the knees to level their heights and thrust into her. "I like to think of it as riding the rails."

She gasped with the force of his entry and the wild euphoric pleasure pulsing through her. She clutched his shoulder and hung on as he pounded deep into her. The animal force of it was intoxicating. The scent of his perfume confusing as it mingled with hers. The way he looked like the sister he didn't have disconcerting. And the bra and fake boobs comical.

Making love to her ex-husband the woman in a train bathroom should have been the last thing from sexy. And yet, she was hot and tight for him and the pleasure built with unstoppable force. He was insistent and passionate in a way that spilled over to her.

There was a knock on the door. Before either of them could answer, it swung open. A middle-aged woman gasped. "I beg your pardon."

Tate slammed the door in her face and turned the lock.

"That was ludicrous," Mal said.

"Scarring." Tate rocked into her again. "She'll never recover." He kissed Mal.

When he released her mouth, she closed her eyes and rocked her hips against him, gasping and moaning with every thrust, trying to hold back the inevitable climax, wanting to hang on to the build and the passion. To the joy of bonding. No man had ever made her feel like Tate was making her feel right then, and always had. She was waiting for him, even while she sensed he was struggling to hold back the release with as much fight as she was.

The wave of passion grew too large and crashed over her. She moaned his name with each wonderful wave. "Tate, Tate, *Tate!*"

He squeezed her tight and came with her.

The force of their climax was so strong she went weak at the knees. She leaned against Tate and he against her. It took each of them holding the other to prevent them from collapsing onto the toilet just behind Mal.

When Mal opened her eyes, Tate was staring at her with a look she couldn't place. And then he smiled as if he'd seen something he'd been looking for for an eternity and finding it exhilarated him.

They were both breathing hard and glowing with the pleasure, the exertion, and the heat of the confined space.

"Wow," Mal mouthed.

"I love you," Tate said, which was the most ridiculous thing.

"You always say that. *After.*" She studied him, wondering again if he meant it.

He tipped her chin up. "I mean it. Whatever happens, never forget it. *I love you.*"

Tate was behaving oddly. Too sentimentally, especially for him. Maybe playing a woman had gotten to him. It didn't have to be more than just sex between exes, even though she desperately wanted it to be and it felt like so much more to her.

She smiled. The situation was too intense. And Tate looked ridiculous with his lipstick smeared, his wig askew, his bra over his rippled abs, and his erect male member still between her legs.

She adjusted his wig and tucked a lock of his fake hair back. "Think of the scandal. That lady will never be the same."

He laughed. "Probably not. But what do we care?"

"Let's hope she doesn't talk. We're supposed to be sisters." She leaned up and kissed him again.

He whispered very softly in her ear. "Marry me again, Mal."

"What?" She couldn't believe what she was hearing.

She must have looked shocked. She was shocked.

Tate had amazing staying power. He was still inside her, giving her ideas of another round. She was so stunned, she tried to take a step back, but he held her tight, the two still one.

"Think about it, at least." He eyes pleaded with her. He gave a gentle, teasing thrust.

"You're using unfair tactics. I can't think straight with that thing between my legs."

He grinned. "You know me better than that—I never play fair."

She didn't know what to say. The first time he'd proposed, she hadn't hesitated. Tate had planned everything down to the most romantic detail and presented her with the most gorgeous ring she'd ever seen. Now he was proposing in a train loo while dressed like a woman after mind-blowing sex? On the spur of the moment, or so it seemed. With no ring at all. It seemed crazy, crazily romantic. Yet she stalled.

All the reasons to say no ran through her head. Kayla, most important. They couldn't keep dragging their child through the ups and downs of a series of marriages and all their ons and offs. "Yes."

The answer surprised her as much as it appeared to have surprised Tate.

"Yes, yes, or yes you'll think about it?"

He was giving her an out and yet she didn't take it. "Yes, yes."

He grinned, looking superiorly happy. He kissed her again and thrust deep inside her. "Say it again, Mal."

He thrust again and again until she moaned, "Yes, yes, *yes*!" And climaxed again, almost as powerfully as the first time.

"That's what I like to hear," he whispered in her ear, and pulled out as she caught her breath. "As a side benefit, now we won't have to lie to the press."

She was still breathing hard and stunned as she stared at him. "*What* press?"

"The press who published a picture of us in bed together in Cheltenham." He didn't even look sheepish as he spoke. "Sold to them by a RIOT photographer. Who also fed them the false intel that you're Sophia, a known terrorist that I'm sleeping with." He explained about the RIOT plot to ruin him, both as a spy and a government software supplier and businessman.

Her mouth fell open. "Have you seen the picture?" Her first thought was, *What if Kayla stumbles on it?*

Kayla didn't even know where babies came from yet. How would Mal ever explain what was going on? Would it scar her for life? Her little eyes certainly didn't need to see her parents in bed together, ever. A new host of doubts assailed her—what was Tate really up to?

"Don't look at me like that, Mal." Tate's tone pleaded with her to believe him. "The story may be a precipitating event. But we're damn *good* together. These years apart have taught me that we're horrible *apart*. I really do love you. Enough to promise I'm going to give up the playboy cover life and turn into a staid old married man. You're the only woman for me."

She swallowed hard, wanting to believe him. "If this is a scam," she said, "or a convenient lie so you can be the hero of this mission—"

He put a finger to her lips. "It isn't. Trust me." He grinned, which was more like him. "Now put your shirt back on and button up or I'll never get this damned crotch-control girl-maker back on."

She stared at his still erect member. He was right. She grabbed her shirt and pulled it back on as Tate struggled with the garment of torture. When they were both dressed, she fixed his hair and touched up his makeup as well as hers as she processed the situation in silence. She wasn't an exhibitionist. The thought of pictures of her naked and in the throes of passion going public made her ill.

"How bad is it? I want to see it." She had to know what she was dealing with.

"The picture?" He tipped her face up so she couldn't look away. "Revealing, intimate, sexy as hell. I'm going to have to beat the guys away."

"Tate—"

He pulled out his phone, brought up the photo, and handed her the phone as she held her breath and steeled herself to take a look. She let her breath out as she stared at it. He'd described it perfectly. The picture was too intimate. The expression on her face gave everything away—she was clearly in love with Tate. She gasped. "How?"

"Probably had a hidden camera on the ceiling." He pried the phone from her and held her tight, wrapping her in his arms. "I'll take care of it. Cox's legal team is already on it. We'll get it pulled down."

Which was a moot point. Digital was forever no matter how hard you tried to eradicate it.

"I'll demand a retraction. Threaten to sue. Whatever it takes." His voice was gentle, reassuring, apologetic. "But you see how we have to make a stand together that that's you in the picture? And that we're back together. It's the only way."

He paused. "I know what I'm asking. It would be easier and a lot less embarrassing for you to let Sophia take the rap. Maybe even easier for her in some ways. I'm sure RIOT ordered her to sleep with me and the whole thing was a setup. It would look like she'd followed orders. But since they want to kill her anyway . . .

"Mal? What are you thinking? Without your help, I'm ruined."

She nodded. "I'm thinking I don't know what it is about you." Mal pulled away enough to look him in the eye. "I never thought I'd accept a marriage proposal from another woman."

He smiled and kissed her tenderly on the lips. "Thank you."

She nodded. "What are we going to do about Sophia? She's either a double agent or a dupe. Either way, this mission was obviously a setup to frame and ruin you. Can we trust any intel she gives us?"

"The chief wants us to bring her. Now that she knows she's expendable, she may cooperate and spill what she really knows. She may still be of value to us."

"Do we confront her with what we know?"

Tate didn't hesitate. "Of course."

Mal nodded. "What do we tell her about us?" Mal hesitated. "I don't know about love. If she feels it, it's a sick love. But she's dangerous and unpredictable."

He agreed. "We won't tell her we're really back together, no." He grinned. "Why provoke a woman scorned?"

Mal nodded. She had to agree with him. "We tell her we're faking it for damage control?"

"Exactly."

She nodded. "Okay. Let's do it. And we really have to stop meeting in the bathroom like this."

"Do we?" His eyes twinkled and he grinned. "I like it."

As they returned to their seats, the woman who'd walked in on them in the loo shot them a nasty look. Mal ignored the woman, who turned to whisper to her traveling companion. When you walked in on someone, you got what you got.

Lash was doing a good job of babysitting Sophia when they returned to their seats. Sophia's eyes lit up when she saw Tate, although she did an adequate job of not throwing herself into his arms and at least attempting to stay in cover character.

Tate whispered something to Lash. Lash nodded and pulled out his phone. Within minutes he had upgraded them to first class and their own compartment, an extravagance that hadn't previously seemed necessary. Like every other intelligence agency, MI5 was facing tight budget constraints. As they settled in in their new digs, Lash mumbled something about how the expense report for this mission was going to be a bloody nightmare.

Sophia clutched Tate's arm as he filled Lash and Sophia in on the latest developments. Mal had to hand it to Tate. He handled the whole thing admirably, using just the right tone and attitude with Sophia.

"I didn't know what they were planning!" Sophia dug her nails into Tate's arm. Her eyes were wild with fear.

But is it genuine? Mal wondered.

"You have to believe me. They used me. But now I really want to escape. I couldn't go back to them now even if I wanted to. When they approached me for this mission, I agreed." She swallowed hard and stared at Tate, ignoring Mal and Lash. Somehow she'd determined Tate was her best, most sympathetic bet.

"Not that I had any choice. Either you do what they say or they kill you. That's the way RIOT works. But you know that.

"There were many girls they could have chosen for the job. But they chose me for two reasons. They knew I'd been following Tate's career and had what they called a crush on him. Which gave them the confidence that I would have no trouble following their orders to seduce and sleep with him."

Mal couldn't believe she had to listen to this.

"And, as a happy coincidence, I resemble your ex-wife." She shot Mal a look full of hate. "The only woman who's been able to really capture your heart."

That should have been a compliment. Would have been maybe if Sophia hadn't practically spat it out and shot her a look meant to kill.

"They set up the plan, tempting you with a beautiful woman who was desperate for you and had valuable intelligence, two things you couldn't resist.

"The science festival came up and it was the perfect opportunity. They knew that you two had fallen in love in Cheltenham and hoped to capitalize on my similarity and your sentimentality.

"I was supposed to sleep with you and disappear." She licked her lips nervously. It was prettily done and no doubt meant to be seductive.

She kept pleading with Tate. "They knew you and your ex weren't on the best of terms. And that she never goes into the field. My handlers never considered that your chief would send her into the field with you.

"But he did. And I screwed up the night of Lord Witham's dinner. Thanks to her." Again, she flashed the death glare at Mal. "I showed up in your bed, wearing only a bow around my neck like I was your gift." Venom filled her voice as she pointed at Mal. "She chased me away at gunpoint."

Tate flashed Mal a mild, amused look, and cocked a brow.

"So I had to try again—in the parking garage. And she ruined that, too."

Mal shrugged. She'd been right all along to distrust the RIOT bitch. "Bygones."

Sophia's glare hardened. "I didn't know they were going to photograph us. They never told me a single detail of what they planned to do. They just issued orders that I had to follow without question.

"I failed. I'm expendable. They've proven that. They'll send their SMASH assassins after me as soon as they realize they killed a dummy, not me."

Although Mal could argue that for all her intelligence, Sophia was a dummy, too.

"They won't stop until they kill me." She appealed to Tate again with a trembling smile and all her feminine wiles on exhibit meant to invoke the hero in him. "You have to save me, like you promised. If you do, I'll tell you everything I know."

Mal thought Sophia looked patently ridiculous clinging to Tate's arm while he was dressed as Kate and making lovesick puppy eyes at him/her. She was a cover-life artist's worst nightmare. She really couldn't stick to a cover to save her life.

Sophia loosened her death grip on Tate's arm and stroked it with her free hand. "I love you, Tate. I really do. Please believe me. Please *save* me."

CHAPTER TWENTY-TWO

"We proceed with the plan and get Sophia out through Northern Ireland." Tate looked to Mal and Lash for confirmation. "From there we'll take her to our top secret safe house that's in the U.S.'s jurisdiction."

Lash nodded. "The deal still stands as far as Great Britain is concerned. You share what you learn from her with us in return for our cooperation and help. Nothing's changed."

Mal didn't say anything. Tate could tell she was pissed at Sophia, but hanging on to her professionalism.

"Another of our agents will meet us in Liverpool and accompany us on the ferry across to Belfast," Lash continued. "Especially given the situation, we can use all the backup we can get."

Tate explained that Mal and he were faking a reconciliation to control the intended damage that picture was supposed to cause. Mal's expression was masked. But he had the feeling she was seething at Sophia.

"RIOT will be furious and ready to retaliate when they realize we've neutralized their attack." He flashed Sophia what he hoped was a comforting smile. "If it's any consolation, heads will roll over this failure. Likely literally. Whoever planned this and planned to use you will pay the price."

That's when Tate got a glimpse of the real Sophia. She looked pleased by the thought in a criminal way, like she was a Mafia don extracting vengeance and loving it. Not at all like a sweet, innocent pawn of a girl who would be relieved, but horrified at the same time.

Sophia was very good, Tate determined. Much more skilled at deception than she led them to believe. He didn't trust her. But he was more expert than she was. He'd seen through her façade to the hard core beneath. That look in her eyes didn't fan ardor in the male breast. It annihilated it. If she were going to fashion herself as a femme fatale she'd do well to learn to mask it. He kept that bit of advice to himself.

"What about our covers?" Sophia asked.

Mal answered for him. "They remain the same. And you'd do well to keep your hands off your sister."

Tate forced himself not to smile at the irony of Mal's command. Just talk to the lady who'd seen the two sisters going after each other like horny teenagers in the bathroom. Speaking of which, he wondered if there was any way to neutralize her and keep the gossip from spreading. Not that it really mattered. But he didn't like loose ends and cracks in the plan. If the wrong person heard about it, his female cover could easily be blown and it was tenuous enough as it was.

They arrived in Liverpool an hour and a half later after an uneventful, but tense, train ride. Tate talked to Cox Software's legal and publicity teams and got an update that things were proceeding. And he'd ignored three texts from his mother demanding to know whether it was true that he was getting back with Mal. Did the woman never rest? What time was it in the States anyway?

Somehow she managed to infuse her texts with the tone of her unending displeasure. Lenora Cox was not a happy camper. In her opinion, daughters-in-law were mere son stealers called by a different name. She'd get used to the idea sooner or later. And once she calmed down, she might even realize she might get more time with Kayla.

They shared a taxi to the Liverpool ferry terminal, Lash playing along as if he was their new fast friend. It wasn't unusual for them to be continuing on to the same destination. There were a number of passengers who had bought a train/ferry package. Which made Tate nervous. Onboard the ferry to Belfast, they'd be sitting targets, not to mention the possibility of a car bomb, which could take out a lot more people than just them.

They made their way into the terminal, up the escalator and into the waiting lounge with its red and blue seats, view of the port, and yellow walls painted with the words SAIL WITH US TO THE EMERALD ISLE.

They met their new contact easily enough. He was seated facing out looking toward the port and the sunny blue skies. He delivered the verification code and struck up a polite conversation, but kept his distance. The cover called for the new agent, Walburn, to be only a passing acquaintance so he could cover their backs at an appropriate distance.

The terminal was full. The ferry totally booked. It held just under one hundred cars and nearly a thousand people. A thousand chances for an assassin to be aboard, less the five of them.

Tate was still hauling around the book-gun copy of *War and Peace,* pretending to read it, actually reading it, and figuring out how to use all its special features at regular turns. The bulletproof shield was small. In a pinch, Tate would have to make a snap decision whether to shield his head or his heart. Even now he wondered which was his more valuable asset.

Even though he was trying to keep a low profile, he

was attracting a fair number of stares and leers from the men around him. Men could be such pigs. He had to force himself not to smile at the sentiment. He was getting his fair share of stares from women, too. Most of them hostile rather than curious. He couldn't decide whether they'd found him out for the man he was and were miffed he was impersonating a woman and hoping he didn't try to use their loo. Or they were just jealous of either his looks, makeup, or hair. The looks were his. Mal had done a fine job with everything else.

He was used to woman falling all over him, not shooting him daggers. Well, only occasionally literally. Like that time in Spain. But with their eyes, no. Women loved him because he loved them. And then there was his money.

Next to Tate, Mal flirted with Lash and Sophia was jumpy and trying not to be. Her eyes darted around as if looking for a menace in every newcomer and every unexpected noise startled her. Mal teased her about being afraid of sailing and offered her an antiseasick pill, probably hoping with any luck it would knock Sophia out for the duration of the trip. Tate noticed it wasn't the less drowsy version.

Tate flipped to a page of *War and Peace*. A phrase caught his eye: "We can know only that we know nothing. And that is the highest degree of human wisdom."

He concurred. Tolstoy had pretty much summed up the spy biz in a few sentences.

Tate checked the weather report. Storms predicted after midnight. Damn. The ferry ride took all night. They wouldn't dock until around six A.M. He wasn't a born sailor. He got up to buy his own antiseasick pills, the less drowsy kind. He needed his head.

"I'm going to check out the shops," he said.

Mal cocked a brow and looked like she wished she'd thought of it. And there was a hint of "don't leave me alone with this bitch" in her look, too. She had Lash to help her.

He wandered into the shop and found the pills easily enough, throwing in a pair of sea-bands, too. Added protection was never a bad thing. A rack of tourist T-shirts caught his eye and so did his image on a security camera. In the privacy of their cabin on the ferry he was going to change into something more comfortable for the ride, like men's clothing.

He bought a men's T-shirt, lamenting aloud that he had such a hard time finding ladies' sizes that fit. The men's cut didn't show off his figure in the best light. Like hell. He looked good in men's clothing, especially when he wasn't wearing fake boobs. See? What was Mal thinking? He could maintain a cover as well as any agent.

He paid for his purchases and joined his group. Mal eyed his bag.

Tate shrugged. "We're clear. I didn't detect any problems."

Their ferry arrived. After dispatching its passengers, the boarding call sounded. The four of them boarded together with Walburn bringing up the backside. The three "sisters" were sharing a sleeping compartment. Lash had a single berth in a compartment across from them. Walburn was down the hall.

They checked into their four-berth cabin. Thankfully it had en suite bathroom facilities. Tate availed himself of them. He thought about stripping off his bra and fake girl-maker/fake hip device of torture. *After dinner,* he thought. *When we've settled in for the night.*

When he came out of the loo, the girls were each sitting on a lower bunk. The upper ones needed to be pulled out.

"We've called dibs on these." Mal was smirking. "We both decided you get the honor of being on top." Her voice was full of innuendo.

He arched a brow. "The old missionary sleeping position trick." He shook his head. "I don't know. You girls might get a peek up my skirt."

"You aren't wearing a skirt." Mal eyed his crotch.

Yeah, she was trying to get a rise out of him, which would hurt like hell. "It was worth a try."

He stretched. The cabin was small, but roomier than the train. It was going to be a long, boring crossing. At least he hoped so. He needed a drink. "It's an eight-hour overnight trip across the Irish Sea to Belfast. Let's get something to eat before we settle down for the night." And the storm hit. "I could use a nightcap."

"Good idea." Mal grabbed a laminated menu from the small fixed desk and flipped through it casually. "The menu looks pretty decent. Let's hope the cook's skill lives up to the food descriptions." She handed the menu to Tate and stood. "Let's go. I'm starved."

Sophia had been quiet. "No!" The word exploded from her into the small room like an earthquake. She shook her head. "Order in if you like, but I'm not going out there. It's too dangerous. You don't know RIOT."

"I think we do." Mal's brow furrowed, peeved.

Tate bet she was. Sophia had been fighting her at every turn.

"We've been battling them for years," Mal said.

"It's not safe. The odds are against us." Sophia crossed her arms. "I have a Ph.D. in mathematics. I can figure odds better than anyone. I'm not going."

Someone had to stay with Sophia. They couldn't take the risk that she'd run.

"Go," Tate said to Mal. "Get yourself something. We'll order in."

"And trust that no one tries to poison your food or that the steward who delivers it won't try to kill you?" Mal's voice was flippant, but only partially facetious. "I'll bring something back for you. What do you want?"

Mal was happy to escape the confines of the cabin and Sophia's company. Not so happy about leaving Tate alone with her. She didn't trust that mathematician. It was just past nine in the evening. The sun was low over the water with a hint of wispy clouds on the horizon. It was threatening a gorgeous sunset. Mal made her way to the bar and grill, which was decorated in deep, nautical sea blues and brass, very modern and sleek.

Lash waited for her at a table. Walburn was seated a few tables away.

"Our little fugitive wouldn't come out of her cabin?" Lash stood as Mal approached and took a seat.

"No. She doesn't trust our ability to protect her."

"And you trust her alone with Tate?" Lash asked.

Mal arched a brow. "What do you mean by that?"

Their waitress stopped by. Mal ordered a chocolate martini. Lash ordered a second whiskey. The waitress left to fill their order.

"Cox's team is top-notch," Lash said. "They're already demanding a retraction from the tabloids and touting your happy reunion."

"That's all just press. Smoke and mirrors."

"Is it?" Lash smiled at her.

A cocktail waitress returned with their drink order.

Mal sipped her martini. "Reunions don't have to last forever."

Tate told Mal to take her time and enjoy herself. There was no need to hurry right back. He wasn't particularly hungry.

Tate bolted the door behind Mal, made sure *War and*

Peace was close at hand, and grabbed the TV controller. Sophia excused herself to use the bathroom.

They were in an inside cabin with no porthole. It felt both safe—an intruder could only enter through the door—and claustrophobic. If someone did manage to get in, however, they were done for. There was no backup escape route.

Tate's gift shop bag caught his eye. While Sophia was occupied and Mal was out, it was time to get comfy and lose his female garments of torture. His bra was digging into his shoulders and he was tired of the boy being bent uncomfortably back. He pulled off his frilly T-shirt, tossed it on the desk, and discarded his bra. He really was better at removing women's undergarments than putting them on.

He stretched and flexed and rolled his shoulders to get the kinks out. He unzipped his girlie jeans and pulled them off, piling them with his other discarded clothes. He shrugged out of his fake hip/crotch control garment and tossed it aside with disgust. That was the least sexy piece of lingerie he'd ever seen.

As he pulled his boy back into its normal free-hanging position, the door to the bathroom opened. He was caught with his hand in his pants.

"Now there's a sight I've been aching to see." Sophia stood in the doorway, leaning provocatively against the frame with one slender arm curved upward. She was completely naked except for a bow around her neck.

The sight reminded him of finding Mal in his bed wearing nothing but an identical bow. Damn, involuntary memories and bodily reactions. He went hard and erect.

"Almost as good as you. Naked. Perched over me," she said.

Mal's dinner arrived—a grilled salad of Atlantic prawns served with lemon and coriander salsa. Lash had green chicken curry and jasmine rice. Mal placed two orders for curry boxed up to take back to Tate and Sophia.

"The sunset is breathtaking." Mal took a bite of salad.

"Indeed it is. Unfortunately, it portends rough seas later."

Mal frowned. "Really?"

"Yes, sadly."

"Good thing I took my seasick pill before we boarded. Though, surprisingly, I have very good sea legs."

"You're a sailor?" Lash asked.

"Sometimes. I grew up on the water. I have a small sailboat I take out when I have time, which isn't often. How's the curry?"

"Very good. Tate won't be disappointed."

Mal laughed. "I doubt he'll enjoy it one way or the other. He probably won't even taste it. Unlike me, Tate is not a sailor. He'll be afraid it will come back up. Why do you think he was so gallant and let me go out for dinner? He's afraid of eating right now." She winked at Lash.

He took a forkful of curry and rice and laughed. "Are you enjoying the fieldwork?"

Mal shrugged. "I would be. If it weren't for Sophia. Honestly? She's a pain in the butt. Fights me at every step. At times I wonder if she really wants to be rescued." She rolled her eyes.

Lash set down his fork and picked up his drink. "I can take care of her for you and make sure she never causes you another problem." His tone was so sinister.

Mal couldn't help laughing. No more Sophia—it was a pleasant thought. "I'm sure you could." She watched the sunset for a moment. "Have you ever thought of taking a foreign assignment?"

"You think they're more interesting?" Lash said.

"Generally speaking they're more exciting."

Lash appeared to consider what she said. "You don't think I'm a coward?"

"No, absolutely not. I've never even hinted at it."

He nodded. "Someone has to guard the home front. We have our share of excitement."

"I'm sure you do." She smiled at him.

CHAPTER TWENTY-THREE

Dressed, Sophia was a stunner. Naked, she was perfection. Temptation of the flesh of the highest order. Beautiful pert breasts with their rosy nipples tightly budded with desire. Eyes that sparkled with lusty promise. A narrow waist, gently flaring hips, and smooth, perfect skin.

A year ago, hell, a couple of months ago, Tate would have found her simply irresistible. Now the stakes were higher. He didn't want bodily perfection. He wanted Mal. It was as simple as that.

Sophia licked her lips and took a step forward before he could tell her to get dressed. She was on him and coiled around him as quickly as a cobra strikes, rubbing against him.

He grabbed her wrist as she stroked his cheek. "I think you can safely ignore those RIOT orders to sleep with me now."

"What if I want to make love with you, Tate? What if it's all I've dreamed of since I met you?" She slid her free hand down his chest and grabbed his erection.

His mind rebelled against the thought of her. But his body had a mind of its own.

"You want me. We can make each other happy."

He dropped the one wrist and grabbed the one around his erection, squeezing her until he felt her pulse.

She didn't wince, but met his eye. "We can play rough if you like. I'm completely unarmed."

"Don't think you have the upper hand because you have me in hand. Even nearly naked, I'm in control." He stared into her eyes, making his voice and expression serious. "Let go." He squeezed her wrist until it turned purple, giving her a chance to comply before he bent it back and snapped it, forcing her to drop him.

People sometimes got the wrong impression about him. He was civilized and cultured when he needed to be. But he was as skilled in self-defense and killing as the next spy and not hesitant about doing what he had to to live and complete the mission. Sophia was trying his patience.

Still staring at him, she slowly unwrapped her fingers and dropped him.

"Get your clothes on."

"Spoilsport." She made a very pretty pout before turning slowly toward the loo.

He took a deep breath and sat down on the bunk. That was his mistake. She turned and pounced on him, knocking him onto his back and straddling him. "I don't give up, not when I want something as badly as I want you. Make me happy and I'll tell you everything I know about RIOT." She slid his briefs down as she bent forward to lick his nipples.

Twilight had fallen outside. Mal glanced at the clock. "I'd better get back to Tate and relieve him of sole babysitting duty." She pushed back and grabbed the curry boxes.

"Let's do this again," Lash said, standing.

She smiled. "A mission? Or dinner?"

"Either," he said. "Or both."

She laughed. He didn't offer to walk her back.

"You're not heading back to your cabin? We could walk together." She stood and pushed her chair back in.

"I think I'll take a walk around the ferry."

"Guard duty? Making the rounds?"

"You caught me."

"Take care."

She walked quickly back to the cabin, stuck her key in, and swung the door open. "It's me. I'm back with your dinner—"

Sophia was naked on a berth on top of Tate, obviously humping him. She turned and looked back over her shoulder to smile cruelly and triumphantly at Mal.

"Damn it, Tate!" Mal dropped the curry on the floor with a satisfying splat. "Sorry to disturb you."

She spun and grabbed the door.

"Mal—"

She slammed the door, cutting off any pleas as she stormed down the corridor. Tate was still Tate. Why had she thought he'd changed? She took a deep breath, trying to regain control, personally, professionally. Enough control that she didn't kill someone, namely Tate. Or maybe Sophia. That was the age-old question, wasn't it? Who do you kill—the cheater or the one they cheated with?

It would be easy enough to explain why to the chief. But she'd be damned if she'd be responsible for Tate earning his gold star on the Agency wall for giving his life in the service of his country. And think of the reputation he'd have—killed in the act of making love to a gorgeous enemy agent? He'd go down in Agency mythology as the personification of James Bond.

No way!

With tears of anger and hurt blurring her vision, she hurried to the upper deck. A breeze had kicked up and grew stronger as she strode around the deck, power-walking unconsciously, cursing Tate. Trying to think.

* * *

"Mal!" Tate shoved Sophia off him onto her pert little conniving ass and onto the floor. "Mal, wait!" He got to the door a second too late.

Mal was already through it and slamming it in his face. He spun around and glared at Sophia.

She smiled back, looking both triumphant and angry at the same time. "You're still in love with her." It wasn't a question. She stood, breasts bouncing, and rubbed her naked butt, striking a pose that was meant to entice.

Tate's anger blinded him to any charms she may have had. He grabbed those damned women's jeans and pulled them on, ignoring her.

Great timing—Mal had to walk in at the very worst moment. He still wasn't sure how Sophia had ended up straddling him naked. He'd grabbed his shirt and sat down to make sure Sophia got dressed. With the move of a master black belt, she was on him, shoving him back onto the bed and straddling him as if she was going to give him the ride of his life. And damn, he'd still had his briefs on and his fly closed. But Mal couldn't see his innocence from her angle.

"I can make you forget her." Sophia curled around him as he pulled his shirt on.

He stared at her. "Like hell. No one else has."

"Let me try. I really do love you, Tate."

He stared at her. "You love something, but it isn't me. You don't even know me."

"Does it matter? I can make you happy."

He pulled her off him. "I'll do my duty and get you safely to the U.S. But that's the extent of it." He grabbed her clothes from the bathroom and shoved them at her. "Get dressed."

He slipped on those girly lavender flats. Yeah, this was really going to make him invisible.

He watched Sophia as she pouted and slowly put her

clothes on, doing a striptease in reverse, still hoping to entice him. When she was finished, he got into Mal's bag of tricks, grabbed a pair of handcuffs and then Sophia, and tossed her on the bed. He grabbed her wrist and cuffed it to the berth rail.

"You're a hard man." She looked as if the thought turned her on.

"Stay put."

"I'm not going anywhere."

He grabbed his cell and called Lash to come babysit. He turned and strode to the door.

"You're leaving?" Her voice was small, almost touching in its vulnerability.

"Lash will be here in a few minutes to keep you company." He shouldn't leave her alone even a second, but he had to find Mal and explain.

"I hope I'm still alive when you get back. You're leaving me vulnerable."

In the time it took Mal to complete her first turn around the ferry, the breeze had grown in strength and become a full-force wind that whipped her hair into her face. A tempest was brewing on the Irish Sea to match the one storming inside her.

She brushed the hair out of her face and turned into the wind, leaning on the rail as she watched the approaching storm and collected her thoughts.

Electricity charged the air as the promised storm approached at startling speed, glorious and frightening as the sky on the dark horizon burst bright with lightning and thunder roared. Waves pounded against the ferry.

Mal should have been afraid. Instead, she felt a kindred spirit with the storm—raging, pounding, desperate. She took a deep breath and blinked back tears. Secret agents didn't cry on the job, unless their cover demanded it. Crying revealed a damnable, exploitable, dangerous weakness of character any good enemy agent would use against her.

Damn Tate! Dress him as a woman and he still can't keep it in his pants. And worse—women still can't keep their hands off him.

It grew colder and more furious on deck. The wind whipped stronger. The waves lapped higher against the sides of the ferry, rocking the boat. The smell of the approaching heavy downpour overcame the smell of the sea. A clap of thunder roared. The storm was very near now and Poseidon was on a tear, roiling the sea.

Bring it on, Mal thought. Seasick pills would have a hard time prevailing against these seas. Tate deserved a bout of seasickness. When she got back to Langley, she was going to make him pay.

She was angry for more than herself. She was furious for Kayla and the dashed future of their family. And worried about the example Tate was setting as a man and father—

"Ma'am, ma'am!" She realized with a start that someone was talking to her and she was shivering. From the cold, not just anger. She hadn't grabbed a sweater. Or an umbrella.

She turned to the voice with a hand on the gun in her purse. It was a good thing she hadn't realized she'd had it on her when she'd found Tate with Sophia.

The deck was empty. When had that happened? She was vulnerable, a sitting secret agent with a target on her back. She assessed the threat. Nothing.

Just a worried crewman staring at her. "There's a storm coming. You'll have to go below. Captain's orders."

She nodded. Overhead lightning clapped cloud to cloud and then streaked to the water spectacularly. Thunder boomed almost immediately. The young seaman walked her to the stairs and made sure she went below before he disappeared.

What should she do now? She was in no mood to go back to the cabin. Lash. She'd find Lash and warn him about this new complication. Make sure he kept his eye on Sophia. With the two of them watching her, they should be able to spot her manipulating Tate.

The boat rocked back and forth. Walking without losing her footing and crashing into the wall took some effort. On the way to Lash's cabin, Mal passed Walburn's. She paused in front of his door. It wouldn't hurt to chat with him a minute and see if he'd noticed any threats onboard. She knocked on his door. It swung open on its own. Someone hadn't latched it properly.

"Walburn?" She poked her head inside.

Walburn wouldn't be answering her any time soon. He lay spread on the bed with two to the head. His eyes were open.

Mal pulled her pink gun from her purse and did a quick once-over of the room and the loo. They were empty.

She took a step closer to inspect Walburn and frowned. Something was off. He looked surprised. Why? That didn't jibe with the mission. He would have been on his guard.

Blood trickled down his face and stained the pillowcase. It hadn't started to coagulate or dry. The cabin held the sickly, rusty smell of blood and death. The faint odor of gunpowder hung in the air. This was a fresh kill.

Mal's heart pounded. She had to warn Tate, Lash, and Sophia. She only hoped she wasn't too late.

She grabbed a tissue from her purse, turned on her heel and pulled the door until it latched shut. Heart roaring in her ears, she raced toward her cabin as fast as she could without attracting any unwanted attention.

She spotted Lash ahead of her, hurrying down the corridor to his room, withstanding the listing of the ferry surprisingly well. "Lash! Hold up."

He turned and frowned when he saw her. She cursed to

herself. She wasn't keeping her emotions in check. Everything must be showing on her face.

She caught up with him. "Walburn is dead," she said without preamble. "Shot execution style by a pro. RIOT is onboard. We have to warn Tate—"

"I'll take care of it," Lash said.

"I'll go with you."

"No." Lash caught her arm. "Fieldwork isn't your area of expertise. Go to my cabin." He handed her the key. "Lock yourself in and wait for me there. Don't answer the door until you get a text from me. Not for anyone, and that includes Tate. It could be a trap. Do you understand?" He looked her intently in the eye.

She nodded.

"If I don't return within half an hour, notify your people, MI5, the captain, and the authorities and get the boat on lockdown." He took her by the shoulders. "You're our last line of defense." He pointed her toward his cabin and gave her a gentle shove. "Go!"

CHAPTER TWENTY-FOUR

Tate couldn't find Mal. He looked everywhere. One crewman seemed to remember seeing her on the top deck taking a walk. She wasn't there now. The deck had been cleared as the storm bore down on them. The wind howled. The ship rocked. And Tate's stomach lurched. He decided to return to the cabin. Mal would have to return eventually.

He opened the door and slid inside the cabin, closing the door behind him as he looked for threats within. "Mal?" A guy could hope.

Someone had dimmed the cabin lights. Sophia was free from the handcuffs and lying on her berth, sleeping so soundly she didn't stir at his entrance or the bouncing of the ferry in the waves.

There was something unreal and frightening about her position and unflinching slumber. In two steps, he was next to her, taking her pulse as his own roared in his ears, drowning out the wind. She didn't stir when he took her wrist in his. Her pulse was sluggish.

Damn! She was drugged. Where was Lash?

Tate heard a footstep behind him and swung around. Lash stood between him and the door, holding a pistol with a silencer aimed at Tate's head.

He was grinning. "Expect you'd like to know what this is all about?" Lash's educated upper-crust accent was gone, replaced by a lower-middle-class private-school kind of accent.

"I expect I know," Tate said, stalling. "You're not MI5, are you?"

"What gave me away, old man? Is it the gun aimed at you?" Lash, or whatever his real name was, laughed again. "Hand over your weapon or I'll shoot. And I'm not ready to kill you just yet. Another fifteen minutes, maybe less, and we'll be in the full teeth of the storm.

"No one will hear a struggle or a thump or a shot being fired. It will be the perfect time for a killing." Lash's eyes sparkled with excitement. The man was a psychopath who enjoyed killing. It was written all over his face.

"SMASH, I presume." Tate tossed him his gun, stalling for time, hoping to find an opportunity to disarm him. Now wasn't that moment.

"Yes. I'm one of their best. You should be honored they sent me to kill you. I'm only sent after the most valuable targets." Lash wasn't dumb enough to bend to retrieve Tate's weapon.

He kicked it away, making sure it was out of Tate's reach without losing eye contact with Tate for even a fraction of a second.

"Does this honor come with a trophy? Maybe a commemorative plaque?" Tate inched closer to his side of the cabin. If he could get his hands on that copy of *War and Peace* . . .

"Don't move." Lash's voice was hard. "I have a hair-trigger reflex. Don't force me to cut your life shorter than it needs to be."

Tate nodded toward the berth opposite Sophia. "At least let me sit."

Lash nodded.

Tate moved to the berth and sat, waiting for his opportunity. With any luck, the tilting ship would knock his book gun right into his lap.

"I'm afraid this honor comes without a star on Langley's wall for your service."

Tate stared at Lash and cocked a brow. "Really? You're a magician, are you? I believe we thwarted your plan to discredit me. Even as we speak the Agency and my PR and legal teams have mitigated the damage."

"Temporarily."

"That's really my wife in those pictures and video, you bastard." Tate was livid that RIOT had dragged Mal into this.

"Yes, I know." Lash's gaze flicked to Sophia. "She almost failed us."

"Where's Mal? If you've harmed her—"

"Don't look for her to help you. She's safely locked away. Alive. *For now.*"

Tate instinctively leaned forward, aching to take a swing at him.

"Careful." Lash drew a bead on Tate. "I almost shot you just now. No more sudden moves."

Tate had to keep Lash talking and distracted. "All right. You're dying to tell me, so spill it. What's going to happen to all of us? Why won't I get my star? Start with Sophia. Did you poison her?"

Lash smiled as Tate tried to assess just how crazy the bastard was. "Just drugged. For now. I had to keep her quiet. She really is crazy for you." He shook his head. "Some guys have all the luck."

"I think that's called charm," Tate said dryly. "You were saying that you're somehow going to discredit me?"

"Yes."

The storm was picking up. The boat rocked along with Tate's stomach. The last thing he needed was to lose his lunch now. The smell of curry that they hadn't eaten filled the room, adding to his nausea.

"The story," Lash said. "It's simple, really. Sophia will have one bullet to the head. Shot at the height of the storm when no one will hear. To the back of the skull, execution style, like she was killed by a pro. A bullet from your gun." Lash's eyes glowed with sick excitement. "You'll be found with one in your heart. Murder-suicide."

"Very nice," Tate said, inching toward the book almost infinitesimally. "But why? And what about Mal?"

"Impatient? I'm getting there. Did I mention this is a double murder-suicide? A nice, juicy love triangle?"

Tate went cold. He had to force himself not to flinch or show any signs of panic.

"Oh, you don't like the plan? That's really too bad. We've been working on it so hard at SMASH for the last six months. It's been our goal to embarrass the CIA and take out one of their agents."

"And the honor fell to me." Tate kept inching. "Did you pull my name out of a hat or was it a consensus thing?"

"I have no idea how they picked you, old man. Someone higher up the chain in RIOT than me made that decision. I'm merely tasked with carrying out the plan they concocted. You must have angered someone."

"Yeah, I imagine I have." Tate smiled. *War and Peace* was nearly with reach. "Back to the plan."

"Yes. It's very simple, really. We know how you love the ladies. We searched through the organization until we found just the one to dangle before you, a prize you couldn't resist. The head of SMASH found Sophia. She's your type and she resembles your ex rather strikingly. What a happy coincidence. It gave us a chance to take out another adversary in the process, two agents. You see," Lash paused dramatically. "You see, we know you better than you know yourself. And we know the Agency equally well.

"We knew you'd jump at the chance to rescue a girl in trouble, especially a gorgeous one who reminds you of the only girl you ever really loved. We also knew the Agency would send your ex out as part of the exfiltration.

"She's a valuable target, too, and hardly ever in the field. We couldn't count on you falling for Mal again. That's just gravy. But that didn't matter to us anyway. We could spin it to our needs.

"You think you thwarted us by letting the world know the woman in the pictures we splashed all over the Internet is your wife? That fuels our story and gives it authenticity and depth.

"Here's the tale as it will be known to the world. You and your ex sneak off to Cheltenham, the place where you fell in love, to try to make a go of things a second time around. You both realized you made a mistake, and for the sake of your child, you decided to give it another shot.

"While you were there, the paparazzi found you and took those pictures which they sold to the press. Ah, but the course of true love never did run straight? Isn't that the phrase?"

Tate shrugged, using the opportunity to get closer to the book. The ferry rocked, sending it to the very edge of the nightstand next to him. One more good wave and it would fall into his lap.

"And so, by an unfortunate quirk of fate, while in Cheltenham, you run into a woman who is like your ex, but young and impressionable, and without all the baggage. And she has something you want—intel that will help the CIA and MI6 bring down a top secret enemy."

Tate had a good idea where this story was going.

"There will be a letter in Sophia's purse detailing how you promised to marry her if she'd provide intelligence for you. In it, she describes how you used her and her body. It's lurid, juicy stuff. Just the kind of scandal the public loves.

"On her phone is a string of texts between you. Lovers' stuff. The promises you made. And a little video of her naked, straddling you, riding you while your ex-wife is out.

"So here's how it plays out—Sophia has followed you onto the ferry where she confronts you about your betrayal. You kill her to stop her from ruining your career and stuff her body beneath the berth. Where it will eventually be found.

"In the meantime, Sophia has sent Mal the video. Mal confronts you. You fight. The gun accidentally goes off. She's dead, too. Distraught, you kill yourself."

"Very nice. Sounds like prime-time evening drama material. I hope you'll let my estate have the movie rights. I have a young daughter to provide for, even after I'm dead."

"You're funny, Tate. Too bad you're on the wrong side. We might have been friends."

Tate highly doubted that. Tate nodded to Sophia, feeling foolish and duped. But not as duped as he might have been if it hadn't been for Mal. "Was she in on the plan? Did she set out to make a sex tape?" He had to know whether Sophia was telling the truth about that.

Lash shook his head. "She has no idea about the tape.

"The intel Sophia has supposedly imparted to you is what you Americans call icing on the cake. As soon as you're dead, I'll use your phone to transmit a program to your CIA servers. Once NCS downloads it, it will launch a cyberattack on their system the likes of which they've never seen."

Lash kept grinning. "It's unstoppable. And part of the story. One of NCS's best men involved with a sexy terrorist. The letter, which is hot stuff. He commits a double murder, kills himself, and then the cyberattack hits. How will the Agency ever recover from the scandal? It will be in the media for months. Heads will roll. Emmett Nelson will at last be taken down with his favorite agent. You can see why you don't get a star."

"That's a nice bedtime story." Tate was running out of time and turning greener by the minute. "You took a chance by joining us."

"Not really. MI5, MI6, and the CIA, none of them pay attention to the small people. We find the weak, underpaid programmers and either bribe them or torture them for the code word of the day generators. We're good. We can infiltrate at will."

"And the real Lash?"

"Dead."

Mal was safely locked in Lash's cabin, yet she was nervous. What was taking Lash so long? She worried he was dead. SMASH assassins were the best in the world, next to the Agency's. What if something had happened to him?

She paced the cabin, trying to determine the best course of action. Her cell buzzed. She grabbed it up, expecting Lash. Instead it was a call.

"Mason?"

"Mal, thank God. Is Tate with you? I've been trying to reach him."

"No." Her heart raced. Mason sounded worried. "What's wrong?"

"Where are you? Get someplace secure."

"I'm in a cabin. I'm fine."

"Can you talk?"

"Yes. I'm alone."

"We just got a call from Scotland Yard. They found one of our agents murdered."

"What? They found Walburn already?" Mal couldn't believe it.

"Walburn? What are you talking about?"

"The MI5 agent you sent to back us up." Mal swallowed hard. "He's dead. Freshly. Less than half an hour ago if that. I found him myself. Who are you talking about?"

"Lash."

"What!" Now she was really freaked. "I just saw Lash. He was heading out to help Tate. You mean he's dead?"

"No, he's alive."

"You just said he's dead."

"I said Lash is dead. The real Lash. A passenger found his body stashed in the train station in Reading."

"What? But how—" Mal's brain wasn't working right. She wasn't processing. Nothing made sense. "Then who's on the ferry with us?" But she knew without asking.

"One of RIOT's top SMASH assassins, near as we can figure."

"Oh, no! He's with Tate. I have to warn him."

"Mal, Tate's not picking up his phone."

"I have to help him." She pulled her pink gun from her purse and headed for the door.

"Be careful. Use extreme caution. I don't need to tell you how dangerous he is."

She was already reaching for the door. She grabbed it and yanked and almost slammed into it as she took a step forward expecting it to open before her. "I'm locked in. But how?"

She was still on the cell with Mason.

"Where?" he asked. "Where are you?"

"In Lash's cabin."

"Get out of there. Now!"

"I can't. I'm somehow locked in."

Just then the ferry listed to the side. Mal screamed as she lost her footing and fell against the wall.

"Mal! Mal!"

"I'm fine. The ship just pitched. We're in the middle of

a raging storm." She struggled with the door. "I can't get out, Mason. Somehow Lash has jammed the door from the outside."

"You have to get out. For your own safety. If Lash comes back, you're done for."

"There's no way out. Just the door. It opens in from the hallway. I'm tugging as hard as I can and it won't budge."

"He's probably used a shim and wedged it from the outside. Are you on the inside or in an outside cabin? Is there a porthole?"

"A porthole! Yes."

"I can give you instructions on how to pry it open and climb out. Hang on. Let me call up the ferry schematics. What cabin are you in?"

She told him the number.

"I'm looking to see if there's a ledge outside."

"Mason, did you hear me? We're in the middle of a gale-force storm. I can't climb out the window onto a ledge. I'll be blown off into the sea."

"Not if you rope yourself in. The life jackets are stowed beneath the right-hand berth. Get one out and put it on. There should also be emergency rope."

She put her Bluetooth headphones on, tucked her phone in her pocket, followed his instructions, and lashed herself to the rope.

"Here's the plan—you're going to go out your porthole and into the one in the cabin next to yours. It's only a six-foot walk along the ledge to the next porthole. You'll pry that one open. Climb in and dash out. Easy."

"For you maybe."

"You can do this. You have to. And you have to hurry if you're going to save Tate and Sophia. And yourself."

"If it isn't too late already. Lash has been gone over ten minutes." She was going to kill Tate herself if she climbed out that window into the storm and he was already dead.

"I'm going to talk you through this. I'll be with you every step." He guided her through a trial run of opening the porthole from the outside as she'd have to do from the ledge. The porthole in her room opened like a window. Lash had overlooked that fact. Or maybe he didn't think anyone was crazy enough to climb out it in a storm. Or egotistical enough he thought she wouldn't discover he was a RIOT assassin until it was too late.

"Here goes nothing." She pulled it loose. A gush of water surged in along with a burst of rain and wind.

"Courage."

She'd already tied one end of the rope to one of the berths. She stood on the berth, took a breath as her hair blew in the wind and the rain plastered it against her head and climbed out. Once she was outside, she could barely hear Mason. The wind and the roar of the sea drowned him out. She climbed onto the ledge and hung on, inching her way in the darkness toward the light of the next porthole.

A wave pounded the ferry. It rolled, nearly knocking her into the sea. She nearly lost her grip. She was drenched now and shaking with cold and fear.

Just remember your boating skills, she told herself. She'd been sailing in rough seas before. This was like being hiked out in rough water with her back barely skimming above it. Only she didn't have to wrestle with a sail, just a rope and her fears.

She inched her way along the ledge, finally reaching the porthole. Inside the occupants were watching TV, oblivious to her plight. They couldn't hear her outside over the noise of the storm as she worked to loosen the porthole with the tools she'd brought with her. A wave caught her. She swung over the side and screamed.

Mason was yelling in her ear, just a buzz in the tempest of sound and fury around her. She managed to get a grip on the rope and hoist herself back onto the ledge, but she'd lost her screwdriver in the process. She pried the porthole loose with her bare hands around the rim. It gave way suddenly, nearly sending her tumbling off the ledge again. She caught herself just in time and threw herself through the porthole, ignoring the startled gasps of the couple inside.

"Pardon me. I'm just passing through." She was dripping and windblown. Her T-shirt clung to her body and had gone nearly transparent. Rain blew in from outside as she threw off her life jacket and unlashed herself from the rope. "Sorry to interrupt. Carry on." She raced through the room and out into the hall toward Tate's cabin, praying she wasn't too late.

The storm was blowing at full force, knocking the ferry around like a toy on the seas and creating enough racket for Lash to get away with as many murders as he cared to commit.

Lash looked at his watch. "How time flies when you're waiting to die, Mr. Cox. Sounds like our storm is sufficiently vicious." He aimed his pistol at Tate's heart.

The ferry pitched. Lash stumbled. *War and Peace* fell into Tate's lap.

Lash recovered quickly and took aim again. Tate counted on the accuracy of Lash's aim and just had time to cover his heart with the bulletproof book. Lash fired. The bullet hit *War and Peace* with enough force to knock Tate back and bruise his ribs.

Damn! That hurt like hell.

The force of the bullet impact took Tate's breath away. Gasping, he had just enough time to aim the barrel-spine of the epic novel at Lash's head. This was definitely war.

Tate fired just as the ferry rocked again. A hole pierced the spine of the book. Lash stumbled. Tate's shot went wild, just nicking Lash's gun arm. Tate cursed the storm. He ordinarily wouldn't miss at this close range.

Lash barely flinched. In the fraction of a second he took to look at his bleeding wound, Tate took aim again. The boat listed to the other side. Tate took a step back to brace himself. Lash charged him, lunging for the book.

Tate knew every self-defense and offensive move there was. So did Lash. They were evenly matched in strength, size, and skill. A betting man would lay even odds on them. Tate wasn't as optimistic.

He aimed a kick at a pressure point in Lash's leg that would bring him down. Lash blocked it. He threw a punch. Lash deflected it.

As they struggled, Lash scratched Tate across the arm. A trickle of blood beaded up. Tate ignored it and tried to bang Lash upside the head with *War and Peace*.

Lash deflected it again. They continued struggling. Tate realized he was on the offensive while Lash was playing defense. This wasn't typical SMASH behavior. For some reason, Lash thought he could outlast Tate, wear him down and then strike.

Tate had to get in firing position. It was tricky. He couldn't risk hitting Sophia with friendly fire. The ferry and the storm fought him every time he got close.

He cocked his arm and got *War and Peace* against Lash's temple.

Tate's ears began to ring. His limbs were going numb. He was having a hard time getting his finger on the trigger of the book. He couldn't feel his hand to pull the trigger.

Lash grinned. "Feeling sleepy?" He knocked Tate's book arm, dislodging the gun from Lash's temple.

Lash got his pistol in position, pressed against Tate's gut, which was nauseated with the motion of the ferry. In a second Tate would throw up.

So this is how it ends, Tate thought as he struggled. *It's*

going to look like I was a coward who lost it at the end.
His stomach clenched.

Lash smiled as if he was enjoying the fight tremendously. "Good-bye, Cox. And good riddance."

The door to the cabin flew open. Mal charged in armed with her girlie pink gun. She pointed it at Lash and fired.

Lash crumbled to the floor. Tate threw up all over the dying man and fell to his knees.

"My sentiments exactly." Mal held a smoking pink gun.

The room smelled faintly of gunpowder and an awful lot like vomit. Like a lot of other cabins probably did at the moment.

Tate clutched his stomach. The room was growing dim. He was weak and having trouble focusing on Mal. "You took a big chance. You could have hit me."

"Yeah? I thought about it. You probably deserved it." Mal walked over and studied Lash. "One to the head. I'm good."

She was soaked. Her T-shirt was plastered to her body and transparent. Her mascara was running. Her hair was wild. She was the best sight he'd ever seen and might be the last one. "Is that wet T-shirt just for me?"

"Shut up." Her voice was tender. "I've just braved the outside of the ferry and gale-force winds to rescue you and you're thinking about wet T-shirts. Some things never change."

He tried to grin, but his lips weren't working. He had to get it out. He had to tell her what he felt. "Like how much I love you. And always will." He took a deep breath, feeling as if his lungs were shallow. "Mal, about earlier—it's not what it looked like."

He was getting double vision and trying not to heave again. The room was rocking.

Mal looked calm. "I believe you." She looked at his arm. "What happened there?"

"Lash poisoned me. And drugged Sophia." Tate swayed on his knees. "The symptoms are like RIOT's usual poison of choice." He took a rasping breath as the world was closing down. "Tell Kayla I love her, too. Don't let her grow up to be a spy."

And then his world went black.

CHAPTER TWENTY-FIVE

Tate woke up surrounded by bright lights and the beeping of medical equipment. There was a window and greenery outside. This certainly wasn't hell. Someone was holding his hand, squeezing it reassuringly.

"You're back." Mal smiled at him, looking more relieved than he deserved.

"You're here." His throat was dry. His tone came out raspy.

"I am. And have been all along."

"Where is here?"

"Dublin."

He frowned, trying to remember. "I thought we were going to Belfast?"

"We were. But Dublin was closer. They airlifted you here from the ferry in the middle of a whopper of a storm in the Irish Sea. It was quite the operation. You owe some brave emergency workers your thanks.

"You've been in the hospital for two days. The doctors didn't think you'd make it." She smiled and squeezed his hand. "I never gave up. I know how tough you are."

"I shouldn't have made it. That poison—"

She smiled at him. "I took a chance and administered the antidote that was in my bag from Sir Herbert. We're lucky RIOT isn't more creative in their choice of poisons.

Once I knew I was dealing with one of their top assassins, I was pretty sure the antidote would work. They have to stop worrying about signature kills. It gives away the cure.

"Once I injected you with the antitoxin, you stabilized and they airlifted you here."

"Sophia?"

"Still worried about her, are you?" Mal was smiling and her voice was tender with no signs of jealousy. "Lash, well, whoever he was, I don't know what to call him."

"Lash will do."

She nodded. "He had only sedated Sophia to keep her quiet until he shot her and framed you. The paramedics checked her over. She slept it off and continued to Belfast where Mason met her. The two of them took our place on our plane for the States. She's safely in custody now. Mission accomplished.

"I'm sorry to be the one to tell you, but I think her case of hero worship has transferred to Mason. He's terribly attractive and there's no complication of an interfering ex-wife and child to worry about."

"Almost ex-ex-wife. You promised to marry me again."

"I did, didn't I?" Her smile deepened. "I'm a woman of my word. I guess I'm stuck. I'll just have to become the ex-ex-Mrs. Cox. If only to keep the gossip media at bay." She stroked his cheek. "We recovered the incriminating files and letter that RIOT had planted on Sophia. And we covered our tracks, though the cleanup crew wasn't pleased with the mess you made on Lash's body."

Tate laughed. It hurt his throat. "Set a date for the wedding. Kayla can be our flower girl this time."

"She'll love that, especially if she can have a long pink dress."

"I seem to remember you dripping wet with your nipples showing through your T-shirt. It was quite erotic.

And something about crawling along the outside of the ferry. Was I hallucinating?"

"Nope. Your memory is spot-on." She leaned over and pulled something from her purse. "Lash tricked me into waiting for him in his cabin. Then he used this shim from the outside to lock me in. I climbed out through a porthole, walked along a very narrow rim, and burst through a porthole in the next cabin. I'm very proud I was able to remove it, but I lost a good screwdriver in the process."

"Did you?"

"Right into the sea."

"That's too bad."

"Yes, and I arrived looking quite the fright."

"You were a sight for sore eyes to me." He pulled her close. "Would you put on a wet T-shirt for me again? I didn't get to take full advantage of it." He pulled her into a deep kiss.

She kissed him back until the monitors he was hooked up to went crazy, beeping and whirling. Mal eyed the heart rate monitor. "That's enough of that until you get your strength back."

"What?" He grinned. "Where's that shim? Why don't you use it to lock us in? Then I'll show you who has his strength back already."

She kissed him lightly. "It only works from the outside."

"Improvise. I'm due for a stress test anyway. You can play doctor."

STINGER

Emmett Nelson sat in his office at Langley, happy that another mission was accomplished successfully. And now he had two fewer agents with exes to worry about. Sophia had given them much valuable information. NCS now had valuable insight into the minds of the RIOT programmers and how they were planning future attacks.

Relations with the Brits were stronger than ever. But Emmett's nemesis, Archibald Random, RIOT's chief, was getting bolder and more personal in his attacks all the time. It was no accident RIOT had gone after Tate.

Emmett tried not to play favorites among his agents. They were all dedicated and damn good at what they did. But he couldn't help favoring Tate. Tate was his godson. And his son.

Tate had no idea Emmett was his biological father. And Emmett had no intention of telling him. The question was—had Random found out?

Random was testing Emmett, seeing just how much he'd risk for duty. Worse, he was going after those Emmett loved.

A wrapped gift sat on Emmett's desk, which reminded him. He asked his admin to call Tate and Malene in.

He smiled as he waited. They arrived together.

"You wanted to see us, chief?" Tate said.

They looked happy, which warmed Emmett's jaded heart.

Malene noticed the gift. "Going to a wedding, sir?"

"Yeah, yours," Emmett said. "I thought you'd want this present early. It's not something you want to open in front of a crowd."

"Ours? You didn't have to do that, sir." Malene looked worried. "You gave us a gift the first time around. We're not expecting anything from anyone this time."

"This is better than the first one." Emmett indicated the present. "Go ahead. Open it."

Tate handed the gift to Mal. "You do the honors."

They sat in the leather chairs opposite Emmett's desk. Malene opened the present gently. There are two kinds of unwrappers—those who tear through the paper and those who try to preserve it. Malene was the second kind. She carefully set the ribbon aside and pulled the wrapping off in one piece. Beneath the paper was a plain white box. She slowly removed the tissue and set it aside.

Emmett watched with delight as she gasped and held up an expensive crystal picture frame that framed the famous shot of them in bed together. "For your eyes only. So you never forget what you two have together."

Malene blushed.

"There's something else," Emmett said. "There's a small data card in there with what we believe is the last remaining copy. Our techies searched the Internet and scrubbed it pretty clean. I can't guarantee there isn't a copy somewhere. But if one surfaces, we'll get it down."

Malene shot Tate a loving gaze. When she turned her smile back on Emmett, it was radiant. "Thank you, Emmett. You're right—this is a better gift." She reached across and squeezed Tate's hand as if getting his confirmation. "In fact, it and the mission are the best gifts I've ever received."